new york times best selling author

NICOLE WILLIAMS

Teri,
Never a victim.
Always a survivor.
Love wins.
N. Willi

love
is fragile

collared

Collared
Copyright © 2016
Nicole Williams

ISBN-13: 978-1-940448-11-4

Cover Design by Paper and Sage Designs
Editing by Joy Editing
Formatting by JT Formatting

Dedicated to all the lost souls,
the broken spirits,
and shattered hearts.

Wear your scars proudly
for you've chosen to embrace life
rather than try to escape it.

One

THIS IS THE happiest moment of my whole life. I know it.

Of course I can't tell Torrin that since he's got a whole theory that those happiest moments are usually followed by the worst moments. He's a little biased after what happened to his dad—not that I can blame him. I'd probably feel the same way if the day I'd scored the winning goal at the state championship was the day my dad had been killed by a drunk driver in the middle of a crosswalk.

So instead of telling Torrin about my happiest moment ever, I curl a little tighter against him and wedge my head under his chin. I like this spot. A lot. I can hear his heartbeat at the same time my head rises and falls in time to his breath.

His heart's still beating. His lungs are still working. I don't know why I find this so comforting—such a relief—but maybe Torrin's happy moment theory is starting to rub off on me. My leg slung over his hips tightens around him.

My arm stretched across his stomach does too.

"What are you thinking right this very second?" His body stirs a little, like he's just waking up, but I know better. We might be in his bed, but we weren't using it for its general purpose. He tilts his head down toward me when I stay quiet. He's probably making sure I haven't fallen asleep.

My thumb scrolls down one of his ribs. I can't tell him the truth, so I tell him what I would be thinking if it wasn't for the happiest-feeling-ever thing.

"That I just lost my virginity to the boy next door." My voice sounds the same as his—like we've both just woken up from a nap or are about to fall into one.

"You make that sound so lackluster—losing it to the boy next door—and technically, I'm not the boy next door."

I hear the smile in his voice, which makes my own form. Torrin's got one hell of a smile—the kind that makes a girl's stomach wring dry—but I'm too happy nestled on his chest to lean back and check it out. Besides, I memorized that smile years ago. Perks of growing up next to Torrin Costigan.

"The house beside mine has been empty for years, and the one beside you is owned by an eighty-three-year-old widow." My smile stretches when I see where Torrin's jeans landed—over the top of the lamp on his nightstand. "You're the boy next door, Torrin. *My* boy next door."

"I'm your whatever you want me to be. How 'bout that?" His hand combing through my hair stops at the ends to give them a soft pull.

I melt a little more. Whatever was left of me to still melt at least. "What are *you* thinking?"

Torrin's both an open book and a book of secrets. Some days I feel like I know everything there is to know about him, and others I wonder if I've barely scraped the surface. Losing his dad messed him up for a long time, and even though he says that's behind him, I know better. It never will be—people can't just put that kind of thing behind them. Some days it's just more in front of him than others though.

"That all I want to do is fall asleep like this and wake up and do it all over again." His chest opens like he's stretching, but both of his arms stay tightly around me.

"I like your idea. That's what I'm thinking now." My leg stretched across his hips slides lower.

I feel something stir inside me again when I feel him. We just finished. Not even five minutes ago. This was my first time. I should be sore and tired and maybe even freaking out a little—according to my friends who ditched their virginity cards before me. Why do I want to do it again? Why is it the only thing I can think about?

I know the answer though. It's the same reason as always—I can't get enough of Torrin. I know it isn't a one-sided feeling either. My friends say being this into a guy when I'm only seventeen isn't healthy. My parents have threatened to move across the city and put some distance between us if we don't slow things down. No one seems to get it. We get it though. When you love someone, you love them. You can't "slow that down" or portion out whatever "healthy" doses your peers deem acceptable.

You love them as hard as you can, as best you can.

"I thought you were coming over to yell at me for covering for Caden again." His voice is quieter. I know why.

"You mean for taking the fall for him? Again?" My voice is louder. He knows why. "Actually, I *was* coming over to do that, but then I saw you, and you gave me that sad smile of yours with that apologetic little shrug, and my emotions got crossed, and I decided this was the night." I have to pause to take a breath. When I exhale, I notice the skin stretched across his chest just below my mouth rise. I love knowing I have this kind of an effect on him—even if I was just exhaling. "It felt right."

His hand buried into the curve of my spine presses deeper. It feels like it's dissolving into me. "Thank you." He kisses my hairline.

"For finally being ready to have sex after being to-gether the past two years? Yeah, no problem." I laugh as quietly as I can.

Torrin's mom is working tonight, but I don't want to wake his little brother, Rory, who's probably asleep in his bedroom next door. I also don't want to give Caden, Tor-rin's older brother, a reason to remember we exist. Usually he's happy to pretend we don't, but when he does, life's rather unpleasant for those few minutes.

"I would have waited for you no matter how long you took. A month, a year, an eternity." My body lifts with his when he shrugs. "I would have waited."

"You would have waited an eternity? You know what that is, right?" My toes press into the side of his leg.

They're cold, and he's warm. It's strange how whatever I need, Torrin has. Or how whatever he needs, I have. Cold toes and warm side of a leg included.

"Forever?" he answers all innocent-like. "Yeah, I know its general definition."

"And you'd be willing to wait forever for me to be ready?" My eyebrow lifts. Not because I don't believe him but because a girl's brow should rise when a boy proclaims he'd wait for her forever. My family believes in fairy tales like they believe in the possibility of world peace.

I'd rather be whatever Torrin and I are.

"There's only one you." He shrugs again. My body bobs with his again. "Of course."

Another laugh escapes my lips. "You used to hate me."

He groans. "I didn't hate you. You just annoyed the crap out of me."

I probably should check the time on my phone, but I'm too happy. This moment is too perfect to end with something as trivial as a curfew. "Because I was faster than you, scored higher on tests than you, and kicked your butt in every game of one-on-one?"

"Exactly. Annoying." He tugs on the ends of my hair again.

"Yeah, well, you used to annoy the crap out of me too," I fire back, pinching his side.

"You're welcome." He says it like he's proud of it because, you know, annoying the crap out of a girl is medal-worthy or something. I guess it worked out for us though.

"So how does a guy go from hating a girl to loving her?" I tip my head back just enough that I can see his face.

His chin is barely stubbled from not shaving today. His dark hair is scattered all over his face and pillow. His light eyes are alive—almost as though the ones I'd been looking into for twelve years had been dead in comparison. In the soft light of his lamp, with his face flushed from what we just did . . . God, he's the most beautiful thing I've ever seen.

I never want this moment to end. Even though I know it has to, I want it to stretch into my next three lifetimes.

"For the millionth time, I didn't hate you." He sounds annoyed, but nothing about his expression matches that feeling.

"But you do love me?" It's a rhetorical question. I know. I've *known* for a while now.

"Damn straight I do." His words come out like they were dipped into steel—strong and weatherproof.

That's when my phone resting on the edge of his nightstand vibrates. I've started setting an alarm when I'm with Torrin because time just kind of gets away from me when we're together. I wouldn't worry about setting an alarm in the first place if my dad wasn't a police chief who carries a gun twenty-four-seven and who also carries an impression that the Costigan boys are the type of people who end up in the back of his cruiser, not holding hands with his firstborn.

"Eh, I'm late." I sigh because this is my second

alarm. The one that means I'd better haul ass and get home if I'm not there already. I distantly remember the first one going off fifteen minutes ago, but I was a bit preoccupied by something else at the time. Or preoccupied by *someone* else. "My parents are going to be pissed."

"You just got here." Torrin reaches for his phone settled beside mine.

"Yeah, I just got here two hours ago." He's shifting beneath me, but I'm not ready to move yet. I'm not ready to let go of him.

"What? Really?" He snatches his phone off the nightstand and flips it around. His eyes widen when he reads the time. "Shit."

"Time flies when you're having sex for the first time."

His eyes are the palest blue I've ever seen, but they darken when I say that. Might have something to do with my leg holding him in place when he tries to slide away.

"Is it true for the second time?" Now he isn't pulling away—he's pulling me closer. He rolls my body on top of his, and my legs straddle his narrow hips. He's all muscle and skin—he's got the classic soccer body. I'm not exactly "soft," but when my body's pressed against his, I feel that way.

"Only one way to find out." My hands cap his shoulders, and I feel the muscles roll beneath my fingers.

"When?" Torrin's hands settle on the peaks of my hips, and I don't know if he means to, but he makes my lap burrow deeper into his. My stomach feels like it's been filled with lava.

"Now?" I ask, but my body isn't really asking. It's more along the lines of telling.

I feel him beneath me. I know he wants to. He knows I want to. So I'm not sure why he clenches his eyes closed and grinds his jaw like he's trying to restrain himself.

"I thought your dad was going to lock you away in some tower and lock me up after the way he found me kissing you last week in the hallway. He finds out about this"—his finger waves between us—"and I'll be in some unmarked grave decomposing under a pile of lye."

My nose curls at the thought. "Ugh. How do you know about that stuff?"

His eyes are still closed, but his jaw relaxes a little. "This beast known as the Internet and morbid curiosity."

His eyes open a second later, right before he gently shifts me off of his lap and slides off the mattress. He snags his jeans from the lampshade and pulls them on. I know I tore off a pair of boxers earlier, but who knows where they landed.

"How can you be that restrained?" I flail my hands at him right before he roams his room, rounding up his shirt and my clothes, which had wound up just about every-where except for dangling from the ceiling fan. "I'm na-ked, in your bed, practically begging you to make love to me again, and you're pulling on your shirt."

He drops the pile of my clothes in my lap but twirls my white cotton panties in my face. I grab them but throw them into the rest of my pile. I'm not ready to get dressed. I'm ready for something else.

"I'm this restrained because I happen to really, *really*

like making love to you and I'd like to continue doing it."
He cups my chin when I continue to sulk in his bed, and
his thumb traces the seam of my lips. He isn't making it
any easier to crawl out of his bed and get dressed. "I also
happen to know that's not going to be an option if you get
home past curfew after leaving my house."

His hand drops, and he rolls the blankets down to the
foot of the bed like he's hoping that will coax me out. Torrin's sheets started out navy blue years ago but are more
periwinkle in color now after being washed a thousand
times. They're soft though, and they smell like him. Why
would I want to leave his bed? Ever?

When he sees I'm still not moving, he holds his
phone up in my direction and points at the time. I'm already three minutes late. If I stall for another three, my dad
will come marching over here and pound down Torrin's
flimsy bedroom door, and I know Torrin's right—he probably would wind up under a pile of lye if my dad found us
the way we are now. That's what finally pries me out of
his bed.

"You've got the restraint of a priest," I mutter as I
slide on my underwear.

"Okay, talking about priests after what we just did
feels all kinds of weird." He'd been about to throw on his
soccer flats but stopped when I started dressing. He's
watching me, smiling again, but this one's crooked.

When I slip into my bra, I go a little more slowly than
usual. When I slide my hair over one shoulder before fas-
tening the bra at my back, he swallows.

"Oh please, like you're the good little Catholic boy

who was saving himself for marriage." My eyes trace back to his bed where I can still see him hovering above me, all of his muscles slicing through his skin as he restrained himself, moving slowly so he wouldn't hurt me. The image makes me wish I was taking my clothes off instead of putting them back on.

"Hey, I've been at Sunday mass every week for the past seventeen years of my life."

I make myself look away from his bed. It's not like that was our last time in it. There's tomorrow. And the day after that. And every one after that too. We have time. "Only because you'd have to answer to your mom if you didn't show up."

After I wiggle into my skirt, Torrin snags my old Cons from his floor and crouches beside my feet to tie them on while I wrestle into my shirt. "Details." When he's done tying the second one, he kisses the outside of my thigh and grabs my hand. "We've got to hustle."

I know we do. I can practically feel my spidey senses going off. If Dad isn't already rounding our front gate, he's a minute away from it. I follow Torrin into the hall and jog down the stairs with him.

Unlike his bedroom, which is relatively tidy for a seventeen-year-old guy's, the rest of the house is kind of messy. Cluttered. Six months past being in need of a deep cleaning. I know he's embarrassed to have me over— that's why we usually spend most of our time at my place or somewhere else—but after the heated making-out-against-the-wall fiasco last week, Torrin's been banned from my place. Indefinitely.

I'm not embarrassed to be here though. Not ever. His house wasn't always like this. Things started to change after his dad died five years ago and his mom had to take on two jobs. Torrin's dad was kind of the anchor of the family, and once he was gone, it seemed like everyone and everything just kind of floated off in different directions.

We're almost down the stairs, and I want to stop and tell him how much I love him and how I could never be embarrassed by anything when it comes to him and how I can't imagine a better place than his bed for our first time, but we're both startled by the sound of something shattering from somewhere in the kitchen.

I'm pretty sure I know what it is and who's responsible for the glass—a.k.a. beer bottle—shattering, but Torrin has to check. His little brother is upstairs asleep, and even though he's the middle brother, Torrin has stepped into the role of man of the house as best as he can. They're big shoes to fill. Impossible shoes to fill if you ask Torrin.

Half of the ceiling lights are burnt out in the kitchen, but it's impossible not to see what's going on. I've witnessed this scene so many times I've committed it to memory. It's one of the reasons my parents don't like me hanging out at the Costigans'.

Everyone took it hard when Mr. Costigan was killed, but Torrin's older brother took it the hardest. Probably because he was the reason why Mr. Costigan was out late that night. He never would have been in the middle of that crosswalk when Sherry Gates—whose blood alcohol level was point three—went blasting through it if Caden had been home when he said he'd be home.

11

Guilt's a strange thing—how it strangles the life out of people. Mr. Costigan was the one who died that night, but Caden has been dying a slow death of his own ever since.

Not that that earns him much sympathy in my book, because Caden's a prick. The leader of them. He was before his dad died and has become an even bigger one since.

"If it isn't my little brother who seriously saved my ass today," Caden announces to the kitchen filled with a half dozen of his loser friends. You know the ones who showed up to first period either drunk or hungover most days? The ones who couldn't fill a thimble with honor between all of them?

Caden was supposed to graduate last year, but he failed so many of his classes that he has to redo his senior year, which really sucks since that puts all three of us in a bunch of the same classes.

"Thanks for taking the fall for me, Torrin. I owe you." Caden holds his hand above his head, waiting for Torrin to smack it.

Torrin's hand tightens around mine instead, and his other stays stuffed into his back pocket. "You can pay me back by not drinking on school property again and leaving a trail of beer cans that lead up to my tailgate."

I stiffen. I'd heard that Torrin had told Principal Thierry that the beer cans were his, but I hadn't heard that Caden had pretty much left a trail of Natty Light crumbs to Torrin's truck. Coward.

"You got it, bro." Caden waves a lazy salute, but by

the glassy look of his eyes, it's pretty damn clear he's already downed another half case. "And sorry about you getting suspended from the team for five games. Thierry's a serious hardass."

I spin on Torrin, but my hand stays tied in his. "You got kicked off the soccer team?"

Behind me, Caden pops off a "Busted!" to his friends, which is followed by a few chuckles, but I don't care. All I care about is Torrin. Soccer is his life—or at least a big part of it. He's good at it too. He's started every game since his sophomore year, and word is he's in a good spot to land a solid scholarship if he keeps averaging two goals a game . . . which can't happen if he has to sit on the bench for the next five.

I'm suddenly so pissed at Caden that I want to punch that smirk off of his face. Even though he kind of looks like Torrin, except for his eyes being dark brown and his body being more stocky than lean, I can't help but feel murderous things when I look at him.

"I was going to tell you." Torrin looks right into my eyes. He doesn't blink. "I just got kinda . . . distracted." His cheeks color just a little. He's lost most of his tan from the summer, so it's more obvious.

"You two were up in your bedroom for a good two hours, and I can make out the sweet sound of a mattress bouncing from a mile away." Caden fires off a wink at Torrin. "I *bet* you were a little distracted, brother."

Torrin's hand tightens around mine, his eyes narrowing at Caden.

"You're a dick, Caden." I face him and step closer.

Caden's a classic coward, and you don't back down from a coward when they throw a punch—you throw one right back. "Grow up and own up. Stop letting your little brother do it for you."

Torrin tries pulling me back to him. When that doesn't work, he steps up beside me. He knows better than to move in front of me or angle his body in that direction. The last time he tried that, we got into a serious fight. I get that he has this instinct to protect me, but he has to get that I can protect myself. He has to understand that it's my job, not his, to look after me. He's getting there. Slowly, but he is.

"Ahh, Jade." Caden crosses his arms over his big barrel chest. His eyes move down me. "You kiss my brother with that filthy mouth?" He tips his chin at Torrin. "Lucky guy."

Torrin flinches, but he stays where he is. I can tell it's almost killing him to let me handle this on my own.

I raise an unimpressed brow at Caden. "Bite me."

Caden snaps his teeth together a few times. "I'd love to. Right in that nice round ass of yours." He chomps his teeth together once more. "Are you tapping that yet, Torrin? Or is she still holding out on you?"

Caden drops his hand on Torrin's shoulder. Torrin shrugs out of it and pulls me back with him. I decide to overlook the manhandling moment.

"That girl's never going to marry you, little brother, so you might as well take what you can as many times as you can get it."

An angry shudder rocks Torrin's body. The muscle

running down his jaw looks ready to snap.

"Why don't you go drink yourself into a coma, Caden?" I pull Torrin back a few steps because I don't have a lot of faith that this isn't going to turn into brawl if Caden doesn't shut his trap before I get Torrin out the front door. "You'd be a lot more useful."

Something flashes in Caden's eyes, then he slams his bottle on the counter. I keep pulling Torrin out of the kitchen. From the look on Caden's face, I know this will drop from ugly to violent in a few more words. Distance is a good thing. Especially when it comes to flailing body parts and compacted fists.

Caden sniffs. "And you'd be a lot more useful if you shut your mouth and opened your legs instead."

Torrin lunges toward Caden, but I was expecting it. I have just a solid enough hold on him to keep him from getting too far. "Torrin, stop. He's just trying to get under your skin. Not worth it."

Torrin stares down Caden, not blinking. "So worth it."

When Caden crooks his finger at Torrin, I give his arm another yank before he can get very far.

"Come on, brother. Defend your girlfriend's honor," Caden says.

"My honor's just fine, spank you very much, asshole." I wave my middle finger at Caden while still managing to hold on to Torrin with both hands.

"Not with the dirty things I'm doing to you in my head." Caden lifts his eyes to the ceiling as he taps his temple. His twisted smile tells the rest of the story.

Torrin makes another lunge, this one strong enough he drags me halfway across the linoleum before I manage to get his attention. "Stop it! Now! This is what he wants. Don't give it to him."

Torrin stops, but the muscles banding down his forearm I'm gripping quiver. He takes a few deep breaths, staring down Caden the whole time. I've seen these two get into it enough to know it's a pretty even match, but after the last one had left Torrin with a black eye and so many bruises dotting his chest I was sure he'd broken a few ribs, I swore I'd do anything to keep him from getting into another one. Caden and Torrin aren't boys duking it out for fun anymore—they're men out to draw blood.

After another minute, Torrin raises his hands and backs up a few steps. "I'm good." When I don't let go of his arm, he glances at me. His eyes go right back to Caden. "I'm good."

I loosen my grip, testing him. He doesn't break loose and go all caged gorilla in Caden's direction, so I loosen my hold a little more. By the time I've totally let go of him, Torrin's breathing's back to normal. His expression's still lethal, but he's good.

"Let's leave these monkeys to their ass scratching and shit throwing." I nod toward the front door. "Come on."

I take the first step out of the kitchen and wait. Torrin follows me.

"Hey, Jade?"

My shoulders tense—why can't Caden just know when to quit?

"You need any help with the leg opening thing, you

know where to find me," he says.

I spin around as fast as I can, but I'm too late—Torrin's already on him. Torrin isn't just known for making goals. He's as well known for his speed getting up and down the field—or in this instance, across the kitchen.

"Torrin!" I shout, but I know he can't hear me. He already has Caden on the ground and has gotten in two punches before I can shout again. "Stop!"

Caden's friends close in around the two of them, but none of them charge in to help their friend, who's getting his ass kicked. Nice friends. Not that I'd let them get close to Torrin. The moment any of them put a finger on him would be the moment before I snapped it.

Caden's laughing, hit after hit, but Torrin's quiet. Eerily quiet. His hits are concentrated, focused almost. It doesn't look like he's going to stop until Caden shuts up.

I don't think Caden's trying to fight back, or if he was, Torrin's beat it right out of him, so when I notice the first splatters of blood rain across the linoleum, I step in. I can't count the number of these "brotherly" brawls I've broken up. At least Rory, the youngest Costigan brother, is more lover than fighter. Once Caden moves out of the house, things will quiet down.

"Enough, Torrin." I don't have to shout this time because there isn't much noise anymore.

Other than the smack of Torrin's fist connecting with some part of Caden, the room is quiet. He's finally stopped laughing.

"Torrin . . ." I step up behind him. He scares me when I see him like this. Not because I'm scared for myself but

17

scared for anyone who crosses him. Torrin doesn't back down once he's committed. "Enough."

Even though my words aren't stopping him, the moment my hand curls around his shoulder, his whole body goes still. Other than his chest rising and falling with his rushed breathing, he doesn't move.

I squeeze his shoulder. "Come on."

He stays straddled over Caden for a few more seconds, but slowly his arms lower to his sides as his fists fall open like they're exhausted. Caden's nose is bleeding, and a couple of Torrin's knuckles look split open—*again*—but I don't think there are any broken bones or stitches required. Torrin was holding back. Sometime this past year, he became stronger than his older brother. The roles have shifted. From the look in Caden's swollen eyes, he knows it too.

"You talk to Jade like that again, and we're over. Through." When Torrin speaks, his voice is controlled, but I don't miss the tremor that runs down his spine. "Now sober up and clean up before Mom gets home. I'm tired of cleaning up your messes."

He stares down at Caden for another moment before standing up beside me. He flexes his fingers, popping his knuckles, then grabs my hand and steers me out of the kitchen. Again. Hopefully for the last time tonight because it's a damn miracle my dad isn't already beating down the front door with the SWAT team covering him.

"Blood's thicker than water, little brother!" Caden calls after us, spitting out what I guess is some blood of his own.

"Yeah, let me know when you figure that out. Big brother." Torrin makes the last part sound like an insult as he throws open the front door and ushers me out first. He wants to make sure to keep himself between his brother and me.

Under most circumstances, I'd call him out for that, but he's just kicked his brother's ass without Caden getting a single punch in. He already has a lot to deal with without me going all independent woman on him.

The cool fall air does a decent job of clearing both of our heads, so by the time we've bounced down the front steps and are rounding onto the sidewalk, he almost looks back to normal—or as normal as Torrin Costigan is capable of looking because on a typical day, Torrin's an intense person. A guy who looks like this world and the next one over is riding on his wide shoulders. It's what I like about him. It's also why I worry about him. Intensity's good to a point . . . that point where it breaks a person. I never want to see Torrin broken.

"You shouldn't have hit him," I say as we wander down the sidewalk. Neither of us are in a hurry to separate.

"I know." Torrin stares at the sidewalk, slowing our pace until we come to a standstill. "But there are only a few people I love, and you're at the top of that list. If I don't take care of you, what good am I?"

I feel the dreaded ball wedge into my throat again. Torrin somehow feels partly responsible for his dad's death too. As if all twelve-year-old ninety pounds of him could have stepped out in front of that speeding minivan and crushed it before it crushed his dad. His thought process makes no sense to me, but that doesn't change that it makes sense to him.

"I can also, you know, take care of myself."

I glance down at my house. The lights are still on in every room but my little brother's. It's just past ten o'clock, and usually my parents go to bed at nine thirty on the dot. Except when I'm out with Torrin. They stay up until I get home every time, scanning me like they're checking to see if my top is twisted around or my skirt is still bunched up or something. Having a police chief as a dad really sucks when you're a teenage girl.

"Yeah, I remember." Torrin rubs at his cheek, trying not to smile.

He likes to rub it in whenever he can that I once took a swing at him at recess in fourth grade. I'd expected him to dodge it, but he hadn't. He stood there, unflinching, and took it. He deserved it though. He'd accused me of cheating on a spelling test, but he was just pissed because I scored one point higher than him. Like usual.

"How much longer are you going to keep covering for him?" I ask, rolling my eyes when he starts popping his jaw like I did permanent damage. "I know he feels responsible for what happened to your dad, and I know you feel bad for him because of that, but you can't let him ruin your life at the same time he's ruining his."

I glare at Torrin's house. I want to go back in there and make Caden's nose bleed again when I remember the consequences Torrin has wound up with because of him. Yeah, I know Caden would have been suspended for good if he'd chalked up another infraction, but so what? He's dug his grave as far as I'm concerned.

"I know. I'm done with it." Torrin exhales and looks off into the distance. Whatever he sees there makes his eyes narrow. "I don't want to lose you because I'm trying to save him."

I tug on his hand until his chest is brushing mine. "You won't lose me, Torrin." I wait for him to look at me. When he does, his light eyes are finally starting to clear. "I guess I'm just hoping you'll figure out one day that you can't save everyone." When the skin between his brows creases, that damn ball in my throat doubles in size. "Sometimes you have to just let go."

His arm stretches around me, pulling me closer. "I'm a sucker for a hopeless case."

When his smile starts to move into place, I exhale. "Good thing you're so cute." I smile back at him, slipping my thumb through one of his belt loops.

"And I might, you know, be pretty decent in bed?" His brow lifts at me.

My stomach knots as I think about how decent he is in bed. "I need to collect additional data before I make my final conclusion."

His face flattens as he holds out his arm. "Hey, consider my schedule cleared. Time, place, I'll be there."

The seriousness in his voice and his face makes me laugh—loudly enough that Mrs. McCune's little terrier starts barking at the front window.

"Jade Childs!" My dad's voice echoes from where I guess he's stationed at the front porch.

I wince. My dad's voice has a way of doing that. Torrin's expression doesn't change. He's immune to it or something.

"Coming!" I shout back, which only makes Roco at the window go even more nutso.

"Come on. I'll walk you home." Torrin shoves his hand in his pocket and starts leading me down the sidewalk.

I don't move. "No, better not. After what happened in the hall last week, you're lucky your man parts are still connected . . . and functioning rather impressively if I do say so myself."

I bite my lip and try to contain the blush I feel creeping up my neck. Much to my parents' dismay, I'm not the demure girl who blushes and could be voted Miss Congeniality. I'm the girl who lives in band shirts and rolls her eyes at cheerleaders. They've been calling me a strong-willed child since I was a toddler, but while they admit that with disappointment, it's a point of pride for me. I know who I am and what I want, so why in the hell would I let a bunch of other people try to tell me who I should be and who I should want?

Torrin has to scrub at his crooked smile before he can reply. He's practically gloating from my compliment about his nicely functioning manhood. Guys . . .

"I'm not letting you walk home in the dark by yourself. Nice try." He tries moving down the sidewalk again.

I stay where I am. I'm a pain in the ass as far as girlfriends go, but he puts up with me. He's a pain in the ass as far as boyfriends go, but I put up with him. I guess that's the way it is with love. Everyone's a pain in the ass in their own way. The goal's to find the person whose pain-in-the-ass is worth putting up with. I've found mine.

"It's ten o'clock," I say, blinking. "I live half a block away. We live in one of the safest cities in the country. What are you afraid's going to happen?"

He scans the neighborhood around us like there are things I can't see. "What I've been afraid of from the first day I knew I loved you." His hand tightens around mine. "That I was going to lose you."

The breath I'd been taking gets stuck in my lungs. As misguided as his fear of losing me is, I know where it comes from. I guess most kids who lose a parent at a young age probably feel the same way. They've experienced firsthand the fragility of life and how quickly it can be extinguished. It doesn't matter how many times I've told him I'm not going to leave him; my words never seems to take root.

Instead of trying for the hundredth time to convince him, I go with something else. "Here. Take this." I pull the chain I've worn around my neck for ten years out of my shirt. I don't even take it off when I shower. It's become as much a part of me as my ears and toes.

When I slip off the necklace and hold it out for him, Torrin steps back. "I can't take your grandma's ring."

"Yes, you can." When he doesn't reach out for the necklace, I slip it over his head. "Hold on to it for me. As long as you have it, you have a part of me. And as long as you have a part of me, you can never really lose me."

The necklace is shorter on him. The ring falls just below my chest, but on Torrin, it swings just above his heart.

He looks down at where it hangs. His forehead creases. "It's a family heirloom. I can't take it."

I study it on him too. My grandma specifically wanted me to have it. She picked me over my five girl cousins, and I'm not sure why. Now that she's dead, I guess I never will. But I love that ring something fierce, and I love this person something fierce, so it's right where it needs to be.

"You can give it back to me one day," I say, shifting. It takes a lot to make me shift, but I guess hinting at exchanging rings one day is up to the task. "You know, when the time's right."

I hear the screen door at my place whine open again. I've already earned myself a weeklong grounding by being what I guess is fifteen minutes late. I don't want to tack another week on by being another minute late. "Good night. And thank you."

I pop up onto my tiptoes and press a quick kiss onto his mouth before jogging down the sidewalk toward my house. After tonight, I feel more like I'm floating though. Run-in with Caden aside, this has been the best night of my life. It always will be. I know it.

He cups his hands around his mouth and shouts at me, "Wave at me when you get to your house, 'kay?"

I flash a salute back at him. "Yes, sir."

I'm in front of the vacant house beside mine when his voice rolls over me again. "Jade?"

"Yep?" I spin around, continuing to back down the sidewalk.

The look on his face stops me.

"Will you marry me?" Hands stuffed in his front

pockets, barefoot, and his dark hair shining in the moon-
light, he smiles at me. It almost looks apologetic. Almost
but not quite.

"What?" My voice breaks over that one syllable.

He doesn't blink. "You heard me."

My heart starts firing like it's trying to escape.
"We're seventeen. I must have misheard you."

Right? I can't have heard what I think I did. *Right?*

He shakes his head once. "You didn't. I'm asking you
to marry me."

My throat runs dry. I'm not sure I can reply. "Torrin
. . ."

"Not today. Not tomorrow." His voice is so calm, like
he's been planning this for years and has been certain of
this for decades. "But someday. I love you. I want to spend
the rest of my life with you."

A breeze rushes over me, playing with the hem of my
skirt and the ends of my hair. I know my answer. I know I
want him. I'm not sure if I'm supposed to know this at this
stage in my life, but I do. I want to spend the rest of my
life with him too.

But I can't just say *Yes* or *I do* or *I will* or whatever
girls in this kind of a situation do, because I'm seventeen
and I'm me and Jade Childs can't be a teenage bride. She
can't even be a teenage fiancée. Can she?

God, I'm so confused. But I'm not confused about
Torrin or loving him or wanting him forever. That's the
clearest thing to me in the whole world.

"Are you just asking that because we"—I clear my
throat—"you know and the good Catholic boy you're not

is making you feel all guilty?"

He's at least fifty feet away, but I don't miss his smile. I couldn't miss it if we were an entire solar system apart.

"No." He pads a step closer. "I'm asking you to marry me because I've never been so sure of anything in my life."

The wind keeps playing with me, toying with my mind the way it's messing with my clothes. "Not today. Not tomorrow."

Torrin's head shakes. He steps closer. His eyes never leave mine. "Someday."

When the next rush of wind hits me, I move. Toward him. Before he can get a few footsteps forward, I throw myself against him. He falls back a few steps then steadies himself.

My legs wind around him and my arms rope around his neck, then I'm kissing him. For anyone to see. For everyone to see. Right here on the sidewalk I grew up riding my bike down, drawing chalk hopscotch squares on, scraping my knees on. I kiss Torrin like my life depends on it, and in a way, it kind of does. Our lives have been tangled together for a long time—this is when I know that they'll always be tethered together.

This moment, right here, is somehow even better than the one we just shared upstairs in his bedroom because this is when I feel it. Forever. It's right in front of me. *He's* right in front of me.

"JADE CHILDS!!!" My dad's shout echoes up and down Madison Boulevard.

A few more dogs are yapping in yards and front windows now.

Torrin keeps kissing me, but eventually I pull back. My heart is pounding. My lungs are straining. Everything else is floating.

"Gotta go," I whisper against his lips, breathing him in one last time, hoping I can hold in his scent until I see him before first period tomorrow morning. I unwind my legs from around him and kiss the corner of his mouth.

Just as I'm about to charge back down the sidewalk, his hand snags mine. "You never answered me." His forehead's lined as deeply as I've ever seen it.

My smile crawls into place as I glance at the claddagh hanging from his neck. "I thought I was pretty damn clear with that kiss."

With a wink, I give his hand one last squeeze before turning and running. I don't want to run away from him moments after his question and my answer, but I know the next time my dad steps out onto the porch, he'll be coming out with his shotgun. My dad will freely admit that he's a cop but that he's a father first. Thus, the shotgun.

When I reach the short white gate in front of my house, I look back. He's still there, waiting. I know that if I asked him, he'd spend the night waiting right there. I know he'd wait longer. I wonder if any length of time's too long for him.

I open the gate latch and wave at him. Home safe and sound. Torrin waves back, but he doesn't move to go back inside. He stays there, watching, waiting. He probably won't go home until he's heard my screen door close.

I feel like I'm dancing up the walkway. I know better than to explode into the house with a crazy grin or my parents' radar will go off hardcore, so I pause to collect myself. It's hard to do. I just had sex for the first time. With the guy I love. He just asked me to marry him. Someday. One day. I just agreed to it in the form of a kiss that felt like it melted all of my nerves.

I need more than a pause to collect myself from all that.

It's dark as nights come, but that can't touch me. I feel like I'm glowing from the inside out, and nothing can dim it. Nothing.

Giving myself two more breaths to compose myself, I pull the screen door open. Just as I'm about to shove through the front door, I hear something behind me.

It might be late and something's making funny noises in the bushes, but it doesn't raise the hair on my neck. This is one of the safest blocks in the whole country. Nothing even remotely exciting happens here. People don't even speed five above the limit.

I let the screen door close before I climb down the front stairs. "Here, kitty, kitty," I call, approaching the bushes slowly.

The honorary cat lady who lives a few houses down adopted a new cat who's under the impression the world is its litter box. Dad's threatened to shoot the poor thing the next time it takes a sideways look at Mom's rose bushes, so I want to shoo it away before Dad and his shotgun show back up at the door.

"Go on, kitty, get out of here if you want to save your

28

skin." I slide a few steps closer and clap, but when that doesn't do the trick, I shake the bush a few times. Sure enough, one surly-looking orange tabby goes flying from the bush. "You can thank me later," I mutter, patching up the dislodged earth before my dad sees it.

I'm just about to head back inside when I hear a car crawl to a stop in front of our house. My dad has lots of random visitors from the police station who show up at all hours of the night. Usually the visitors who come this late don't have good news.

I walk around the bushes toward the gate. The car stopped in front of our house is an older white van, not the cruiser I'm used to seeing show up late at night. I can't see who's inside. The van's still running, so maybe the driver just pulled over to make a call.

The driver's window rolls down, and a man's face pops out the window. He's clean-cut and middle-aged—he could be a cop, but I know he's not. I've met all of the cops in my dad's precinct.

"Excuse me, ma'am. Is this Driscoll Avenue?" the driver asks, spreading a map over the steering wheel.

Lost. It happens a lot. Our neighborhood's tucked back behind one of the main commercial parts of town, and out-of-town business people get lost in here all the time.

"Eh, no, this is Madison Boulevard," I say. I'm pretty sure I just heard Torrin's front door close. It's a sound I memorized a few summers ago. "Driscoll is back a couple of miles. Off of Hemlock Street."

The man nods and consults his map again. "Hemlock,

Hemlock . . ." He skims the map apparently unsuccessful-
ly.

Who still uses maps? There are these handy things
known as cell phones with built-in maps and navigation
and everything. They make life really easy. Speaking of
phones . . . I left mine on Torrin's nightstand in my hurry
to get home. Great.

"I don't see it on here. Must be an old map." The man
frowns and rubs his chin, still studying it.

Opening the gate, I step out onto the sidewalk and try
looking at his map. I can't see it from this angle though.
"Hemlock's an old street. It should be on your map."

He holds it up for me to see, and I take a couple steps
closer. Glad I can be this guy's personal MapQuest

"There, there it is." I land my index finger on the grid
where Hemlock Street runs into Driscoll. It's only a mile
or so back. "You're not too lost at least."

That's when I feel a sharp prick in my wrist. That's
when the hair on the back of my neck finally rises.

Why is a needle hanging from my wrist?

I snap my arm back, but I feel like I'm moving in
slow motion. I feel like my entire body has been dropped
in a pool of Jell-O and I'm trying to move.

The man's hand seizes my wrist before I can step
back. "No." His voice is different now, less friendly. "I'm
not lost at all."

I'm floating and sinking at the same time, and before
I know what's happening, I'm being thrown through the
van's door and sealed shut behind it. I can't move. I can't
scream. I can't do anything but think of him. The way he

looked in bed with me tonight. The way he looked on the sidewalk after asking me to spend my life with him. The way he'll look tomorrow when he finds out what has happened.

"Torrin . . ." It sputters past my lips barely loud enough for me to hear, then the darkness creeps in.

It sucks me under until I can't remember my name. It takes me down until I'm not sure I want to remember it.

Two

THE DARK ISN'T as black as it used to be. Not because it's changed any but because I've changed. I've gotten used to it. What once was dark isn't so suffocating. What once was black isn't so consuming.

That's the dream I wake up from. Weird.

I stretch my legs and arms and sit up on the couch. So I guess it isn't really morning anymore. A quick check of the clock hanging above his recliner reveals it's almost twelve thirty. Lunchtime.

I roll my neck to get out the kinks. Sleeping on an old couch with a flat pillow isn't exactly comfortable, but it's a lot better than what I used to sleep on.

I stand up slowly to test my legs. If I stand up too quickly, I fall right back down. I've learned that lesson more times than I care to count. I hear the television upstairs in his room, the usual show on at this time of the day. Just in time for the usual lunch. The usual.

Every day is predictable because every day is the

same. There was a time I would have hated living with a rigid schedule, but that girl is gone. This one, whoever she is, likes knowing what to expect because it doesn't feel like so long ago when I couldn't predict anything. This is better.

Sometimes I have to remind myself of that, but most days I'm content with the mundane schedule. Today's different though, at least a little. Instead of moving toward the kitchen because it's 12:20 and lunch is to be on the table at twelve thirty, I find myself lingering beside the couch. An emotion flares inside my chest, one that starts out small as a seed then blossoms into something so large I feel like it's going to break me open.

I had a lot of these days at first, but they've decreased in frequency and intensity. This one's different though. As intense as any I've had—maybe more than any of them. Of course the dream's to blame for that. The dream of him.

I can still see his face that last night, the way the dark shadowed half of his face and the moon illuminated the other half. The way he looked at me like I was everything. The way he smiled like we shared a whole lifetime of secrets.

God, those dreams are painful. Too painful. Part of me wishes they'd go away so I wouldn't have to feel as if my ribs are being cracked from something growing inside my chest. Another part never wants to stop dreaming about him because that's all I had left of him—dreams.

It's a poor substitute for the real thing, but it's a better alternative than losing him totally.

As I move toward the kitchen, my legs feel weaker

with every step, almost like the muscles have atrophied. There's probably some truth to that. My legs aren't nearly as strong as they used to be. Neither is the rest of my body. That's part of his plan of course. The weaker I am, the stronger he is. The frailer I become, the more powerful he grows.

I try to shove all of those thoughts away before I make it into the kitchen. They don't do me any good, but they could do me harm. That girl, that life—that boy—they're all gone. Another life.

This is my life.

It's not a bad one. It could be worse. At first, it was, but now . . . it's not too bad. He told me that so many times at first it started to cycle through my mind involuntarily. Somewhere along the way, I adopted the same belief. This life isn't so bad.

And when the dreams remind me of the life I had, I convince myself that it's nothing more than a dream. I'm more convincing now than I used to be.

I flip on the overhead kitchen light, and sterile florescent light floods the room. It's too bright, but at least I'm allowed to turn on lights whenever I want to. I feel like I lived in the dark for years. The kind of dark that was so disorienting I lost my sense of what was up and what was down. My eyesight had paid a price. Being stuck in that kind of dark for however long I was messed with my long-distance vision. I probably have the eyesight of an eighty-year-old now.

That's okay though because now I can turn on the light whenever I want. I sleep with the light on too.

I try to ignore the framed photos hanging on the wall behind the small dining table, but I'm never successful. As I reach for the white loaf of bread in the cupboard, I find myself staring at those two photos. I move to the old tan fridge to grab the pack of bologna and bottle of yellow mustard, still staring at those photos. I've made this bologna sandwich so many times I can do it and still keep staring at that wall.

Behind the glass of those brass frames are the faces of two girls. Well, one girl if you ask him. I guess most people would look at the two girls and believe they were the same, one photo taken a few years before the other. Hell, there have been days I've convinced myself of that to see if it makes things easier. Sometimes it does, at least for a while—until another one of those dreams shatters that feigned reality.

The younger girl has the same light brown hair that lightens in the sun that I have. The same green-blue, wide-set eyes. She even has the same bone structure. That girl is smiling, the kind that's real because it hits her eyes. It's clearly a school picture with one of those swirly bluish backgrounds. She's wearing a lavender shirt and a matching headband.

The older girl in the photo a few inches to the right is wearing the same kind of shirt and matching headband. Her hair's draped in front of her shoulders, the same as in the other photo. The same background, the same hair, eyes, and face . . . the only thing that's different is the smile.

The older girl is smiling, but it doesn't hit her eyes. In

fact, that girl's eyes look dead, like whatever lights used to burn behind them had been blown out like a birthday candle.

I force myself to look away because I have the urge to throw the chipped white plate I'm making the bologna sandwich on at the photo of the older girl in the hopes that the frame will shatter. The girl in that picture's broken—it seems unfair that the photo of her would tell a different story.

I hear the floor creak upstairs as he moves across the room. This is an old house. I don't know for sure, but I guess it's at least a hundred years old. It creaks a lot. In a storm, it makes so much noise it feels like it has a life of its own.

A minute later, as I'm portioning out a handful of plain potato chips on the plate, I hear the rush of water through the pipes snaking through the walls. The news on at twelve, bathroom break at 12:25, lunch at twelve thirty.

I remind myself that predictability is a good thing. Knowing what to expect is better than knowing nothing.

I pad back across the weathered wood floors to the fridge and trade the bologna and mustard for the gallon of milk. Always milk. With every meal. With every snack. Milk. So much milk I've had nightmares of drowning in it.

I pour him a tall cup of it and slide the almost empty jug back in the fridge. He can't go without his milk, which means he'll have to make a run to the store soon. He leaves the house sometimes. Usually once a week. It's only for a couple of hours at the most, but those are my hours. The ones I can do what I want without the fear of

36

him peeking over my shoulder and not liking whatever I'm in the middle of.

The last time he caught me doing something he didn't approve of, he had me make a fire in the wood stove and forced me to rip apart the picture I'd spent the last week of nights sketching. He made me watch each piece go up in flames while I repeated over and over that that was my old life—ripped to pieces, burned apart, nothing but a pile of charred ashes.

Now when I draw, I make sure to keep one ear tuned to the stairs that lead upstairs to his bedroom. At the slightest creak, I gather everything up and stuff it into the very back of the game cupboard because I know he'll never look there. He doesn't like playing games. At least the kind on boards.

There's an old box television in the living room, but it doesn't work anymore. It used to, and sometimes when he left, I'd flip it on and tweak the antennas enough to get reception on a channel or two. It was usually always a news channel though, and the news was just too depressing. Especially when, for those first years, the faces of my past were there, talking about not giving up hope or holding my photo at some candlelight vigil with tears in their eyes.

It might have comforted some in my situation to know that they weren't forgotten—that people still cared—but it did the opposite for me. I didn't want them to keep looking, because I knew what they didn't—I'd never be found. He'd never let it happen. He'd told me so. He hadn't just told me that—he'd shown me. He'd been showing me for years.

People could look for me, but they'd never find me.

His lunch was ready. I set it on the table, at the same chair as always, tucking a paper napkin under the right side of the plate.

"Dad!" I call upstairs. "Your lunch is ready!"

I hear the floor creak upstairs again.

"I'll be down in three minutes, Sara," he replies.

His voice is kind of high for a man's but rough. Like each word has to be processed through a tunnel of gravel. At first, that voice terrified me. Eventually I got used to it, and now . . . it's the only voice I ever hear. Now, it's almost a comfort.

I wander to the sink to wash my hands. My fingers are greasy from handling the chips, and I can't stand the smell of bologna on my skin.

"Sara?"

The water from the faucet is blasting as I scrub my hands with dish soap. I hear his voice, but it takes a few minutes to process.

"Sara!" This time his voice is less patient, more like I remember it at first.

It makes me stand up straighter and turn off the sink. "Yes?" I call back, reminding myself for who knows how many million times that I'm Sara.

Sara Jackson, Earl Rae Jackson's daughter. I'm his daughter. He's my father. That's the way it is. I can't let things like dreams of the past mess up that reality or else I'll wind up back where I started. In the closet. The one so sealed up that not even a stream of light came through the cracks.

It's been years since I've spent any hard time in it, and I only have to occasionally visit it whenever a random person shows up at the front door. It doesn't happen often, only once every few months or so. Like a couple of days ago, when that solar panel salesman showed up and Earl Rae practically threw me in the closet after plastering a strip of duct tape across my mouth and another around my wrists.

I suppose I could have made noise. I could have kicked at the walls. I could have thrown my body against the door. I could have tried screaming through the gag. I could have tried to get help, but I know what Earl Rae has been telling me from the beginning is true—I'm beyond help.

It's been too long. Too much of me has been replaced by Sara. Too much of me has been snuffed out by Earl Rae. Help can't help me.

So I stopped looking for ways to escape. I stopped searching for the cell phone I know Earl Rae must have somewhere. I stopped looking for metal cutters to free myself. I stopped watching the driveway for the police cruiser I prayed would show up one day. I stopped hoping.

It makes things easier.

"Dad?" I call again after he doesn't say anything back.

I can't hear the creaks from him moving around upstairs. It's quiet. The television has even been turned off, and a quick check of the time shows it's only 12:28—he still has another two minutes left of the afternoon news. He never turns it off early.

I move toward the stairs leading upstairs. "Dad?" I shout louder.

My heart's speeding up. This isn't normal. This isn't predictable. This isn't part of the schedule. Earl Rae lives and dies by his schedule. By default, so do I.

My pace picks up as I move across the kitchen floor. Something's wrong. I slow when I reach the bottom step because I know I've reached it—the end of my lead. When I twist my neck to peek up the stairs, the cool kiss of hard metal cuts into my throat.

I wince but don't cry out. I've gotten better about learning how to turn my head so it doesn't pinch or dig into my skin, but every once in a while, I'm reminded by the thick metal collar cutting into my neck.

I feel a couple of warm trickles trace down my neck. I've broken it open again—the perpetual scab that never seems to heal, the one I sometimes tear open when I forget.

At first, my neck spent more time bleeding than scabbing, but I've gotten used to it. I sleep with the collar on. I shower with it on. I walk on the old treadmill with it on. I've gotten used to it the way people get used to a wedding ring. It might feel foreign and strange at first, but eventually, you don't even know it's there. Eventually, it just becomes a part of you.

"Dad?" I'm screaming as loud as I can because I know something isn't just wrong—something is *very* wrong.

I angle myself so I can look up the stairs, but I can't

see him. I can't see anything but more stairs. I've never been up there, but I've drawn pictures in my mind of what it looks like.

That's when I hear it—the sound of feet pounding up the wooden steps to the front door. This can't be some lost delivery man trying to find one of Earl Rae's fellow reclusive neighbors. This can't be some door-to-door salesman trying to sell windmills and water tanks to the off-the-grid types drawn to these kinds of remote locations.

There are too many footsteps. They're too loud. Almost like a herd of wild horses have been set loose and are about to charge through the front door.

Since I'm getting nothing from upstairs, I rush through the kitchen toward the living room to see if I can tell what's going on. I hear shouts, but I can't make them out. Still more pounding. How many people are out there? There could be a thousand from the sounds they're making.

Earl Rae keeps the windows sealed up, but there's a peephole at the front door. I don't want to get that close though. I feel safe here, not too close to the front door. I don't know who or what's on the other side of that door. I want them to go away. I want the noise and shouting to stop.

Other than Earl Rae's voice and the household sounds, I haven't heard anything in years. The feet pounding on the porch and the fists pounding at the door and the voices shouting outside probably aren't as loud as they seem to me.

I can't make out what they're saying, but it doesn't

sound friendly or like they're asking. They're telling. Ordering. I know that tone. It was the only tone I'd heard for months.

Finally I can make out sounds upstairs. He's moving around the room, quickly from the sounds of the creaks the floor makes.

"Earl Rae?" I don't wince in anticipation of what he'll do to me for using his real name. What's banging on the front door is scarier than any punishment he can dole out.

He doesn't answer.

More frantic noises come from upstairs.

More angry noises come from outside.

More panic surges inside me.

"Earl Rae!?!?" My lungs strain. I haven't screamed this loud since the beginning. I haven't screamed half this loud since then.

What I hear next, I want to pretend I don't. I want to pretend I don't know what it is. But I do. Once upon a lifetime ago, someone close to me was a police officer, and the sight and sound of guns have been embedded in my head. I'll never forget the way a gun sounds when firing. The chilling sound a shotgun makes when being pumped. The explosion it makes when it goes off.

Up until today, I'd only experienced those sounds in a gun range, with sound-cancelling headphones and targets downrange. It isn't until today I hear the sound it makes to the unmuffled ear when it goes off a floor above you. The sound a body makes when it crashes to the floor a moment after the blast.

The feeling that pools in the stomach of the person left behind.

"Earl Rae!" I scream, but I know it. I know he'll never reply again.

That's when the front door bursts open behind me in an explosion of wood shards and dust. I crawl across the kitchen floor and huddle beneath the kitchen table as far as I can go before the chain gets tangled up in the chair legs and I become stuck.

Stuck.

I've been trapped in the same small square for years, but I've never felt so stuck.

What seems like dozens of men in black outfits, helmets, and bulletproof vests storm through the front door, all of them holding guns. Most of them fan through the house, some ducking into downstairs rooms and some sprinting upstairs. Their guns are all aimed forward, ready. Four large white letters are stamped across their vests, and even though I have a distant memory of what they mean, I can't quite remember. It doesn't stop me from being scared of them with all of their guns and all of their shouts.

I wrap my arms around my legs and curl into as small of a ball as I can. I've never been tall, and I've gotten so thin Earl Rae's brought me back children's sized clothes from thrift stores whenever I've needed something new. I imagine becoming so small they won't see me. I imagine becoming invisible so that once they're done doing whatever they're doing, they'll leave and never find me.

I've been taken once by a man I didn't know. I don't want to be taken again by a bunch of men I don't know.

I've almost convinced myself they won't find me when I notice two dark shadows kneel beside the table. I shiver and try crawling farther under the table. The collar cuts into me, and I cry out in pain.

The two men don't crawl under the table after me. Instead, they stay where they are, one of them taking off his helmet slowly. I don't recognize his face, not that I would. I'm not sure I'd recognize my parents' faces anymore.

The man beside him also removes his helmet. One is older, the other younger. They both have clean-cut faces and look friendly enough, but I know from Earl Rae that these kinds of faces aren't to be trusted.

"Jade Childs?" the older man says, lifting his hands when I try crawling away again.

The collar tears at my scab as I move. I feel more warm trickles wind down my neck, soaking into the collar of my sweater.

Both men look at me like they're having to try very hard to keep a brave face. The younger one has a harder time with this. Each time his eyes drop to my collar, the length of chain trailing off of it, he diverts his eyes like the sight is too much for him.

I don't blame him though. The first time I saw my reflection in the mirror— that metal collar fitted around my neck—I threw up. I didn't stop until my stomach was empty and my throat felt raw from the acid.

When I don't say anything, the older man lowers his hands and digs something out of the front pocket of his vest. It's a photocopy of a picture of a girl. Not the same girl whose photo is hanging on the wall beside me.

"Are you Jade Childs?" he asks me, turning the photo toward me.

I stare at the picture for a minute, trying to remember her. I stare at it for another minute, trying to remember what she liked and who she was and what her dreams were. I can't though because that girl's gone. The life and soul was choked out of that girl years ago, compliments of the collar still around her neck and the man who locked it there.

The men are waiting for my answer, so I shake my head and look away. "No, I'm not her. I'm Sara Jackson."

Three

I EXPERIENCED A living nightmare once. I'd hoped life would spare me a repeat.

My head is foggy from the drugs they've pumped into me. My body's numb from the same. When I tried ripping out the IV so I could attempt to invoke one clear thought of my own, my hands were confined. They keep telling me I've been saved and am safe, but so far, none of this feels any different from what Earl Rae did to me.

He burst into my life and took me without my consent as they did. He confined me to a small space, pumping me full of drugs as they are doing. He punished me when I didn't do what he wanted as they have. He restrained me when I resisted, taking away my freedom, just as they have.

If this is what being saved means, I want a pass. I want my old life in that small house in the middle of nowhere back because at least there, I'd gotten used to it. I had a schedule. I had fifteen feet of freedom inside a house instead of being strapped to a small hospital bed.

I've been told I'm at Seattle Mercy Hospital in Seattle, but I'm not sure how long I've been here or really much of anything else. The nurses and doctors whisk out as quickly as they whisk in. With the drugs pulling me under every few minutes, I've probably only been here for hours instead of the days it feels like.

I could ask. They probably would answer me. I could ask what happened to Earl Rae. I could ask where I've been living for years. I could ask just how many years I've been missing. I could ask any one of the million questions I have, but I don't because I know the answers can be summed up in one phrase—I don't want to know.

If I want any chance of making whatever kind of life a person like me can have going forward, I have to bury all of the past and pretend it doesn't exist. The only way to have a future is to murder the past. To cut its throat, let it bleed out, and bury it in an unmarked grave.

The machines surrounding me beep every few seconds. I guess that means I'm alive, but I've never felt so dead. Well, other than those first few months after Earl Rae took me. The machine on my left shows my heart's still beating, but it isn't. Not really.

The room is dark and quiet. They gave me a private room when I was whisked in, and I'm thankful for that. My life has been so small for so long I'm not sure what would happen if I were thrown into all of the stimulation of the outside world all at once. The light, the noise, the smells, the people . . . I panic just thinking about it.

My head's melting into my pillow again—the drugs are strong—when the door opens. At first I think it's a man coming in, but when the person moves closer, I can see it's a woman. She has short hair, is tall enough to play in the WNBA, and is in slacks and a button-down shirt. She isn't dressed like the doctors and nurses. She isn't in a SWAT uniform either. She's wearing normal clothes—the first person I've seen in them.

She moves slowly across the room after closing the door. Her shoes barely make a noise on the tile floor. "Good evening. I'm Dr. Argent. I'm a psychiatrist who works with the hospital in certain instances. Is it okay if I sit down and talk with you for a minute?"

I can only imagine the things she wants to "talk" about. I'm not sure what her clinical term for me would be, but I know what the layman's term is—a head case. I've been kidnapped and held captive, and I actually tried evading rescue when a team of police officers came to "save" me. She's probably already working on a book deal for this mess of a case.

"Certain instances?" My throat's dry because of the drugs. In the closet, I spent what felt like a year with severe cottonmouth. It isn't a feeling I associate with pleasant memories.

"Exactly." Dr. Argent moves closer, still slowly, and reaches for the pitcher of water on my bedside table. She pours some into a glass.

"Certain instances being a girl who's been found years after her kidnapping?"

She doesn't commit to my assumption. Instead she rolls her hand. "Anyone the hospital staff feels could benefit from talking with me."

She holds the glass out for me, but I don't lift my head. Cottonmouth's uncomfortable, but not as much as drinking from a cup being held by a shrink because my hands are restrained.

"I don't have much of a chance for a normal life, do I? After all of this?" I shake my head when she tips the cup in front of me. "I know the stories of other girls who were taken and held for years. They don't acclimate back into society very well."

She shrugs in a suit-yourself kind of way and sets the cup back down. "True, some don't adjust back into what you call normal life well. But some do. That's why I'm here and why I'm hoping you'll be receptive to speaking with me."

"*Some* do?" I repeat. "Don't you mean most don't?"

"And if some—even one person—have done it, that means it can be done. That means you can do it too." She pauses like she's hoping those words will wind their way inside me, but that door, the one receptive to optimism, was sealed shut years ago. "You don't have to let what happened to you define the rest of your life. You don't have to tell yourself you have no chance for a normal life, because guess what? There's no such thing as a normal life. You can make a new life for yourself— however you want to build it."

My throat itches. I need to scratch it, but I can't with my wrists restrained. I try twisting my neck around on the pillow, but that's useless. "I already built the kind of life I wanted. Years ago. I want that life back."

"And why can't you have it back?" she asks gently.

I haven't had a conversation with another person in forever. Even with Earl Rae, we never really conversed. We exchanged words and a sentence here and there, but we never sat down and just talked. I feel out of practice. I don't recognize the voice or words or edge of bitterness in my tone. I'm the one talking, but it feels like someone else is calling the shots as to what's said and how it's said.

"Because the girl who created it is dead," I say at last.

"No, she's not. She's lying in this bed right in front of me."

I exhale loudly. "You know what I mean."

"No, I don't." Dr. Argent shakes her head. "I believe we're all free to create whatever kind of life we want on whatever day we choose. I believe, yes, you are going to have more challenges getting there than most would, but I one hundred percent know you have a chance at a new life. A *good* life."

"A good life like becoming a hermit afraid to leave a house? Scared to wake up each day and realize there's no waking up from the nightmare? Unable to have anything close to another loving, trusting relationship ever again?" I turn my head away from Dr. Argent. "That kind of good life those other girls are just reveling in?"

"No, the kind of life you want, not the one that comes easiest. The one you have to work really hard for. *That* kind of good life, so when someone else in my shoes has to sit down with another girl like you someday in the future, she can say *some* girls have risen above what happened to them and mean it. So the next girl can have a little more hope that it's possible."

I look at the ceiling as she slides into the chair beside my bed. I can't keep talking about new lives and possibilities and overcoming the odds. I can't talk about all of that positive shit because it's just too damn depressing. Because I know . . . I'm too fucked up to even hope any of that's a possibility for me now. "Aren't you supposed to be like, I don't know, understanding? I've been through something most people, a psychologist especially, would be sensitive to."

Dr. Argent lifts her hands like she's holding something in them. "You know how medical doctors have those electric paddles to bring a person's heart back to life?"

My eyebrows move together. "Yeah?"

"I like to think of my 'unique' approach as those paddles that jolt your psyche back to life." She lowers her hands and shrugs. "What you do after this is up to you, but at least it's back. You can feel it, can't you?"

My psyche? My soul? My feelings? I'm sure what she's talking about specifically, but I do feel something stirring. I think it's irritation more than anything, but she's right—at least I can feel something. "You're kind of crazy . . . and I'm supposed to be the crazy one."

Dr. Argent leans in like she's about to tell me a secret. "Life is the great maker of crazy. No one's immune."

I'm not sure if that's more reassuring or depressing, but I know it's true. After everything, I'm starting to wonder if the whole point of life is to see how much each person can take before they break.

"I'm sorry you got stuck with me," I say because how frustrating must working with me be for a person whose profession is to help piece back together a person's life? Mine has been totally and irrevocably obliterated.

"Actually, I requested your case. I couldn't wait for the chance to meet you."

I would have laughed if my throat wasn't burning. "It's such an honor to meet the stupid girl who managed to get herself kidnapped by a total stranger a whole twenty feet away from her front door, right?"

Dr. Argent crosses her legs and folds her hands in her lap. She doesn't have a pen and notepad like I would have expected. You know, so she could make notes for her book deal. "It's an honor to meet a strong woman who managed to survive ten years of captivity with a severely mentally ill man. It's an honor to meet a survivor."

This time I do laugh. It comes out ragged-sounding though. Like I've spent most of my life puffing on a cigarette. "Yeah, well, I didn't really have a lot of choice in the matter. He kind of kept me chained up for ten years"— *God, has it really been that long? I guessed closer to eight.*—"and it wasn't like he starved me or beat me senseless, so I didn't really have a choice in the whole surviving part. It was kind of forced on me, because that wouldn't have been my choice."

My eyes shut. After those first months spent locked in that dark closet, the months—or hell, years—that followed were dark ones. I held on to too much of the old part of me, and I wanted to die. If I had been given the opportunity, I probably would have taken it. It wasn't until I forced myself to strangle the life out of the girl I'd been that life got better. I could be Sara Jackson more easily when Jade

Childs was dead. The life I had wasn't so bad when I didn't compare it to the one I'd had before.

"Do you know how old you are, Jade?" Dr. Argent asks. "Or would you prefer I call you Sara? That's what you told the officers your name was when they found you."

"My name's Jade. You can call me Jade." I open my eyes and stare at the ceiling tiles.

"That doesn't necessarily mean that's what you want to be called."

"I *want* to be called Jade," I say slowly. "The sooner I get back to my old life, the better off I'll be." It's a lie, but I'm telling her what she wants to hear. I hope it doesn't backfire on me because I'd like to pass the shrink test and move on to . . . whatever comes next. "And I'm twenty-seven," I add because even though I hadn't known I was missing for ten years, I can still do simple math. Seventeen plus ten equals twenty-seven.

My God, I'm almost thirty.

My stomach roils.

"That's right. It's June, so you just had your birthday." Dr. Argent's voice stays the same no matter what she says. It doesn't change even when mine does. I guess that's what years of college and hundreds of thousands of dollars in school loans will get you—a level, emotionless voice. "Do you know the name of the man who kidnapped you?"

I barely have time to absorb that I'm in my mid-twenties before she thrusts me into the next difficult topic. "Earl Rae Jackson." My tongue drills into the side of my cheek when I say his name. I don't know why.

"Do you know where you were being held?" She crosses her legs and leans back like she's getting comfortable.

This is one of the most uncomfortable experiences of my life.

"In an old house. Somewhere in the country." I wet my lips and think. How could I have lived somewhere for a decade and have no idea where, in what city in which state, I was?

"That's right. You were just outside of Bellingham."

Bellingham. In the same exact state. So close to home . . . what took them so long? Why couldn't they have found me before I lost myself? Why . . .?

That had been the tenor of my early years with Earl Rae, and it messed me up good—I'm not going back there. Asking why doesn't do anything. It can't fix what had happened. Asking why doesn't belong in the future; it belongs in the past.

"Do you need anything, Jade?" Dr. Argent pauses like she's waiting for me to rattle off some laundry list of things I need.

Maybe I do need plenty of things, but none of those things can be picked up at a grocery store. I let the silence continue.

"The doctors say that, given your circumstance, you're quite healthy. It's hard for them to say until the bloodwork comes back, but it doesn't appear as though you have any vitamin or mineral deficiencies, and with some exercise and time, I'm told you'll be able to run marathons by next summer if you so desire."

I hear the smile in her voice, but I don't understand it. Why is she smiling? What's there to smile about? So I don't have any vitamin deficiencies—I have plenty of others that can't be fixed by pills and sunshine.

"He took care of me. Made sure I had vitamins. Access to a treadmill and some weights. I had to eat healthy, no sugar. He even brought home antibiotics the one time my neck managed to get too infected. I didn't survive ten years because he neglected me." When I swallow, I feel the gauze wound around my neck. It's not too tight, but it feels strange. Foreign. I'm used to something heavy and cold circling my neck, not something light and gentle. It makes me uncomfortable.

"Did he abuse you, Jade?"

Her question hits me hard. So hard I need to shake my head to clear it before I can answer. I'd known this question would come. I spent enough time fantasizing about being rescued that I'd run through what my life would be like after being found. Questions. Morbid curiosity. Everyone telling me they wished me the best but secretly believing I didn't stand a chance. No one able to look at me without seeing me as a victim. No one able to not wonder what Earl Rae had done to me.

"Are you asking if he raped me?" I don't flinch. I just blink at the ceiling and wait.

"I'm asking if he abused you."

"If he raped me."

Dr. Argent is quiet for a minute. I'm not making this easy on her, but she isn't making this easy on me either.

"There are more abuses than rape, Jade."

I don't need her to tell me that. Actually, it upsets me, pisses me off that this person who's studied books is telling me how abuse works.

"The answer is no. He never touched me like that." I swallow because my throat is on fire. From the drugs and now the emotions clawing at it. "I was his daughter. He never raped me. I'm fine . . . so you can move on to another patient who needs you."

I'm Sara, your daughter. I missed you, Dad. I'm so glad you found me. I love you. Those phrases have been so programmed into me I'm not sure I'll ever be able to forget them. In a way, they're the words that freed me. Once I finally gave in to playing the role of his daughter, I was allowed out of the closet. I moved from the dark to the light. I went from being a prisoner to a priceless family member.

"He didn't rape you, but he did kidnap you, held you against your will for ten years, and kept you chained up." Dr. Argent lets that hang in the air. She isn't waiting for me to respond; she just wants to make sure that gets good and embedded in my head. Since clearly my head wasn't messed up enough. "This isn't something a person can just get over, Jade. It's not something they can just be 'fine' from a day later."

I wish the drugs would carry me back under again, but my adrenaline's probably burning through them too quickly. I want to fall asleep and wake up to find that I'm all ready to move on and my scars have faded away.

"Well, I can." My voice breaks, and I look at the cup

of water. I wet my lips again. "I just want to forget it all. I can't do that if you keep asking me questions, okay?" My fingers tremble. I ignore them. "I just want to forget the past ten years of my life."

"You know that isn't possible." Her harsh words are spoken softly.

"I know I can *try*." I shift in the bed, but my body feels limp. Kind of the way it felt for a couple of days after he drugged me the night he took me. "Is he dead?"

My voice is so quiet I'm surprised she hears me.

"Earl Rae Jackson?" She just barely nods. "Yes, he's dead. He shot himself."

Something squeezes at my heart, and when I swallow this time, I can't. Something's stuck in my throat. "What are they going to do with his body?"

"I don't know, but I can find out if you'd like." Dr. Argent uncrosses her legs and crosses them the other direction.

"Will they have a funeral?"

"I'm not sure. Would you like me to ask?"

I shake my head, and it's only then that I realize I've started to cry. They're silent tears, but they come one right after the other, feeling as though they're carving canyons down my temples. "No, I don't care what happens to him."

I want to wipe the tears away so I can pretend they'd never been there. I want to swipe them away so she can't see them. I want to stop crying altogether because I learned a long time ago that tears do nothing but make a person feel worse.

Dr. Argent's quiet for a second. Then she clears her

throat. "You know, it's very common for victims in your situation to form some sort of attachment to their captors."

I close my eyes, but really, I want to cover my ears. I don't want to hear any of this.

"It can happen in a matter of days, and with you being under his control for a decade—the only person you had contact with—it would be very normal for you to feel some kind of bond with him."

The tears don't stop. They come faster. "He took my whole life away. I hate him."

Dr. Argent scoots the chair a little closer. "You're crying."

I laugh a few notes. They don't sound like most laughs though. "In case you missed it, it's been a rough decade for me."

"You weren't crying until I mentioned Earl Rae."

Goddamn shrinks and their being all observant and forming conclusions. I've dealt with enough in my life—I shouldn't have to put up with this bullshit. She can't ask me a few questions, witness a few tears, then leap to the opinion that I fit the mold of this case study she read about or that one her college professors discussed once upon a time.

I'm a person—not a diagnosis.

"Could you please just leave? Now?" I manage to swallow the mass lodged in my throat. "I don't want to talk about what happened. I don't want to talk about him. I just want to get on with my life."

There's a knock at the door, and someone pops their head inside. I don't know who it is, but Dr. Argent clearly does. She lifts her hand to indicate they should wait, and the person disappears and closes the door.

Her attention lands on me again. "Ten years have gone by, Jade. You can't just go back to being a high school senior. Your friends will have changed. Some might be married and have families." Her shoulders lift like that was that. "You can't go back to that same life, but that doesn't mean you can't make a new one that's just as good."

I twist as much as I'm able until my back's facing her. "Please go."

She doesn't say anything for a moment, but she doesn't get up and leave either. "Your family's here. They're waiting outside."

My lungs deflate. My family. I spent the last decade pretending to be someone else's family until I almost stopped thinking about my real one at all. It hurt too much.

"I asked them to wait for me to talk with you before the doctors let them in."

I imagine my body being cast in steel until I'm certain nothing can penetrate it. That's a trick I learned when I was with Earl Rae—if I built strong enough defenses, nothing could get through. "Let them in."

"Do you remember their names, Jade?"

I look back at her, insulted. That look fades when I realize I don't. At least not right away. Not automatically like everyone else in the world can list off the names of their family members. One name is still there—it never faded—but I can't say his name because his is the one that hurts the most.

I bite my cheek and search my memory. They're there. I know they are. Earl Rae tried to strangle them out of me, but he didn't get all of it. "Mike and Eleanor Childs—my parents' names. Connor and Sam—Samantha—are my brother's and sister's names." I want to say his name. I want to know if she's seen him. I want to ask if he's here.

I want him back . . . but that was another lifetime. The girl who loved him is gone. The girl he loved is gone.

"That's right, Jade. Good. They're all here. They came in as soon as they heard you'd been found. They're anxious to see you."

"Then why aren't they in here with us?"

Dr. Argent looks at the ceiling like I am doing, probably to see if she's missing out on anything. "I've worked with others like you, and most find it overwhelming to have everyone all at once just burst back into their life. It can be a lot to take in."

I feel my eyebrows lifting. "You're drilling me about what Earl Rae did to me and pressuring me to be the second girl to rise above, and you're worried a reunion with my family will be overwhelming?"

"Nice summation. Your mental acumen seems in good shape too."

She's trying to make a joke, I think. It's been forever since I've heard a joke—Earl Rae didn't have the talent for them.

"I had books, loads of books, and nothing but time to study. As my body weakened, I tried to keep my mind strong."

Dr. Argent nods. "That's good, Jade. That will make

acclimating back into everyday life that much easier." Her stare moves to the door. "Back to your family. There's nothing wrong with needing a little more time before seeing them. I know they'll understand. They want what's best for you—whatever that is."

I squirm in the bed. "They're my family."

"And as good as their intentions are, chances are they'll revert to treating you like you're the exact same girl you left them as. You can't move on when everyone's treating you like you never changed."

She stands and pulls a pair of large nail clippers from her pocket. She cuts through the tie holding my left wrist. Then she moves around the foot of my bed and does the same with the right. She doesn't ask if I'll leave my IV in if she cuts me free. She doesn't warn me that if I try it again, my wrists will be rebound. She just cuts me free like that's all there's left to do.

"I'd advise you to ease yourself back into your old life. Little bits at a time, not the whole thing all at once." She unwinds the second restraint and tosses it into the garbage, pocketing the clippers again.

I rub my wrists for a second, then I reach for the cup of water. I sit up and drain it in one drink. I may not be ready to see them, but if I wait until I am, it might never happen. I have to pick my life up where I left off. As best as I can. This is part of that process.

"Let them in."

Four

I HAVEN'T SEEN them in ten years. The ten minutes I wait for them feels like another ten years.

Before she left, Dr. Argent told me I'd gotten to Seattle Mercy around three in the afternoon. It's almost nine o'clock at night now. A lot has happened in the less than twelve hours since I've been rescued. Tests have been run. A shrink has "shrunk" me. I'm about to be reunited with my family.

It's a lot to take in all at once, like Dr. Argent warned me, but I'm not about to tap the brakes. I'll be okay. I've dealt with a lot. I can deal with this. I can deal with whatever comes. I'm strong.

These are the things I feel like I have to repeat to myself until I've convinced myself of them. *I'm okay. I can deal with whatever comes my way. I'm strong.*

I've brainwashed myself before—I can do it again.

That's what's playing on a reel in my head when a knock sounds outside my door right before it opens. I've raised the back of my bed so I'm more sitting up than lying down, and I've been a good patient and left my IV in my arm where the doctors want it. My wrists still burn a little from the restraints but not so bad a little cream and rubbing can't fix it.

Who's going to come in first? Who will it be?

I feel like I should know this. I lived with these people for seventeen years and Earl Rae only ten. I should know them well enough to be able to figure out who'll be the brave one to slip through the door first.

Dad. That's who it will be. He's always been the head of the household, and we all knew it. He'll be the first one through the door.

I'm wrong.

It's my mom. I don't recognize her at first. It isn't until she half says, half cries my name that I know it's her. She might look different, but her voice is the same.

"Sweetheart . . ." she says-cries next, walking forward a few steps before waiting for everyone else to file in behind her.

Dad comes next. He looks the same. Exactly the same. His hair's still precisely parted to the side, his moustache is as prominent as ever, and he still enters a room like he owns it. Unlike Dad, Mom's hair has started to gray and she's lost weight. Probably as much as I have. She looks . . . old—like thirty years have gone by instead of ten. I wonder if I look the same.

Dad doesn't say anything at first. He just looks at me for a moment, then he has to look away. His hand moves to his mouth, and his back shakes.

"Hi, Dad." I have to remind myself to call him dad. It

NICOLE WILLIAMS

doesn't come naturally anymore.

When I speak, he turns around a little. His hands settle on his hips, and his back shakes again.

"Oh my god, Jade." Mom wipes her eyes. They're raining tears. "Thank god they found you."

She moves a few steps closer, but it feels like they're hanging back. Waiting for an invitation from me or to gather up a little more courage. I don't know. I feel as uncertain what to do and say next as they do.

Two more people come through the door. They hang back by Dad, almost like they're trying to hide in his imposing shadow. I don't recognize them. At first.

A decade has a way of really changing a ten- and fourteen-year-old. My brother, Connor, has a goatee and is wearing a University of Washington tee. He's tall like our dad but doesn't have the same wide shoulders. He tries to smile at me, but it doesn't last long. He rubs the back of his head and leans into the wall.

Sam looks a lot like Mom—or a lot like she had. Sam looks put together and polished, the way I remember her looking as a fourteen-year-old. She can't even look at me but stays an arm's length from the door, shifting from one foot to the next every few seconds.

This is my family. How can I feel this uncomfortable around them? How can they feel so uncomfortable around me that they can barely stand to look at me?

I reach for my cup of water. It's empty. I grab the pitcher. It's empty too.

The longer the silence stretches on, the more I wish I'd taken Dr. Argent's advice and waited on the family reunion thing. I don't know what I was picturing, but this isn't it.

"So . . . how have you guys been?" I ask.

Mom sniffs and keeps moving closer. "Let's not talk about how we've been. Let's talk about what we're going to do now that you're back. Now that you're home."

When she notices Dad, Sam, and Connor still huddled close to the door, she waves them over. Connor moves first, then Dad. Sam last.

"We've missed you, sweetie. So, so much." Mom chokes on a sob.

Dad comes up behind her and rubs her back. I know now why Dad angled himself away from me at first. His eyes are red-rimmed, and his face is puffy. He's been crying. Maybe he still is. I've never seen my dad cry. Never. Not even when he found out one of his men had been killed in action. Not even when he spoke at the funeral. I didn't think it was possible.

Looking at my family hovering at the foot of my bed, I realize I'm not the only one who's suffered. They've been broken too. They might not have been held by a chain for ten years, but they've clearly been tied to other chains that have held them back.

Guilt floods my stomach then, spreading to my legs and arms. This is my fault. My mom looking like she's twice her age, my dad's iron wall crumbling, my brother and sister barely able to look at me—it's my fault.

"I'm sorry," I choke out, biting my cheek so I won't start crying again. There are already enough tears in this room. "I'm so sorry."

Mom rushes to my side first, whipping her head from side to side and reaching for me. "No, Jade. Don't apologize. No, baby," she coos, leaning over me and winding her tiny arms around me like she's trying to hold me the way a new mother might cradle her infant. Kind of awkward at first but carefully. "You're back. That's all that matters. You're back." Mom's arms tighten around me as her head lowers beside mime.

It's too much. Her arms and the hold and her head next to mine and the perfume I smell on her and the fabric softener I smell on her blouse. The words she keeps repeating right beside my ear are no more than a whisper, but it feels like she's screaming. It's too much.

I wiggle beneath her, my arms feeling stuck at my sides. That's when the rest of them move in. Dad leans over me on the other side, and while Mom's tiny arms feel like they're strangling the life out of me, when Dad wraps his giant arms around me and holds me close, I feel like my body's snapping into a hundred tiny pieces. I feel my bones smashing into powder. My organs liquefying. My skin being rubbed raw.

"Stop," I choke out, squirming.

Sam and Connor stay back, but Connor takes a seat on the edge of my bed and pats my leg a few times. It feels like he just stuck a hot brand into my calf.

I cry out.

They don't hear. Or if they do, they take my cries to be the same as theirs—the happy ones from the reunion.

"Stop. Please." My voice is so tight it's not even a whisper.

Still, they keep holding me, smashing me, confining me, screaming in my ear, assaulting my every sense until I feel like I'm burning from the inside out.

"Let go." This time I'm not even sure if I verbalized the words. I can't tell.

I feel something bubble up from my stomach. I'm not sure what it is, but it feels molten hot and explosive. I harness whatever it is and force it to the surface. It feels like all the survival instinct I have left.

"Stop," I plead with a whisper.

No one hears. They just keep suffocating me. Whatever survival instinct I have left, it isn't enough. That's dead too.

My body does the only other thing it can to save itself—it shuts down.

Five

I'D BEEN HAVING a nightmare. I wake up to a nightmare too.

Asleep, awake, it doesn't seem to matter. I'm haunted by things in both worlds.

The shades are open when I wake up, but it's all the way dark outside now. The clock across from me reads two. Five hours have gone by since I passed out. I've experienced the feeling enough to know what happened. I passed out most days after I was first taken by Earl Rae. I think it's my body's way of dealing with extreme fear. Or maybe it's my brain's way of shutting down so it can reboot and try harder next time. I don't know. I just know I don't usually pass out for such long stretches.

The drugs still pumping through my IV probably have something to do with that though.

My family's gone, which I feel guilty for being relieved by. I hadn't realized how hard it would be. If I can't even handle four members of my family, how will I deal with the rest of the world? If I can't handle a simple embrace from my dad and mom, how can I get back to my old life? My life had been filled with people and activities and places and . . . I'm not sure how I can handle it all if the city lights of downtown Seattle glowing through my window are overstimulating.

My mouth's dry again, but my pitcher is still empty.

I'm just pressing the call button when a nurse slips through my door. I haven't met this one yet. She probably works the night shift. Just from the scrubs she has on, I know I'm going to like her better than the day-shift Nurse Ratcheds I've dealt with.

"You awake, honey?" the nurse asks, lowering her glasses down her nose.

I nod, almost smiling when I notice the teddy bears on her scrubs are holding balloon bouquets.

"You up for a visitor? Or would you rather rest? I know it's late."

She doesn't talk so loud that it feels like a scream or so soft that I can't hear her. Her voice is just right. I suddenly feel like Goldilocks finding just the right chair.

I'm about to answer that I'd rather rest when she adds, "If you're going to see any visitors, this would be the one to see." Her dark brows bounce a couple of times. "Trust me."

My head lifts from the pillow "Who is it?" It's been a long time, but I still recognize the sound of hope in my voice. The tone of anticipation.

"I'd be just fine calling him Tall, Dark, and Handsome, but I suppose he's got a name." The nurse looks out the door like he's standing right there.

It's been years, but even back then, he fit that criteria. My heart climbs into my throat. "What's his name?"

Her shoulders wag. "Don't know. Didn't ask." She cranes her head out the door again. "Want me to ask him, honey?"

"That's okay. You can let him in." I find myself trying to get a good look out the door, but other than a stream of yellow light, I can't see anything.

"Good choice." She winks before turning to leave. She stops when she gets halfway out the door. "You need anything?"

I might have needed something, but I'm too nervous to think about it. "No, thank you."

He's here. I don't know how I know that, but I do.

Torrin's here.

Thinking his name makes my heart convulse. I don't know what saying it will do. I can't imagine what seeing him will do to me. Hopefully I won't pass out like I did with my family.

The room's quiet for a minute after the nurse leaves. I should use the time to adjust my hospital gown or comb my fingers through my hair or pinch a little color into my cheeks because I know how pale I am. Lack of sunshine will do that to a person.

Instead, I sit here, feeling like my heart's both swelling and shrinking at the same time.

I lift the head of my bed a little more, and just when I'm wishing I'd asked the nurse for a water refill, I notice the shadow in the doorway. It is him.

My breath stops.

He stays there for a moment, hovering in the doorway, staring at the shadow his body casts on the gleaming tile. I watch his shoulders rise and fall as he breathes, but I can't make out anything else. My gaze automatically lowers to his left hand, but I can't see his fingers with the way he's standing.

A minute later, he steps inside my room. His shoes echo on the tile, making me wonder if he's exchanged his soccer flats for a pair of dress shoes, which makes me wonder what else has changed.

If he's changed anything like I have, I probably won't even know the person he is now.

He closes the door, snuffing out the bright light from the hall. After blinking a few times, I can see him. Better at least. I would have thought spending as much time as I have in the dark would make it easier for me to see in it, but the opposite seems to be true.

Every few blinks, my eyesight adjusts a little more, until I can make out what he's wearing: a pair of dark slacks, what look like matching dress shoes, and a dark green raincoat still zipped up. It wasn't raining earlier. It doesn't look like it's raining now.

His face I look at last, mainly because I know it's going to feel like a wrecking ball's driving through me.

I'm right.

He looks the same. At least other than the decade that's touched him. He's taller, wider in the shoulders, and the boyish softness of his face has been ironed out into square angles and straight lines. He still wears his hair the same—looking like it's a few weeks past needing a hair-

71

cut—and it's as dark and inky as I remember.

And then there are his eyes. How many times have I pictured them since that last night we were together? How many times have I tried to draw them to find I could never get them right? How many times have I concentrated on his light eyes, finding a warmth in them that touched me even on my darkest days?

They practically glow in the dark. When he blinks, it's like all of the light has been siphoned out of the world.

He makes his way farther into my room, stopping when he's in front of my bed, but he keeps his distance. He stays closer to the wall than my bed.

My heart feels like it's pulsing against my tonsils now, and even if I knew what to say, I'm sure I couldn't get it out.

He opens his mouth, but nothing comes out. He tries again, but the same thing happens. Clamping his mouth closed, he rubs the back of his head like he used to when he was trying to figure something out. The familiarity of it makes my body ache.

"I thought I knew what I was going to say." His voice is a little deeper but the same. The ache boils into a throb. "I've been planning it for the past ten years, but now that I'm standing here in front of you, nothing I planned to say sounds right." He continues to rub the back of his head, focusing on the floor in front of him, his brows pinched together like something's hurting him.

"I did the same thing—thinking about what I'd say to you if I ever got to see you again." My voice sounds small in comparison to his, but that line between his brows pinches deeper with every word. I wonder if I'm the one hurting him. Like my family, he's been hurt by my disappearance too. I know that. "None of it sounds right now that you're here."

He nods a few times. His hair falls over his forehead like it used to when he played soccer. Like it had that last night we spent together . . .

"God, Jade." He swallows. His throat bobs as though he's swallowing an apple whole. "How are you?"

That's when he finally looks at me. Like, really looks at me. His eyes stay on mine for a moment, then they lower to my neck. Something flashes in his eyes when he studies the bandages wound around it. Something that makes his expression darken.

I don't want to lie to him. But I really don't want to tell him the truth. He's suffered enough with the rest of us.

"Considering everything that happened"—I wring the blanket covering me—"I'm doing good."

Torrin can't stop staring at my neck. I think he wants to, but his eyes won't let him. Maybe I should have thrown on a scarf or something. I know it's an eyesore—something eyes can't help but be drawn to.

He forces his eyes to mine. They're darker than before. "I'm happy you're back." He shoves off of the wall and moves closer.

The air grows a little thinner. "I'm happy to see you."

It's a play on words because really, I haven't decided if I'm happy to be back. I should be. It's what everyone else assumes I feel, but it's too early to know. I am happy to see him though. That I don't have to think about.

Torrin doesn't miss my twist on words. "I know it's late, and I'm sorry . . . I was going to give you some time before I just showed up, but I was here and I knew you were, and I couldn't . . ." He looks away, his throat bobbing. "Walk away."

I feel a brow lift. "You were just in the neighborhood?"

"Yeah, kind of." Torrin's shoulders lift. "I was visiting someone else in the hospital."

"Hopefully they're in better shape than me," I say, kind of joking, kind of serious.

"Actually, they're dying."

I lift up in bed a little. "God, Torrin, I'm sorry. Rough night for you."

He shakes his head. "I've had lots of rough nights."

"Used to them?"

"More like equipped to handle them."

Heaviness thickens around us. I've drowned in it so many times, but I don't want Torrin to experience it. I don't want him to know what it feels like to have your lungs feel like they're about to explode from holding your breath right before they turn to stone when you lose the battle.

"So what have you been up to the past ten years?" I try to keep my voice light, but there's too much heaviness now.

His tongue drills into his cheek as he stares out the big window. This is hard for him. I wish I could make it easier. I wish I could convince him I'm okay and that I will be and that even when I was gone, I was okay.

I'd give anything.

I feel like I've already given everything though.

"Looking for you." He shrugs. "Living. I wasn't very good at the living part though."

He's trying to lighten the mood too. He's better at it than I am based on the smile I feel wanting to form, but he's lost his knack for it. I don't need to ask why.

"Anything else you've been up to?" My eyes drop to his hands again. I don't see a ring, but that doesn't mean he doesn't have someone. That doesn't mean someone doesn't have him.

My stomach feels like I've dropped fifty floors in one shallow breath.

"I graduated. Kind of." He's still staring at the Seattle skyline, but it's like he isn't seeing any of it. "Then I went to college, and they took mercy on me and let me graduate too."

I wonder what he studied. I wonder what kind of job he has. I wonder if he went to senior prom. I wonder about everything.

"You were always a good student."

A small laugh escapes his lips. "I *was* a good student. Kind of hard to keep that up when I spent most of my time trying to find you."

"You looked for me?" I say it like a question, but I already know the answer.

I'd caught a glimpse of him on some national news station when Earl Rae had slipped out and I'd stolen a few minutes of TV time. Torrin was giving an interview to one of those big news anchors, wearing a T-shirt with my picture on it, and talking about how he hadn't given up on finding me even though it seemed like the rest of the country had. That was two years after my kidnapping.

"Of course I looked for you. Everyone did. Your dad and the department turned this city upside down looking for you. I never stopped looking for you. I'd still be looking for you if they hadn't found you." He pops his knuckles and wanders a little closer.

The air thins again.

"I feel weird talking about myself with everything that happened to you. We should be talking about you, not me."

I shift in bed. I don't want to talk about me. I'd much rather talk about him. "I spent the last ten years in the same house, with the same man, on a fifteen-foot length of chain." The words spill from my mouth like an avalanche, gaining speed with each one. I can't stop them. I can't take them back. "There. Now we've talked about what I've been up to."

He swallows another apple, his forehead creasing. "Jade—"

"I don't want to talk about it, Torrin."

It's the first time I've said his name in months. Maybe years. It seems to hit him as hard as it does me. His eyes seal shut.

"A psychiatrist already talked me to death about it earlier, and I'm going to have to go over the whole thing tomorrow with a couple of detectives. I don't want to talk about it any more than I have to."

His fists curl at his sides. He tries to unclench them,

rolling them a few times, but it doesn't work. "He kept you chained up?" The words come out sounding strange. Like his jaw has been wired shut and he's trying to speak.

"It wasn't, like, in a dungeon or anything," I say quickly. I won't mention the first year when I was kept in a dark, damp closet that could have qualified as a dungeon. He doesn't need to know that. His dreams don't need to be haunted by it too. "I got to roam the kitchen, my bedroom, the bathroom . . . even most of the living room." I'm so concerned about making him feel better that talking about Earl Rae doesn't cripple me like it did with Dr. Argent earlier.

He moves closer and looks at the chair beside my bed. He looks like he's going to take a seat, and at the last minute, he stands taller. "Did he . . ." He has to work his jaw loose to continue. "Hurt you?" His eyes flash again.

"Not in the way you're thinking." My voice wobbles. He notices.

He looks away again, but not before I notice him wince. "I'm so sorry, Jade. God, I'm sorry."

I bite my lip because I'm not going to cry in front of him. I'm not going to let him see me in pain. I'm going to end this nightmare for him once and forever. At least one of us can find some peace.

"I am too," I say.

"I never should have let you walk yourself home that night. I shouldn't have left your side until you were inside safe." He stops to take a breath, but he's going to keep going.

I jump in because I know this path. It never ends.

"This isn't your fault, Torrin." My hand curls around the bedrail close to him. "It's not your fault there are sick people in the world."

He stares at my hand, studying it. I wonder if it looks as foreign to him as it does to me. "No, it's my fault I let my girlfriend get taken by one of them."

"No, don't." I shake my head. "That's all in the past now. Forget it. Let it go."

He turns until his back is facing me. Even beneath his rain jacket, I notice him quiver. "I'll never be able to let that go. He took your life from you. He took my life by doing so." Torrin's knuckles pop when his fists curl again. "He took *everything*. I'll never be able to forget it. Never."

I've known Torrin Costigan since we were five and my family moved in down the block. I know him better than I know my own brother and sister. I feel like I know him better than I know myself now. Something's wrong. Other than the obvious.

There's more. I can feel it. I can see it. He's trying to tell me something, but he can't.

Acknowledging that makes my stomach feel like it's being ripped open. "What's the matter?"

"Besides finding out that this whole time you were two hours away?" His voice is rigid just like his posture"

My legs tingle like they're going numb or just waking up from being numb. "What aren't you telling me?"

He takes a moment to reply. "It's been ten years. Probably a lot."

I wait for him to add something else. He doesn't. He doesn't want to say whatever it is, but I need him to. How can I move on unless I know? He was most of my whole life back then. I need to know if he can still be in it. My eyes drop back to his hands again. No ring. But that doesn't mean anything. That just means he isn't married. It doesn't mean he isn't in love. Someone else could crawl into bed beside him every night, curling around his warm body.

Even if there is no one, just because I'm back doesn't mean he wants me back. A decade's gone by. I'm not the same girl he fell in love with. I'm not sure if even a sliver of her is left in the broken woman lying in this hospital bed.

"Your knuckles. You still pop them when you're nervous, you know?" I say when I catch him rolling them again.

He stops the moment I mention it.

"What's wrong?" I ask, turning in the bed to face him.

He doesn't turn around, but his head drops. "I didn't know . . . I wasn't sure . . . if I'd ever see you again. I never stopped looking—I never stopped *hoping*—but I just didn't know."

I'm falling. I'm falling and there's no end. "I didn't think I'd ever see you again either. It's okay. Whatever you have to tell me, I'll understand."

His head lowers even more, and I know that whatever he has to tell me, it might finish the job of breaking me. "You're comforting me," he says to himself. "You're the one who's been through hell, and you're comforting me. It should be the other way around."

I focus on the exposed back of his neck, the bands of muscles pressing through the skin. "Just tell me, Torrin. You and me, that was a lifetime ago. I'm a different person now. You probably are too." I swallow, but this time instead of flames, ice encases my throat. "It's okay."

When he catches himself popping his knuckles again, he slides his hands in his front pants' pockets. "I came prepared to talk about you . . . to see you . . . not to talk about me."

"Plans change." I'm hinting at more than his conversation agenda, and from the way he tips his head back at me, he knows it.

"I wasn't going to tell you this until later. With everything . . . everyone . . . I didn't want to spring one more thing on you right at first."

He's got someone. He's moved on. Part of me is happy, but part of me feels like I'm losing my whole life all over again. Ten years is a long time—a lifetime for teenagers like we were when I was abducted.

He's moved on, and that's a good thing, I remind myself because I know I can't love him anymore the way he deserves to be loved. I've gone too long without feeling it, too long without expressing it, and learning to love again is not like riding a bike—it doesn't come back naturally.

"I'd rather have it all come at me now than spread out over weeks," I say, my hand gripping the bedrail a little tighter. I'm not sure if it's keeping me from drifting off or falling away, but it's keeping me here, with him, and that's where I need to be right now. "The sooner I know it all, the sooner I can move on with my life."

He lets my words stagnate for a minute, then he exhales. It sounds like he's been holding his breath for the past ten years.

"I'm sorry, Jade," he whispers, like he's confessing a crime.

Then I hear him unzip his raincoat followed by the rustle of him shrugging out of it. His back is still to me, and I'm not sure why. Or maybe I do. He can't look me in the face and tell me what he has to. I can't imagine what could be so bad Torrin can't look me in the eye and confess whatever it is.

"It's okay," I say again because it is. Once upon a time, I had the love of a really wonderful person. That's more than most people can claim.

His shoulders tense at my words as he hangs his jacket over the back of the chair. He's dressed in a dark, short-sleeved shirt. Torrin was never much of a black fan. He used to live in faded jeans and colored tees. It looks like darkness has touched him too though. I wonder how deep its claws have gotten into him.

"I thought you were gone." This time it's not a whisper—the words spill from his mouth like he's cursing them.

The bedrail is sticky from my palm sweating. "I know." I have to pause because those two words feel like I've just recited the Bill of Rights in one breath. "It's okay."

He stares out the window for another minute. The city lights don't seem as bright as they did when I woke up. The sparkle's been taken out of them.

Finally, he turns toward me. Slowly. Like he's fighting a herd of wild horses pulling him the other way. His head is bowed, and his arms are at his sides, his hands open and his palms facing me.

At first, all I notice is how perfect he is. Standing in front of me ten years later. The boy I remembered is inside the man in this dark room with me. His dark hair is falling into his eyes, and his jaw is locked the way it's been most of the night.

It isn't until I lower my gaze from his face that I see it. The collar. His is black with one square of white nestled below his Adam's apple, but a collar is a collar—an object meant to control and restrain its wearer.

Instead of answering my questions, it brings on a fresh landslide of them.

My gaze lowers to the black button-down shirt, the matching slacks, and the dress shoes. I can't make any of it make sense.

"Why are you dressed like a priest?" The words don't sound like mine, but no one else in this room could have said them.

His eyes meet mine. "Because this is what I am."

The world is spinning faster than normal. My room is at the vortex of it. I replay my question. I replay his answer. I can't make them agree.

"No, you're not." I feel my forehead crease.

He exhales slowly and moves closer. "Yes. I am."

My heart is beating against my breastbone so hard, it hurts. "You're lying."

Torrin doesn't stop until he's beside my bed again.

It's the closest he's been to me tonight. He's close enough I can make out his scent, and it's the same one I remember. It takes me back to that last night we were together, when I felt surrounded by that smell as I lay below him in his bed. The way it seemed to envelop me like nothing could cut through it.

"I'm telling the truth." His eyes travel to the monitors on the other side of my bed. His brow furrows at one of them. "I finished seminary a year ago. I'm the priest at St. Marks."

St. Marks. I remember it. I remember driving by it and admiring the stained glass windows and gothic architecture. Never once had I driven past it and imagined Torrin being the priest of it one day.

One part of me hopes the drugs pumping through my veins are strong enough to cause hallucinations because maybe then this isn't real. Maybe he isn't really dressed like a priest and admitting he's one. A hallucination seems more real than believing Torrin has become a priest.

"You had to practically be dragged to mass every week. You'd sneak out of Sunday school to spend it making out with me in the church parking lot." I lift my brow at him. He lifts his own brow back. "I thought you would have become a baby seal clubber before a priest."

He moves another foot closer until his belt is almost touching my bedrail. I want to touch him, but I'm not sure I can. I'm not sure if it's allowed or if I'm even capable of it anymore.

"Back then, so did I, but like you said, you've changed." His shoulders lift. "So have I. This is who I am now."

I don't know what to say. Are congratulations in order? An apology? An acceptance? I don't know. All I know is that I feel like I've been saved from one prison only to be tossed into a different one. Life feels no different now that I've been "rescued." I still feel trapped. I still feel alone. I still feel like I can never trust or be close to another human being. I still feel like the girl I was is dead. I still don't know if I want to spend the next sixty years as the woman I've been forced into.

"Your heartbeat—it's too fast." Torrin's eyes narrow on the machine monitoring my heart. "Try to calm down, Jade." He looks at the door then at the nurse's call button.

I take a deep breath. The beeps don't slow down. "I was found less than twenty-four hours ago and just found out my boyfriend became a priest." I try another deep breath. This one doesn't help either. "It's a lot to take in."

Torrin can't stop watching the heart rate monitor. "I'm upsetting you. I'll leave." He backs up a few steps and stops. "I just wanted to see you. I *had* to see you." His jaw tightens like something I can't see is flashing in front of him.

"Did my parents tell you?"

They were here hours ago, so they had plenty of time to call him. They had to know Torrin would want to know.

He shakes his head. "We don't really keep in touch anymore." His hand curls around the handle of my water pitcher. When he notices it's empty, he heads over to the sink. "I think it was too hard for them with everything and, you know, how you'd been coming back from seeing me when you were taken. Plus, I was kind of a prime suspect for a while after you went missing. I don't think your dad's ever really taken me off the suspect list either."

The water spurts on, and his back's to me again. I feel like he's trying to keep some distance between us, but I'm not sure how much. Did he only come tonight to see me one last time before saying good-bye? Or can we get together for coffee every once in a while?

God. The boy I thought I would marry is now the man I'm questioning if it would still be okay to ask out for a latte on occasion. My life has been decimated.

"I'm sorry they didn't call you," I say, trying to sit up a little higher. "And I'm sorry anyone thought you had something to do with me going missing." I hadn't considered that once. I should have. Those closest to a victim are always first on the suspect list, but it just seemed so preposterous that anyone could think Torrin would do something like that to me.

He shrugs and pours some water into my cup before setting the pitcher down beside it. "I'm sorry it took so long for you to be found." He manages a smile that is all guilt and regret. "I should go. It's late."

My hand moves toward him automatically. He's too far away for me to reach him, but he doesn't miss it.

"Don't go. Please." I keep my hand in the air for another second before dropping it onto the mattress. It's too heavy to hold up. "I know he's dead. I know he's never coming back . . . but I'm scared." I drop my eyes. It's not just Earl Rae and what happened that scares me. It's what's waiting for me tomorrow. It's all the tomorrows after that that scare me.

"Do you want me to find a nurse? Maybe they could give you something."

I tilt my head at the IV bag. "They've already given me everything they've got. Just . . ." *What is it?* "I don't want to be alone. Does that make sense?"

I don't know if it does. I've spent the past ten years virtually alone. Why am I so afraid of being alone for one night?

Torrin exhales, his shoulders relaxing. He grabs the leg of the chair with his foot and pulls it to the edge of my bed. "I don't want to be alone either. I'll stay." He takes a seat and scoots a little closer. He almost looks as relieved as I am that he's not leaving. Yet. "As long as you want me, I'll be here. Right at your side."

His hand slips through the bedrail and finds mine. His fingers tie through mine as his palm slides beneath it. His hand is a little bigger than I remember. It's a little rougher too. My fingers knit tightly around his like he's all that's keeping me from slipping away.

It's so natural, so instinctual, it's like I never stopped holding his hand these past ten years.

"I'll stay awake. Keep watch. Okay?" His chin tucks over the bedrail, and this time when he smiles at me, there's no emotion tainting it.

I smile back, the same kind. "Okay."

I roll a little more onto my side so I'm facing him. With the way his head's resting on the rail, it hides his collar. For a moment, I let myself believe that nothing has changed and he's the same boy who asked me to marry him . . . someday . . . one day . . . barefoot and grinning.

I let myself get carried away by that moment. I let myself feel the only joy I've felt in ten years. I let myself feel it . . . then I take an imaginary pin and pop it.

That life died the night I died to the world. That life is gone.

My eyes drop to our combined hands, and I wonder if I should pull away. I wonder if pulling away now instead of later would be easier because I'm not sure I can be friends with the man I once loved. I think doing so would be like dying again every day.

I should pull away.

But I can't.

"Is this okay?" he asks when he notices me staring at our hands. "Me . . . touching you?"

The way he says it makes me think someone warned him about what happened earlier with my family.

My fingers tighten around his. "This is okay."

His smile stays in place. "Good."

He doesn't say anything after that. He doesn't seem to move. He just sits there, holding my hand and staying watch for whatever we're both afraid will come at us next.

Just before sleep is about to pull me under again, I whisper his name.

"Yeah?" His voice doesn't sound sleepy like mine. It sounds the opposite.

"Are you really a priest?"

A soft chuckle vibrates in his chest. It's the single best sound I've heard in a decade. "I really am."

I curl deeper into my pillow. "Why?"

His exhale comes out sounding like he still holds the weight of the world on his back. "Sleep." His thumb skims down the side of my hand. "We've got time to go over all the whys and whats. Just rest."

For one short second, my eyes open, and I see a look on his face that makes my throat tighten. His head isn't on the bedrail anymore, but it's still close. I can see his collar now though. In the darkness, that square of white is almost blinding.

The last thought I have is wondering if his collar feels as confining to him as mine did to me—keeping him from the people he loves and the life he wants to live.

"I missed you, Torrin," I whisper.

I'm more asleep than awake when I hear him exhale. "I miss you, Jade."

Six

I CAN'T WAKE up. I know I'm having a nightmare, but it won't let me go. It won't let me surface from it. The more I fight, the tighter it binds around me, strangling me.

My neck. It's rope instead of metal, but it's twisted around my neck, constricting tighter and tighter with every step I make to wake up. I rip at the rope, trying to tear it away, but I'm helpless against its pull.

Jade.

A voice creeps through the fog of the nightmare.

You're safe. It's okay.

The voice keeps whispering to me until the black shell hardened around me cracks and I see the faintest dot of light.

Wake up. You're safe.

The dot spreads into a hairline crack. More light creeps in, blanketing me. The rope around me loosens.

"Wake up, Jade. I'm here."

The dark shell shatters, and light floods in.

I wake up like I'm drowning, gasping for air and clinging to whatever life raft I can grab hold of. The closest thing to keep me from falling back under is Torrin's arm.

He's leaning over me with an anxious look on his face. He doesn't move. He just stands there, letting me cling to him until I feel like I can let go.

"It was just a dream. It's okay." He looks a little pale, like he was crawling through that hell with me.

"Just a dream," I repeat to myself and force my fingers to loosen before I cut off the circulation in his arm.

I'm coated in sweat, and my blankets and sheets are twisted like a tornado around my legs. It's light outside, and from the looks of the shadows hugging Torrin's eyes, he didn't sleep at all.

"What time is it?" I ask as I release his arm. I've left angry red marks on his skin.

If he notices, he doesn't show it. He just stays beside me, unwinding the twists binding my legs, one at a time, until I'm free.

"Almost nine o'clock." He doesn't look at the clock.

"I slept that long?" I sit up to check the clock on the wall. I have to blink my eyes awake a few times before I can read it. Even then, the numbers are a little foggy.

"Yeah, mostly." He smooths the blankets over my legs now that they're fixed. "Except for the few times you did . . . what you just did."

"But I didn't wake up?" I can't remember any of the nightmares except for the last one. It's a small mercy I'm happy to accept.

collared

"No, I just gave you my arm to cling to each time, and you calmed down." He twists his right arm to check it out. "Remind me to don armor the next time I agree to sit bedside vigil."

There are scratches, welts, and what looks like the start of bruises on his arm. I never would have guessed the kind of strength necessary to inflict that kind of damage was left inside me. "God, Torrin, I'm sorry. You should have just let me scream and flail. I'm used to it."

The breath he'd been exhaling comes up short. "No, I shouldn't have," he says quietly, then he forces a smile. I can tell because his eyes don't join it.

I swing my legs over the side of the mattress suddenly. "I have to get out of here. I have to leave."

Torrin comes up beside me as I test out my legs. "Wait, like . . . *now*?"

"Now."

"Are you sure that's a good idea?"

He holds his arms out as I stand, but I stay upright. My legs feel stronger—stronger than they've felt in a while. "I'm sure it's a good idea."

Standing up, I realize how much taller he's gotten. He's grown at least a few inches since the last time I saw him. That puts me almost at eye-level with his neck—right in line with that black-and-white collar.

It hits me hard again—as hard as it did last night. "How am I supposed to put what happened behind me when this hospital, these doctors and nurses, all of it reminds me of what happened to put me here?" I can't keep staring at his collar, so I walk toward the window. Seattle

91

is buzzing; everyone's on their way, wherever that way leads. I wonder if anyone down there feels like I do—totally and utterly lost. "The longer I stay here, the longer I hang on to what happened, the worse off I'll be."

He's quiet behind me. "Jade, I don't know . . ."

There are too many sounds here. Too many people. Too many strong smells. The bed's too soft and the temperature's not right and the mealtimes are off and . . .

My eyes close when I realize I'm comparing the hospital to his house. The place I spent the past ten years in. The only home I've known. I never wanted to get used to it. I never wanted to equate it with "home."

I never wanted to be kidnapped either.

Some things in life we get to choose, and some things are forced upon us.

"Well, I do know. I need to leave. I'm *going* to leave. If you want to help, great, but if you don't, it's not going to stop me."

He sighs, but it's more one of giving in than giving up. "Do your parents know you're checking yourself out?"

My head shakes. The floor is so cold here. All of Earl Rae's—the parts I was allowed in—was covered in carpet, even the kitchen. The bathroom was linoleum, but it felt warmer than this icy tile. Spongier too. "No. They'll find out when I show up at the front door." I don't tell him I don't remember their phone numbers anymore. If I did, maybe I would call them to let them know.

"What do you need from me?"

I cross my arms and pretend like I know what I'm going to do with the rest of my life. Like I've got it all planned out and just need to cross things off the list one at a time. "Tell the nurses' station I'm checking myself out."

"Done." When Torrin's halfway to the door, he stops. He looks at me over by the window.

What does he see when he looks at me? A piece of his past? A damaged woman? A girl who needs saving? A duty? I could ask, but I'm too afraid of the answer.

"Will you be okay here on your own?"

His question does something to my chest. "I'll be okay."

He nods and rushes to the door. "I'll be right back."

As soon as Torrin leaves, I grab the plastic bag holding the clothes I came in with and hurry to the bathroom. The hospital smells especially antiseptic this morning, and I can't wait to get out of here.

I hear footsteps echo into my room as I'm buttoning my cardigan, but I don't hurry out because I know it's not Torrin. His footsteps don't sound like that— there's more time between each one; they're gentler sounding.

I check my reflection in the mirror for a second. It's a second too long. Earl Rae had all of the mirrors removed from the house when he found me sawing at my chain with a sharp piece of the bathroom mirror I'd shattered. I haven't seen my reflection in years. The image has changed from the last time I saw it.

My face has sunken to the point all I see are shadows and bones. I look like a skeleton with a piece of skin stretched over the hard bone. My eyes don't seem to possess much color anymore, and my hair, along with everything else, has lost its shine. I'm pale to the point I can see frail webs of veins winding beneath my face.

I look more dead than alive. My face matches the way I feel inside.

Dried blood stains the collar of my sweater from yesterday, and I know it doesn't matter how much time or cold water I use—those stains are never coming out.

I rake my fingers through my hair a few times, splash some water on my face, and rinse my mouth out a few times. Whoever's waiting for me isn't leaving. I have an idea who it might be.

When I slide through the bathroom door, I discover I'm right.

"I just heard you're leaving." Dr. Argent isn't as tall as she seemed yesterday. Maybe that's because my perspective has changed.

I close the bathroom door. "News travels fast."

Dr. Argent exhales through her nose. "I'd strongly advise against that, Jade. You have been through a trauma that would crush most people. You shouldn't be checking yourself out of the hospital the next day and planning on picking up your life right where you left it."

I've been told what to do every day of the past decade. I suddenly feel like I can't take one more person telling me what to do one more time. "Yeah, well, the day you're held against your will for ten years, come find me, and I might take your advice a little more seriously."

She crosses her arms and leans into the foot of my bed. "What are you so afraid of, Jade?"

Nothing. Everything.

How can I say that without sounding like I need a

straitjacket and a Dixie cup of pills at breakfast, lunch, and dinner?

"I'm not afraid," I say because I don't want to be afraid of anything. I don't want to be afraid ever again . . . even though I can feel it pulsing in my veins right this very moment.

"If you can wait a few more minutes, I'll round you up some fresh clothes." Dr. Argent's eyes skim the reddish-brown stain circling my sweater.

I know it looks gruesome, but gruesome's subjective. Some blood on my sweater feels like the least of the worries pummeling me.

"These are my clothes. I'm fine," I reply.

"Actually, those are Sara's clothes."

My teeth grind together. I don't know if Dr. Argent's objective is to piss me off with every conversation, but maybe that's part of her "electric paddling my psyche" approach. "They. Are. Mine."

Dr. Argent sighs, and it's the kind that makes me think she's reached the conclusion that I'm as hopeless as I think I might be. "If you'll let me give you one final piece of advice . . ." She's looking at me, waiting, but I don't look back. "Find an emotional tether. Someone you trusted before and someone you can trust now. A person who can connect you to your past but can pilot you into the future. Someone who can pull you back from the ledge when you find it and from the dark when it finds you. Find that person, hold on tight, and don't let go."

That's when Torrin bursts through the door. He's clearly been hustling since he's breathing a little hard.

"We're good." He doesn't seem to notice Dr. Argent, but he doesn't miss the stains on my sweater. They seem to pull the air straight from his lungs. "I pulled my truck around front too."

My posture relaxes now that he's back. I wonder if he's talking about his old truck, the one that had been his dad's before it became his. It had been old ten years ago. "They let you leave it there?"

Torrin pointed at his neck. "Perks of the collar."

"Well, there better be some if they're going to make you commit to celibacy, right?" I say without flinching.

I'd just been making a joke, but it makes Torrin shift. Yeah, I guess talking about celibacy with the girl you lost your virginity to would be kind of awkward. That should have been obvious. It would have been if I hadn't spent the last decade in forced seclusion. I've become the socially awkward person who doesn't know what to say or when to say it.

"Who are you?" Dr. Argent shoves off the bed and angles toward Torrin.

Torrin clears his throat and finally seems to notice Dr. Argent. "Father Costigan."

Father Costigan. My god, that, more than anything else, drives home the realization that he really is a priest.

From the way she looks at him, I can picture her flipping through the stack of notes I know she has on me in her office. Her eyebrows lift when she remembers. "As in Torrin Costigan? Who grew up next to Jade?"

"The very one." He lifts his chin at me. "The boy next door."

This time, it's his comment alluding to the past that makes me shift.

"You were her boyfriend at the time of her kidnapping, correct?"

Torrin looks at me like he's checking to see what he should say.

I move toward Torrin, watching Dr. Argent. I don't trust her. I don't have a reason not to, but I don't. I probably won't be able to trust people for a long time though . . . if I'll be able to trust them again. "Hey, I thought I was the patient. Leave him alone."

"I'm here to help. That's all," Torrin tells her.

When she looks between the two of us, she doesn't try to hide what she's thinking. Her gaze flickers to Torrin as she moves toward the door. "Just make sure you don't confuse helping her with hurting her." She peaks her eyebrow at him. "Father." When she passes me, she holds out her business card. She waits until I take it. "If you ever want to talk, I'm a phone call away. My cell number's on the back."

I take the card, but I don't have any plans of using it. What happened happened. I'm not about to spend two hours every week dissecting it into tiny, ugly bits. The key to fixing myself is moving on.

"Good luck, Jade," she says before leaving the room.

The room's silent now that she's gone. Until Torrin's footsteps puncture the quiet. "Where are we going?"

I haven't really thought about that. All I know is that I need to leave the hospital. My forehead creases as I consider my options. There aren't many. "My parents', I guess."

Torrin nods and turns around, inspecting the room. "Do you have any bags?" he asks as I move toward the door.

"No. I only came in with what I've got on." I pinch at the faded cardigan that's a couple sizes too big.

Torrin glances at the dark stain ringing around the collar again. His hands go to his hips, and he has to look away. "Sorry. Dumb question." His voice is light, but his expression doesn't match. "There'll probably be a lot of those, and you have my permission to just punch me in the nose when I ask too many, okay?"

As we leave the room, I drop Dr. Argent's card in the garbage. I have enough baggage already. "You've played soccer since you were three and never managed to break your nose." Or at least he hadn't until he was seventeen. I'm not sure what's happened during the last ten years to him. Going to school and becoming a priest is the extent of what I know Torrin has been up to. "I wouldn't want to be the one responsible for finally breaking it."

He holds the door open and lets me pass through it first. "A person can fix a broken nose, no problem."

As we pass the nurses' station, Torrin waves at them. Everyone's already looking at us though. Not quite with morbid curiosity but something that comes close.

"Yeah?" I say, moving toward the elevators a little quicker. I don't like being stared at. I don't like it because most people can keep their dirty secrets from the rest of the world—mine are on display for the whole entire world to learn about.

"Yep. Some breaks are easier to fix than others." He punches the down button when we stop in front of the elevator, and he glances up and down the halls. Kind of like he's looking for someone. Or expecting someone.

I scan the hall with him. Nothing but a couple more nurses pretending they aren't watching me. "Some breaks can't be fixed at all."

Torrin doesn't reply, because I know he's on a first-name basis with breaks that can't be fixed. He learned about those after his dad died. I learned about them after I died to myself.

He holds the elevator door when it opens and motions me inside. I go in easily enough; it isn't until the doors slide closed that I feel panic start to claw at my stomach. Small, confined places. Doors that can't be opened easily. My breathing's picking up, and I feel my hands get clammy. An elevator. I've ridden in a thousand of them, but now I can't travel down five floors without feeling like I'm going to hyperventilate.

From the corner of my eye, I see Torrin glance at me. "Are you okay?"

I nod and grip the railing behind me a little harder. He watches me for another second then slides a little closer. We aren't quite touching, but the warmth of his body breaks across mine. I feel the energy he's emitting. It doesn't put me out of the panic zone, but it gets me through the rest of the ride until the doors whoosh open on the first floor.

I nearly crash out of the elevator.

"Jade?" Torrin comes up behind me, lowering his

face to mine.

"I'm okay. Just give me a second." I lean over a little to catch my breath, wiping my hands on my jeans.

It takes a minute, and I know people are watching me again, but I don't care. They're just watching me because I look like I'm about to have a baby, not because I'm the girl who's just been rescued after being kidnapped ten years ago.

"Good?" Torrin's hand grazes my lower back.

I squeeze my eyes together tightly before opening them. "Good."

I straighten up and give him a smile, but I'm shaken. An elevator just made me lose my shit. What else would be responsible for doing the same? An alarm clock? Rush-hour traffic? A woman tapping my shoulder at the grocery store?

Everything seems scary, which is ironic since I just did a ten-year stint in the mecca of scary. An elevator should feel like a relaxing massage in comparison.

Beside me, Torrin goes rigid, his forearms flexing like he's bracing for something.

"What is it?" I still sound out of breath, but my head's clearing.

He doesn't blink as he stares at something in front of us just outside the big glass doors. "Shit," he mutters.

If I wasn't staring at his collar, I probably wouldn't have thought anything of it. "I didn't think priests were allowed to cuss."

"We're not, but I'm new." His forehead folds into creases as his stare turns into a glare. "I'm still learning."

"Your secret's safe with me." When he doesn't respond, I look to see what's gotten his attention. When I do, I feel like I'm stuck in that elevator again. Times ten. "Shit." I don't mutter it.

"There's got to be another way out of here. I'll pull the truck around and meet you there." Torrin can't stop glaring at the army of reporters waiting just outside the doors, surrounding his truck. I don't realize I'm backing up until he looks back at me. "Wait here. They can't come inside. I'll figure something out."

He starts marching toward the reception desk, but before he can get there, I grab his arm.

"No. Let's go through the front door." A few of the reporters have clearly noticed me now. Camera lights flash, and the buzzing herd turns into a crazed mass. "I want to get this over with."

I don't let go of Torrin's arm. It's the same one I practically clawed to shreds last night, but he doesn't wince or pull away. "You don't have to do this, Jade. Make the vultures wait. Make them wait until they move on to the next story."

I swallow and find myself sliding behind Torrin, using him as a shield against the relentless flashes breaking through the glass. "They won't move on. I know that. You know that."

When he clenches his jaw, it pops. "Give it some time."

I shake my head. "I just want to get this all over with. The sooner they can get their photos, their headlines, the sooner this will pass. I don't want to delay the inevitable. I want it over with."

Torrin watches me for a minute. He watches another minute more. "You're sure?"

Of course I'm not, but I'm not sure of much anymore. "I'm sure."

He sucks in a breath like he's preparing to make a deep dive. "Here, put this on." He holds out his raincoat and waits.

"Why?"

"Just . . ." When his eyes lower to my neck, to the stained collar of my sweater, I know why. "Don't give them anything more than you're ready to talk about."

I nod, and he steps behind me and slides the jacket up my arms and over my shoulders. He even slides the hood over my head before zipping the coat up to my chin.

He lowers his face to mine and smiles. "There. Now you're ready to weather the storm."

I smile back, but I'm a ball of nerves. *Get this over with. Move on.* When I move toward the front door, Torrin rushes up to my side. Everyone in the lobby is still looking at me, but this time it's because they know who I am now. That girl. The one who'd been kidnapped from one of the safest blocks in the country ten years ago.

That girl.

I can almost feel those words cycling through the consciousness of everyone staring at me. That's how people will know me now. As That Girl.

It makes my feet move faster until I'm practically charging through the sliding glass doors. Torrin's truck is only a few meters away, but getting to it is like trying to move through a pool of cement.

Cameras are thrown in my face. Microphones are thrust to my mouth. What feels like hundreds of people close in around me, corralling me, trapping me. In my rush to get outside, Torrin has fallen a few steps behind. Now that we've hit the wall of reporters, it's next to impossible to move.

Lights flash in my face. Questions fire at me one after another.

"Jade, how are you?" I hear that question at least a dozen times. "Anything you'd like to say to the world?"

I don't answer. I just tuck my head down and try to keep moving forward. It's impossible though. They're too strong, and I'm too weak. I can't break free.

"Anything you wish you could say to Earl Rae Jackson if he were alive today?" another reporter shouts, lashing another microphone in my face.

The flashes are relentless. I'm trying not to look at them, but they're blinding me. I can't see. I can't move. I can't talk. I've felt helpless like this before, but never when I haven't been attached to a short length of chain.

"Is it true he kept you chained up in his house for ten years?" a male reporter crows above the rest of them, getting his microphone so close to me it actually bounces off my nose.

I cry out a little. Not because it hurt but because it surprised me.

That's when I hear a loud growl behind me, and I start to feel space opening up around me. Someone comes up behind me, drapes their arms over my head, and guides me through the ocean of reporters.

"I've got you," Torrin says, steering me through them like he's a sharp knife slicing through ribbon.

"What's your relationship to Miss Childs, Father?"

Now that Torrin's come into the picture, the questions are changing. The tone of them is shifting. There's less pity in the reporters' voices, replaced with skepticism.

We're almost to the truck. I can just make out the front tires. I think Torrin has to shove a few cameramen away from the door so he can open it, but he does it without hesitating. He does it like he's moving cardboard boxes instead of grown men.

Once the door is open, he shields my body with his until I'm all the way inside the cab. He slams the door, almost taking off a man's hand when he sticks a microphone in after me.

Now the reporters are focused on him, slamming their mics in his face while cameras pan in his direction as he shoves around to the driver's side of his truck. As soon as he throws the door open, he dives inside and fires up the engine.

"Stay down." He has to shout above the noise, but his hand is gentle as it guides my head forward into my lap. The cameras don't stop flashing.

Torrin blares his horn twice, then he presses down on the gas. I hear shouts of anger as we drive away. I wonder how close he came to running someone over.

It's quiet for a while before he taps my back. "We dropped the reporters. You can sit up now if you want."

I straighten up slowly and glance out the window.

Flashes of buildings and cars pass by. Looking out the window like this makes me nauseated, almost motion sick, so I turn to face forward.

My hands are shaking in my lap. Not trembling—shaking. I stare at them and try to make them stop. I focus on them until I feel my teeth grinding together, but I can't control them.

They won't stop shaking.

I want to cry because I feel like my body is betraying me. I stare out the window again. I'd rather be nauseated than let Torrin see me cry.

He blasts through a light that's more red than yellow and pushes the speed when we hit the on-ramp. The truck still rattles like it's about to fall apart whenever it breaks fifty, but now there's a whine coming under from the hood. This scrap of familiarity is calming. In a world I don't seem to belong in anymore, a familiar truck's engine sputtering and spewing reminds me that there was a time when I belonged.

An emotional tether. Even the way he glances at me from the driver's seat, like he needs the reassurance that I'm still here, is familiar. He's the one I'd tie myself to, but I don't feel like I have anything left to be bound with. How can he tether me when vapor has more substance than I do?

The trip from Seattle to Sammamish isn't a long one. It feels even shorter now.

He breaks the silence when he flies down the off-ramp for Sammamish. "Ready for this?"

"Yes," I say because it doesn't matter if I am or not.

Life's not going to slow down just because I can't tolerate the pace. "Does your family still live in the same house?"

His head shakes. "No. Mom sold it a few years ago and moved into a little condo. After Rory graduated and she finally kicked Caden out."

"How are your brothers?"

He turns down a familiar street. The one our high school was on. "Rory's studying biology at U-Dub, and Caden's . . . being Caden."

"So you're saying not much has changed?"

"Other than me going into the priesthood, not much has."

"That still doesn't feel real." I twist in my seat to look at him.

He drives his truck exactly like he used to—one hand gripping the wheel, the other arm draped over the top of it, his legs spread wide and taking up half of the bench seat. "What doesn't?"

"You." I wave at his outfit. "This."

He glances at his shirt like I just told him he spilled ketchup down the front of it. "Yeah, well, it's kind of surreal sitting here beside you and talking about my brothers too."

"Do you keep in touch with any of our old friends?"

He's just turned onto Hemlock. My hands wring together.

"Not really. I see them around town every once in a while. A few are members of the church, but I think me becoming this . . ." He says it how I did, summing up a handful of words in a single one. "Was a little weird for

106

them. No one wants to have their friend the priest over because they're worried I'm going to tell on them to Jesus or something."

The way he says it makes me laugh.

He smiles at me. "What? It's true. No one wants a priest around when there's a party, but if someone's being born or dying, I'm on speed dial."

I'm still laughing. He's still smiling. The sun's shining, and everything is green and lush. It's the most perfect moment I've had in years.

It ends the moment Torrin turns down Madison Boulevard. My parents' house is a few blocks down, but I can already see it. The street is lined with trucks, and the sidewalks are littered with people. It makes the scene at the hospital seem peaceful and puny.

Torrin curses the same word from the hospital under his breath. "What do you want me to do?"

What I really want is for him to turn around and drive until we've hit the coast. I want to rent a little cabin on the beach that I can make a big fire in, and I want to walk up and down the beach until I can't take another step. I want to walk without a chain dictating how far I can go. I want to walk with him. I want to try to get caught up on the last ten years of his life. I want to laugh again like I just did.

I want to run away.

"I want you to keep going. Pull into the driveway, preferably without running anyone over, and walk me to the front door so I can give you your jacket back."

The truck slows, but it keeps rolling forward. "You can keep the jacket. It'll help you weather the storm, remember?"

"Then I'd like you to walk me to the front door as my personal security guard." My hands are wringing themselves again. God, there are so many of them. It feels like every country in the free world has sent their own crew to my front porch.

"They can't put one foot on your parents' property without their permission."

"And they probably can't bonk someone on the nose with a giant microphone either, but journalists aren't exactly well known for their rule abiding."

When we're half a block away, a few heads turn our way. They know we're coming.

"My God, Jade." Torrin leans over the steering wheel, his eyes wide. "Are you sure about this?"

No. I'm not. "I'm sure."

He presses down a little more on the gas, and the truck speeds up. He's as ready to get this over with as I am.

The cameras are already flashing, and I can hear through the windows the roar of the reporters' shouted questions. I don't duck down this time, but I keep my face forward, my expression flat. I make sure the hood is still over my head and the zipper still pulled to my chin. When we get to my parents' house, the driveway is barricaded by reporters waving their microphones and screaming their questions at me through the windshield.

My hands start to shake again.

Torrin blasts the truck's horn a few times. When that doesn't seem to do anything, he thrusts his palm onto it and doesn't let up. A few of them cover their ears, but no one moves.

I can see my parents' faces through the living room window.

Pulling off the horn, Torrin revs the engine a couple of times before creeping the truck forward. Finally, reporters move. They file to the sides, banging on Torrin's and my windows as we pass them. I feel like a disco ball is flashing in my face from all of the photos being taken.

"Where's the crowd control for Christ's sake?" I wince when I realize what I've just said. "Sorry."

Torrin blasts his horn again, and once it's clear, he speeds up to the edge of the driveway. "It's okay. I won't tell on you to Jesus or anything."

I look into my lap to keep my smile hidden. I don't want to share that with them. Torrin's right; I don't want to give them anything I'm not ready to talk about—the reason the man sitting beside me can still make me smile especially.

I can see from the side view mirror that the reporters stay on the edge of the sidewalk, but a few have one foot in the lawn. I just want to throw the door open and run until I've locked the front door behind me, but I don't want them to see that either. I don't want them to know I'm scared. I don't want to fulfill the profile that's already been drawn of me by probably dozens of shrinks giving dozens of interviews. I don't want to be *That Girl* whose life was ruined.

I want to be seen as the person who survived.

Though it's not a story even I'm sure I believe.

"I'll come around and get you, then we'll make a run for the front door." Torrin puts the truck in park and cuts the engine. "I'll stay on your left side so the only headlines we'll make tomorrow will be about how the Catholic church should really find a new slacks supplier, because these things"—Torrin pinches the material of his pants— "would even make Jason Momoa's ass look flat."

I smile. Again. I don't know who Jason Momoa is, and I don't know about those slacks not looking good on Torrin, but I like the way he's trying to make me comfortable. I like the tone of his voice. I like that I just heard "ass" pass by a priest's lips.

"Well? What are you waiting for? You and your flat-ass-making slacks' two seconds of fame are running out." I curl my fingers around the door handle and wait.

Torrin looks over his shoulder and inhales. Then he shoves open his door and jogs around the front of his truck. I wait until he's standing outside my door before I open it. When I do, the questions being hollered from the sidewalk hit me, almost leveling me to the ground. There are more video cameras than I can count and just as many regular cameras. Dozens, maybe hundreds, of reporters are staring at me, calling me over, practically begging for my attention.

Is this what my life's going to be like? Ducking in and out of doors, evading the media at every turn? Is my story ever going to lose the public's attention? If so, how long until that happens?

I'd been trapped at the house in Bellingham. I'd been trapped in the hospital. I'm still trapped.

The chain might be invisible and a little bit longer, but I'm still bound to it.

Torrin comes around my left side as promised when I crawl out of the truck. His arm tucks around my shoulders as we rush across the lawn. The yard's different now. My mom's rose bushes are gone and have been replaced by river rock. The short white fence has been replaced with a taller chain link version.

I try not to look at the walkway when we pass it. I try not to stare at the sidewalk at the end of the walkway, the very spot where I'd fallen off the face of the planet. I can still see his van parked beneath that old maple tree. I can still see the map he drew me in with. I can still smell the inside of the van before I passed out.

My legs give out without any warning. I'm falling, about to crash into the ground, when Torrin catches me.

"I've got you," he says as he pulls me up, more carrying me up the stairs than guiding me.

The front door flies open when we reach the porch. My mom waves us in, but my dad steps in front of her, blocking the doorway. I look at him, but he isn't looking at me. He's looking at Torrin.

"We've got it from here." Dad reaches for my arm, but I pull it away.

Behind me, the noise level climbs.

Torrin just turns toward me. "If you need anything, give me a call. I tucked my cell number into the pocket of the jacket." His arm is still wound around me like he's afraid I'm going to fall again.

"Will you stay?" I ask him.

My dad's chest puffs out. It's clear he doesn't want Torrin to step foot in his house. I can't imagine this still has to do with the time he found us all hot and heavy up against the hall wall. If it does, Dad has some serious forgiveness issues to work out.

"I want to," Torrin says, angling me so my back's to the street. "But I can't. I've already missed two counseling sessions, one breakfast with the church elders, and a hospital visit. If I miss the eleven o'clock baptism, they're going to go all medieval on me and burn me at the stake or something."

"You're a busy guy."

He nods. "They like to keep us busy for a reason." When I tip my head, he adds, "So we don't have time to regret that whole vow of celibacy." This time, he doesn't shift. He just smiles and winks.

My dad clears his throat. "This probably isn't the best time to have a conversation on the front stoop."

"My God, Mike, invite them in." Mom peeks her head out from behind him and waves us in.

Behind us, the roar grows.

Torrin and my dad have some kind of stare down. I'm not sure who wins, but my dad steps aside to clear the doorway so we can come in. I stay planted on the porch with Torrin.

"I better get going." Torrin backs down the first step. "I'll check in with you later."

I feel a tightness in my chest as he backs away. It's more of a stab than an ache.

"I'm glad you're back." He smiles at me from the

bottom step and waits.

He wants me to get inside. He's not going to leave until I do. I wonder if that has anything to do with the night I was taken.

I turn to face him, and the cameras go off like a swarm of angry fireflies. "Thanks for staying with me last night. Thank you for bringing me home."

Something meaningful stretches across Torrin's face. Then he nods. "You're welcome." Then he lifts his chin toward my parents. "You better get inside."

I know he's right, but I don't want to. I don't want to say good-bye, however temporary it is. I know good-byes have no guarantee that you'll see that person again. I know that good-byes can be permanent even if you don't mean them that way.

When I step over the threshold and pass my dad, I turn to wave at Torrin. He's still there, almost like he's guarding the walkway. He's watching me like he's concentrating, but when I wave, he lets himself smile as he waves back.

His smile is what I'm watching when my dad steps in front of me and closes the door, sealing us inside. It's darker with the door closed. It's cooler too.

"Oh, Jade, are you okay?" My mom moves in front of me and settles her hands into the bends of my arms. She's not barreling at me with a storm of tears and suffocating embraces. Someone must have talked with her about it yesterday, post my meltdown from being touched too much too fast.

Dad steps in around us, but he keeps a safe distance.

He keeps his hands at his sides.

I don't answer her because I think the question was a rhetorical one—a question a mother has to ask her child no matter what's happened, from a sliver in the thumb to a ten-year kidnapping.

I don't see my brother or sister anywhere. It isn't until I find myself looking for them that I realize they don't live here anymore. They've moved on. I'm twenty-seven, the oldest child, and still living here. I never really checked out.

"Welcome home, sweetheart." Mom's eyes are teary when she smiles at me.

I try to smile back, but it's impossible. This isn't home. It doesn't feel like it anymore. When I think about what does feel like home, my stomach churns. I miss the house. I think I might even miss him.

There really is no hope for me.

Seven

NOTHING ABOUT THE house I grew up in has changed. The walls have a fresh coat of paint and my dad's ratty recliner's been replaced by a new one, but everything's exactly how I remember it. All the same.

I should feel right at home, like I'm picking up where I left off, but I don't. This house feels strange, foreign. I feel like a guest in someone else's home, afraid to go through the cupboards or kick my feet up on the couch.

This house hasn't changed, but I have.

It's not really the house that feels foreign—it's me being inside it, like I don't fit. The way my parents have hovered over me all day, it's like they sense it too and are trying to figure out a way to make me fit. No matter how many times they try though, I'll never fit. My edges are too jagged.

It's dinnertime, and the smells of prime rib and garlic have been rolling from the kitchen since this afternoon. It used to be my favorite meal: red meat, garlic mashed potatoes, and sautéed green beans. From the smells alone, I know it's not my favorite anymore.

My brother and sister are supposed to come here, and Mom's even set the fancy china on the table. The good wine's been pulled out, and Dad has on his tweed blazer. The meal has the feel of a celebration, but my heart isn't in it.

I know it should be, but that doesn't change that it isn't.

For my family's sake, I'll pretend to celebrate with them. They deserve their celebration, and maybe one day, once I manage to un-mess up myself, I'll be able to join in.

"Do you need any help, Mom?" I call into the kitchen from my perch at the front window. The sheer curtains have been drawn, but I can still see outside. The media circus hasn't shrunk in the eight hours since I arrived; it's gotten bigger. Now big floodlights extend from the top of news trucks. Some of the stations are familiar local channels, some aren't, and some of the bigger trucks have national stations stamped on their sides.

"No, sweetie, you just relax. It will be ready in five."

She's been telling me to rest all day, but I've spent the past ten years resting. Besides, I've got too much nervous energy to relax. I need something to keep my hands and mind busy.

"What would you like to drink, Jade?" Dad calls from the kitchen.

It's a strange place to find him. Dad used to spend the hour leading up to dinner in his chair, watching the evening news.

I can guess why he doesn't keep that tradition anymore though.

"Water, please," I say.

"I picked up some of your favorite kind of soda."

"Water's good." I haven't had a soda in ten years. It would probably tear my stomach apart now.

"Why don't you take a seat, Jade? Sam and Connor will be here any minute."

I turn away from the window. The cameras are still firing. Not as much, but they're still going off. "Where do you want me?"

"In your usual seat," Mom says as she settles a glass bowl of mashed potatoes on the table.

I stare at the table. I can't remember where my usual seat was. I know it was close to my dad, but was it to the right or the left of him?

Mom catches me staring and pulls out the chair to the right of my dad. "Here you go."

I take a seat and wait. It's so quiet in the house now. Without Connor's alternative music blasting from his room and Sam and her friends giggling behind her bedroom door and Mom's jazz streaming from the kitchen and Dad's nightly news echoing from the living room, it's silent.

Now that I'm home, my parents seem to have no idea what to say to me. I don't exactly know what to say to them either.

"Look at this beauty," Dad trumpets as he carries in a huge roast.

He sets it right in front of me, and I have to scoot my

chair back from the smell. It's almost offensive now. The pools of red-stained grease below the meat have me squirming in my seat.

Outside, the noise level rises right before the front door explodes open. Connor wanders into the living room first, looking a little shocked, but his face clears when he sees me.

"Hey, Jade." He stuffs his hands in his pockets and takes a seat in what I guess is his usual seat. I can't remember that either.

For a brief moment, I look around, wondering who Connor's talking to. I catch myself right after. *Me.* I'm Jade. I spent ten years being called by a different name, but still—searching the room for a Jade when I was born with that name and was probably called it dozens of times every day for seventeen years?

I don't need another confirmation that transitioning into normal life is impossible for someone like me. I've had enough of those already.

Dad claps Connor on the back and heads toward the front door. I hear hushed whispers that sound like Sam and Dad are arguing about something.

I'm sure that something has to do with me.

Dad comes back into the dining room first, his brows drawn in a hard line. Sam follows a minute later. She doesn't look at me at first. Like yesterday at the hospital, she looks totally put-together, like nothing could touch the shine on her shoes or wrinkle the silk of her dress.

"Hi, Jade." Her voice is stilted, but she finally looks at me. For a second.

I've changed into one of my old outfits Mom brought down for me earlier, but everything's too big now. So she pulled out an outfit of hers and let me try that on. I feel strange wearing my mom's khaki trousers and cashmere sweater, and I must look it by the way Connor's staring at me.

Actually, it isn't my clothes he's staring at.

"What happened to your neck?" he asks, studying the fresh bandages.

I'm about to answer him when Mom comes in carrying the green beans. "Connor." She shakes her head.

Just like that, he looks away and takes a drink of his water.

"It's from a metal collar I wore. Sometimes it would dig into my skin and make me bleed. I bled a lot the day they came to get me." I don't realize everyone's gaping at me until I look around the table. Well, Sam's the only one gaping. Everyone else is just kind of wide-eyed.

"Who's ready to eat?" Mom's voice rings through the room, and everyone except me nods.

So I guess they're happy to have me back, but they aren't ready to hear what happened. Maybe they never will be.

Dad takes his station at the head of the table and cuts into the roast. The sawing noise the knife makes as it cuts into the meat makes my stomach convulse. The sight of the bright red meat makes me close my eyes.

I've never been so keenly aware that the chunk of meat I was about to eat came from a living, breathing animal. The blood pooling into Mom's china serving plate is the same blood that kept that animal alive. I'm about to eat its flesh.

I know I'll never eat meat again. I'll never dine on the pieces of an innocent animal ever again.

When Dad puts the first slab on my plate, I shake my head.

"You love roast, Jade," he says, the knife in his hand dripping red grease.

"No." I keep shaking my head. "I don't."

Mom wets her lips across from me and looks at Dad. She doesn't know what to do. I know she planned this meal for me. I know she wanted it to be special. I hate that I'm ruining it for her, but I can't eat that. I can barely stand to sit in my seat with it staring at me.

For ten years, I've eaten food that came from a can or a bag: rice, beans, tuna, peas, green beans . . . I might have liked bloody meat in a different life, but not this one.

"Here, trade plates with me." Connor leans across the table and grabs my plate before setting his empty one in front of me.

I send a small smile his way, and he shrugs back like it's no big deal. Dad goes back to cutting the roast, and I distract myself by scooping a mound of potatoes and green beans onto my plate. I already know I won't be able to eat much of it, but for Mom's sake, I'll try. My appetite has disappeared ever since I was rescued. I don't know why, but it's like I can't stomach anything anymore.

"What are you studying in school, Connor?" I ask as I squirm on the chair, trying to find a comfortable spot. This chair's so hard. Back at Earl Rae's, the chairs had pads covering the seats.

He shrugs again while Dad grumbles.

"A little bit of everything right now," Connor answers.

"Are you a junior now?" I glance at his U-Dub sweatshirt, wondering if he ever sees Rory anymore. They used to be friends, but who knows if that's the case anymore.

"Senior."

"Who should be graduating with the rest of his class in a week," Dad adds under his breath.

"I don't know what I want to be when I grow up yet. It's a big decision." Connor takes a drink of his water. "I'm leaving next week for Europe to spend summer quarter taking a course in ancient Scottish history."

I nod while Dad grumbles, "Because just think of all the job opportunities out there for people who spend a summer learning about Scottish history."

"*Ancient* Scottish history." Connor lifts his fork.

Dad grumbles again.

Sam is silent down the table from me. I feel her anger directed at me, but I can't figure out its source. I've been gone for ten years—what could I have done to piss her off so badly? She can't still be mad about the time Torrin and I turned the sprinklers on her and her friends when they were camping out in the backyard.

"What have you been up to, Sam?" I try a bite of the mashed potatoes. I'm sure it's the same recipe, but I feel like I'm choking down rubber cement.

She tenses when I say her name, then she picks up her fork. "I graduated from University of Oregon three years ago with a double major in International Business and Economics. I work for Boeing in Federal Way as an international liaison. Two years ago, I married Patrick, who I met in college." She lifts her left hand, and a ring sparkles from her finger. "He works for Microsoft in Redmond as a software developer. We had our daughter last year. Her name's Maisy."

Sam lists this all off like she's reading a grocery list, so it takes me a second to catch up. She's married? She has a kid?

"So that means I'm an aunt?" The words sputter from my mouth as I try to work that out.

Sam lifts a shoulder.

"Are Patrick and Maisy coming to dinner too?" I ask, but the table's only set for five.

Sam shakes her head. "Patrick and I aren't ready to explain all of this to Maisy yet." She makes "this" sound like a lurid thing.

"How old's Maisy?" I ask, swirling patterns into my mashed potatoes.

"Fourteen months."

I feel my forehead crease. Explaining "this" isn't why Sam left her family at home. She doesn't want me to meet them. She doesn't want them to meet me. Is she ashamed of me? Embarrassed? Does she think I'm ruined now? A potentially bad influence? A black hole that will suck everything that gets close into its vacuum?

"Congratulations," I say before trying the beans. They go down a little easier, but I know I won't be able to eat more than a few bites.

"Thanks." Sam picks at her plate, but her appetite looks as absent as mine.

"Jade, sweetheart . . ."

Just the way my mom says it, I know she's hesitant to mention whatever she's going to. She's walking on eggshells. Everyone at the table is. I hate it. I just want them to act like nothing happened, to treat me like the same person they remember me as, to not think of me as a victim who was kidnapped but as their sister and daughter.

"When should I reschedule your meeting with the detectives?" Mom asks.

My fork freezes above the beans. "I don't know."

"Next week?" she asks gently.

Dad stops cutting into the roast and sits down.

"I don't know."

"You have to talk to them sometime," she presses.

I nod like I know, but really, I don't. Why do I *have* to talk to them? Why is everyone so concerned about me talking to someone? Earl Rae is dead. I've been found. What more do they need to know?

"I'll let you know." I take another bite of beans as a distraction. This dinner is like enduring slow torture, and I'm not the only one who feels that way. It looks like everyone feels the same. Even my "usual" chair feels like it has sprouted thorns.

"Do you want me to put together a little get-together with some of your old friends?" Mom's holding her fork, but she hasn't touched her plate. The only ones eating are Connor and Dad. "I know they'll be eager to see you."

I can barely remember the names and faces of my old

friends. I know I had some. Good ones. But their faces are blurred out of my memory, their names buried in the attic of my mind.

I swirl my beans around on the plate. "I've seen Torrin."

Mom and Dad exchange a look.

"Maybe some friends who aren't old boyfriends who went and became a priest," Sam says under her breath.

"A lot's changed in ten years, Jade. I know you weren't here to change with it, but you'll have to find some way to catch up."

I know what my dad's talking about. Or *who* he's talking about. He wants me to accept that Torrin's not a part of my life anymore. He wants me to let go of whatever part of him I've held onto.

"Don't worry, Jade, I'll take care of arranging some kind of get-together." Mom glances at my plate. Worry touches her eyebrows. "I was also looking into a way for you to work on your GED so you can start applying to colleges. You could probably even start your freshman year in the fall."

My head spins, and I numb out the rest. My GED. College. Career. I haven't seen the inside of a classroom in a decade. What if I can't pass the GED? What if no college wants me? What if I don't even want to go to college?

I don't know. Up until now, I haven't even considered it possible. Does the person I am now still want to go, or does she want something else?

I don't know—big goddamn surprise.

Mom's moved on to talking about old friends—who

married who and who's off at med school—and I suddenly feel like someone's just come up behind me and wound their fingers around my neck. I can't breathe. I can't talk. The invisible fingers tighten, and I jolt out of my chair.

Everyone stops talking and stares at me.

"I'm going to excuse myself." My voice sounds strained, like those fingers aren't as invisible as I thought. "Thanks for dinner."

I don't wait for them to say anything; I just leave the dining room. I don't miss the way Sam watches me leave though—like I'm a grenade that's pin is gradually being pulled. Or the way Connor stops chewing and looks like he wants to say something but doesn't. Or the way my mom leans her head into her hands and the way my dad looks out the window like he's at a loss.

They're as uncomfortable around me as I am around them. I don't know how long this will last. I don't know if it will ever pass. All I know is that I can't sit in that chair, at that table, any longer.

Once I hit the stairs, I lope up them. By the halfway point, I have to slow to taking them one sluggish step at a time. I haven't climbed stairs in years. The treadmill I used to walk on didn't have an incline option, so the stair climb feels like sprinting up the Himalayas.

When I reach the second floor, I pause to catch my breath before continuing down the hall. I haven't been in my bedroom since arriving home—I'm not sure if it's still "my bedroom"—but it's the only place I can think to go where I can close a door and have some privacy.

I glance in the room that used to be Sam's. It's been

turned into a gym. Connor's room has been turned into a guest room. The door at the end of the hall is closed. My room. I wonder what it's been turned into. A storage room? An artillery room for Dad's gun collection? A sewing room?

I twist the handle and push the door open. Cool air washes over me. The room's dark, so I can't see much, but I can tell that the curtains are the same. I remember them because Torrin opened a can of soda that exploded all over them, and no matter how many times Mom washed them, the dark stains couldn't be totally removed.

I search for the overhead light switch and turn it on.

Light floods the room, and I blink a few times to make sure I'm seeing what I think I am.

My room's the same. Nothing's changed. It's almost like a shrine the way the stuffed animals are still arranged on the rocking chair stuffed in the corner of the room and the way the blankets look like they've been ironed free of all wrinkles. My dresser's in the same spot with the little glass swan figurines I kept on it. The pictures of my friends and family are still there, propped on my vanity. The corkboard with all of my random junk—old movie ticket stubs, bandanas from homecoming games, more photos—is still hanging beside my closet.

It's like a seventeen-year-old girl walked out of this room this morning and was expected back after school. It's kind of creepy. I should feel at ease in my old room, but I think I'd be more comfortable in Connor's-old-room-turned-guest-bedroom.

Something's missing though—or a few somethings.

All have to do with a certain person. The pictures of Torrin are missing from my nightstand. The soccer trophies he gave me are gone from the windowsill. The corsages from the dances we went to together have disappeared.

They held on to me—but they let him go.

Except for the stuffed elephant sandwiched into the stuffed animal pile on the chair. Torrin won it for me at the fair that fall I'd been taken, but they didn't know that.

That's the first place I wander toward. I pull the elephant free of the other animals and look at it. I'm sure it hasn't changed—it's an inanimate object after all—but it doesn't feel as soft. Its face isn't as sweet as I remember it being.

When I hug it, it doesn't make me smile and get ready to fall asleep.

I hear footsteps climbing the stairs. From the lightness of them, I guess they're my mom's. She's probably coming to check on me, but I'm not ready for her. I'm not ready for any of them really. I'm not ready for this.

I close my door before she reaches the hall.

Eight

"**S**HE'S GONE. I can't find her. No one can find her."

That's the first thing I hear as I wake up the next morning—my mom's frantic voice, her footsteps matching.

"We've looked everywhere and nothing. Oh my god, it's happened again, hasn't it? Someone's taken her?" She chokes on her words. "We're never going to see our baby again."

I blink, but it's dark. Except for the slice of light coming from beneath the door, I can't see anything.

Another set of footsteps moves with my mom's. These are less hysterical and more pronounced sounding. I hear them stop outside the door, and I start to sit up. The sleeping bag slides down me.

The door gently slides open, and light blinds me for a second. When I can see again, I see him. He's crouching in front of me, his head brushing the bottoms of my sweaters and shirts hanging in my closet.

"She's here," he calls to my mom, who comes rushing into the room. Her eyes are red, and her foundation's messy from the tears she's crying. He clasps his hands in front of him and smiles at me. "Cozy in there?"

I sit up a little more and rub my lower back. I can practically feel the impression the sneaker left there from sleeping on it for so long. I rest my back on the side of the closet. "What time is it?"

My mom hovers over Torrin, looking at me with her red, puffy face.

"Time to get up and start the day." Torrin checks the watch on his wrist.

It looks like it's almost ten o'clock, which is really late for me to sleep in. Although if you count actual sleep time, I only got five hours.

"What are you doing in there, Jade?" Mom scans the sleeping bag and sees the pillow. She looks almost horrified. "Did you sleep in there? All night?"

I shrug. "Some of it."

"Why?" she asks.

"My bed"—I nod toward it—"was too soft or something. I couldn't sleep."

She looks back at my bed. Nothing's been disturbed on it.

Torrin doesn't look back because I think he knows. I think he understands that I couldn't just crawl into my old queen bed and fall fast asleep on my first night home. It was too open. Too exposed. Right now, the closet is more comfortable than the bed.

"Are you hungry? I saved some breakfast for you."

I haven't really eaten anything since I was found. I'm not hungry though. "No, thanks. Maybe later," I add when I notice her frown. I know she's trying to help—I know she *wants* to help—but the thing is, none of it actually helps. "I'm sorry if I scared everyone hiding out in here. If I'd heard you come in earlier, I would have said something, but I must have passed out pretty hard."

Mom bites her lip, still watching me like I might disappear. Then she straightens up. "I'll give you two a minute. I'll be in the kitchen if you need me." She pats Torrin's shoulder a few times. "Thank you for finding her."

Torrin watches her leave the room. He's in the same clothes as yesterday, and that white square looks extra bright today. They must bleach the hell out of those things because I've never seen anything so white. It doesn't seem possible it could stay so clean.

"You need a cell phone," he says like he didn't just find me stuffed in a closet like a scared little child.

"Why?" I reply.

"Because I called last night to check in, and when I asked if I could speak to you, your dad told me to do something to myself I'm pretty sure would be frowned upon in my profession."

I tore off the bandages around my neck last night, and even though he's not staring at the blend of scar and scab, I can tell he's having to force himself not to. I lift the corner of the sleeping bag and tuck it under my chin. "Well, you made it through the door this morning. No bullet holes from the looks of it."

"I made it in because your dad's at work and your

mom called me when she couldn't find you." He's freshly shaven today, unlike the serious shadow he had yesterday, and for some reason, this makes him seem even more priest-like. "I fully intend to be out of this house when your dad gets home from work because hollow points just aren't a good look on me."

When I smile, he looks kind of relieved. I wonder if he's trying to be careful too—watching what he says and does because he's afraid of upsetting me.

"Hey, I've got a really great idea," he says suddenly. I lift an eyebrow. "We should take a trip to the zoo soon. You know, whenever you're ready to crawl out of the closet and brave the big, bad world again."

"The zoo?" Kind of the last thing that I thought would be his great idea.

"You used to love the zoo. Maybe you still do." He backs up from the closet, waiting for me to peel myself out of it. When I do, he pops up. "Besides, the animals have lots of experience with being stared at by masses of people, so maybe they can offer you some advice."

I stretch my arms above my head. "Good one."

"I'm a witty guy." He stuffs his hands in his pockets, and when he sees what I'm wearing, he turns to look out the window.

My old pajama bottoms wouldn't stay up anymore, and the old boxers I stole from Torrin that I used to sleep in during the summer had disappeared with the rest of his stuff. So I threw on a cotton sundress. It still kind of hangs limp on me, but at least it stays on.

I don't know why seeing me in it makes him uncom-

fortable. Bony knees, knobby elbows, prominent collar-
bones, and boobs that have shrunk to the point that a bra's
just a formality are all that's showing.

"What about today?" I pull a long cardigan off of a
hanger and slide into it.

He stays at the window. "*Today* today? Are you . . .
you know, ready for that?"

I know what he's asking. Am I ready for the people,
the noises, the sights, the damn media? Of course I'm not
ready for any of that, but I doubt I'll ever be ready, and my
life isn't just going to come back together on its own.

"I'm ready for the zoo." I'm surprised by how convincing I sound.

He turns around once he notices my sweater, and he
sits on the edge of the windowsill. "Wow. You're really
taking the bull by the horns, aren't you?"

I roll my hand. "I think you're mistaking that for the
bull prodding my ass with its horns, but yeah, something
like that."

When I head back into my closet to dig through the
pile of old shoes, I have to go all the way to the back to
find the ones I have in mind. I have a million pairs of
Converses, and even though my favorite ones went missing the night I did, I have plenty of backups. I want the
black ones back, but I settle for the navy pair.

"This isn't too much too fast? Busting out of the hospital yesterday and going to the zoo today? The world isn't
going anywhere if you want to take your time easing back
into it."

I hear the concern in his voice. I know I would see it

on his face if I glanced back. He's right—this is too much too fast, but it would feel that way even if I stayed stuffed in my closet for the rest of the day. At least at the zoo, I can enjoy fresh air and be with him.

I work up the only kind of courage I have left—the pretend kind—and slip into my old Cons. "I've got ten years of making up to do. I can't afford to waste a single day."

Nine

TORRIN ISN'T JUST a priest—he's a ninja priest.

I don't think a single reporter figured out I'd left my parents' house—that's how good he is.

After brushing my teeth and hair, I found him sitting on the bottom stair, waiting for me. Mom voiced her protests, but she didn't blockade the door like Dad would have if he were home. I was surprised she hadn't called him yet, with Torrin being there and everything, but maybe she'd noticed how I was most at ease when he was around.

He'd parked his truck down at his old house—he'd cleared it with the new owners, I guess. Then he led me through the maze of fences and yards we had to have run hundreds of times to each other's houses—because why take the sidewalk when this was so much fun?

We crawled into his truck and disappeared down the road without anyone noticing. Torrin didn't stop checking his rearview mirror until we hit the freeway though.

"I didn't think priests were allowed out from behind

an altar, and here you are, taking me to the zoo." The cars whirring by don't make me as nauseated as they did yesterday. I still can't look out the side window for long, but I can stare through the windshield no problem.

"Please, most of my time is spent just like this—with people." He jets into the left lane and pushes the truck faster. I feel like it's about to rattle apart right here in the middle of I-5. "I spend a couple hours a week behind an altar. The rest of the time, I'm out here with the rest of you."

"Helping people?" I guess.

"Trying to."

I look at him. He sees me from the corner of his eye. "You're good at it."

"Yeah?"

I crank the window down an inch to let in the fresh air. It smells good. Like rain and green plants. "Yeah."

"That's one of the reasons I became a priest. To help people." He rolls down his own window a little.

The dueling breezes play with my hair, whipping it around my face. I haven't felt wind in my hair for an eternity.

"What are the other reasons?" Even though I've accepted he is a priest, I'm not sure I understand it. He's still the Torrin I remember, but the priest part just doesn't fit. It would be like me running for politics—totally unexpected. Out of nowhere.

"There are lots of them."

"What's *one* of them?" I press.

He exhales like there's some war being fought inside

135

him. I don't think he'll answer. He has a right to keep his secrets—god knows I should be able to empathize with that.

His hand dangling over the steering wheel curls into a fist. "The woman I wanted to spend my life with was gone. I wasn't in the mood to find a backup."

My chest does that thing again—contracting like someone just hit me in the ribs with a hammer. When Torrin glances at me, it looks like someone's swinging a dozen hammers at him too.

I can't keep looking at him watching me like that. I know we're feeling the same thing—the ache of what could have been. The pain of accepting it never can be again.

I find myself focusing on the dashboard. I don't notice it right away, but when I do, I touch the bright coral smear running down the front of it. "You never cleaned it." I trace my finger down the dried nail polish, reliving the moment like it was happening right now.

"I could never bring myself to." Torrin's eyes land on the stain from the bottle I accidently spilled when I was painting my toenails on a drive to the beach. "I couldn't bring myself to just . . . erase it."

I don't know a tear's slipped out until it falls onto my arm that's still reaching out, touching the stain. It's only one tear, no more are coming, but Torrin doesn't miss it.

He sighs and clenches the steering wheel a little harder. "I'm sorry. I don't know what to say. How to act around you. I don't think I'm doing anything right." His knuckles are white when we exit the freeway. "This is all very surreal. What happened. You being back. I'm totally lost."

I don't know why he's apologizing. The only time I've felt like life hasn't siphoned every last drop of emotion out of me is when I've been with him.

"You're treating me exactly like you used to." My fingers fall away from the dash. The good memories have turned to painful ones, a spilled bottle of nail polish included. "I'd rather have you act like nothing happened and I'm the same person you remember than have you second-guess everything you say and do."

His knuckles loosen around the steering wheel. He rolls his fingers, popping them.

"Just do what comes naturally to you." I turn in my seat to face him. "I'll do what comes naturally to me, and maybe things will get easier."

We're stopped at the light leading to the zoo, and he looks at me. His forehead is folded into creases. "What comes naturally to me?" He doesn't pause long enough for me to reply. "I'm not sure that would be helpful to either of us."

It's not my chest that hurts when he says that—it's my stomach. It's not really pain though—it's something else. I haven't felt it in a long time, and I know I shouldn't feel it right now. Not with him being what he is, me being what I am, and the world being zeroed in on what feels like my every move.

I can't let that look in his eyes keep doing this to my stomach. I can't let the way his chest is rising and falling harder now affect mine.

The light changes, thankfully, and his eyes move from me to the road. The air inside the cab takes a while to clear though despite the cracked windows.

"That's when I started to fall in love with you—after my dad died and you acted the exact same around me. You treated me the same as you had every day before. Still rubbing it in my face when you scored higher on a test. Still knocking on my door and seeing if I wanted to shoot hoops. When everyone was understanding of me wanting to lock myself in my bedroom, you got me to play basketball." He smiles at the windshield like he's watching the twelve-year-old versions of us playing a game of Around the World. "You brought me back . . . when everyone else just kind of left me behind."

I find my eyes drifting back to the nail polish stain. "And when did you finish falling in love with me? When I finally let you win a game of one-on-one? Or was it the night we . . . you know?" Thinking about that night makes me blush. Talking about it makes me shift.

Torrin glances at me for a moment. "I'll never finish falling in love with you."

My chest kind of seizes, and I don't know what to say because I'm not sure what he means. So I stare out the window, and he gets back to looking out the windshield. Torrin winds around the parking lot a few times before settling on just the right place. It's angled right in front of an exit, and he backs into it—he wants to be able to make a quick escape.

"I brought along some essentials." His voice is back to normal, but he's careful not to look at me.

"Like snacks essentials?" I guess.

Back then, Torrin couldn't make it two hours without eating. I used to keep a packet of Skittles in my purse just in case the hunger hit him hard and we weren't within arm's reach of a container of Pringles.

"Like incognito essentials." Torrin dumps the contents of a paper bag onto the seat between us and grabs the sunglasses first. He slides them onto my face, tucking the sides behind my ears carefully. Next he flops one of his old ball caps on my head.

The third item he leaves on the seat.

"The scarf isn't an essential?" After tucking my hair behind my ears, I find myself rubbing my neck. The bandages are off, but it hasn't healed. It never will. I'll always have a thick, uneven purple scar circling my neck to pique people's attention. Some of them will assume I tried to hang myself, and the others will recognize my face and be surprised the scar's as angry looking as it looked on television.

"It's up to you. I wanted to bring it just in case . . ."

I reach for the turquoise pashmina scarf and twist it around my neck. My fingers shake at first when I feel something tightening around my neck, but then Torrin loosens it. Sliding it around and positioning it just so, he finds a way to leave it loose while still covering the scar.

"Thank you." I clear my throat when his fingers brush my neck as he finishes adjusting it.

He smiles his *you're welcome*. I remember him doing that a lot. "There. Now you're free to roam the zoo without having to worry about a swarm of reporters documenting your every move."

"At least one of us is incognito." I lower the dark glasses down my nose and scan his less-than-subtle outfit.

When Torrin looks at himself, he shakes his head. "Just when I think I've got it all planned out."

I smile at him and shove open the door. After closing it, I check my reflection in the window to make sure the scarf's still covering the scar.

"Ready?" He comes around the front bumper and waits for me.

I answer him by strolling up beside him. "Do you always have to wear this when you're out in public?"

I've been to church before, and mass with Torrin a few times, but I don't know the rules. After *do unto others* and *thou shalt not murder*, that's where my church knowledge runs out.

Torrin scans the parking lot as we move through it. Nothing but strollers and frazzled-looking parents. "No, I just think it's better if I do."

I nod. "To help me remember what you are now?"

Torrin's arm stops me when I'm about to step out in front of a minivan. It's been a decade since I've had to use a crosswalk.

"No," he says, dropping his arm. "To help remind myself."

I don't know what to say next, so I just don't say anything. Seems like a better option than asking him to explain. Because I think I know what he means. When he glances at me once we reach the ticket booth, I think he knows I understand what he means too.

He holds up two fingers at the ticket booth and pays for our admission. He pays with a card.

Money. Credit cards. Checks. I have none. I've never written a check. I've never used a credit card. I've never paid a bill.

I feel like I fell asleep as a child and woke up as an adult. The whole world has moved on while I'm still clutching my blanket.

"Thank you," I say, about to tell him I'll pay him back, but I can't.

Unless I ask my parents for money, I can't pay him back, and I don't want to ask them. I don't have a job that earns a paycheck and don't know what I'd be qualified for anymore. What kind of person's going to hire someone who can list their last ten years of experience as making bologna sandwiches and pouring milk while chained to a metal pipe?

"Thank *you*." He nudges me as he passes through the gates. "I haven't been to the zoo since the last time we skipped class the first week of school."

That's another good memory. A painful one now. "Why not?"

Torrin takes a map from an employee handing them out and stops. He's looking at me in that same way again. "Because it wouldn't have been the same without you."

I think I'm looking at him the same way. The sun's out, and it's warming my back, and there are no reporters or hospital staff or family to make me feel like an anomaly. There's no past and no future when he looks at me like that—there's only right now.

The map drops to his side, and he steps closer to me. His hand is reaching for me, and just when I feel his thumb brush the inside of my elbow, an old woman waddles up to us.

"Bless you, Father." She reaches for the hand he's stretching out to me and gives it a gentle squeeze. "God bless you for all you do."

She shoots me a quick smile before going on with her business, but our moment is carried off with her down toward the Arctic Adventure.

Torrin clears his throat and steps back. "What do you want to see first?" He slides his finger underneath his collar like it's too tight and holds up the map for me.

I don't need to look. I know what I want to see first. "The elephants."

"The elephants." Torrin tries to groan, but it's pathetic. Just like it always was when he'd try to grumble over my excitement at the elephants. "Why always the elephants? Why not the lions? Or the gorillas? Or the adorable sea otters?"

"Because," I answer him.

He follows me with another grumble. "They eat. They poop. They trudge. What's so exciting about that?"

"Try looking in their eyes this time, Mr. Lion Lover. If you do, you'll see that there's a soul in there. Not just an animal that's all instinct. Not one who only eats, poops, and trudges."

He makes a face like he's considering that, but he shakes his head a whole five seconds later. "Nope. Lions are cooler."

I roll my eyes and shove him as we wander down the path to the elephants. It's a beautiful day at the zoo, so it's a busy day at the zoo. People are passing by me and in front of me and around me, and I'm trying my hardest not to think about it.

I tell myself that I've got to get used to this again. People. Places. Living in the suburbs of one of the largest cities in the nation. By the time we round the zebra enclosure, I think I'm doing a pretty good job of it. I might be the only person meandering around the zoo with sweaty palms from fighting off an anxiety attack, but at least I'm not succumbing to it.

I've got a headache too. A bad one. I think it's from the sunshine. I haven't been in direct sunlight in a decade, and it's making my brain feel like it's about to explode through my temples. Even the sun hurts me now—just like everything else good from my life before.

Torrin stays beside me, matching my unhurried pace, looking happy. I wonder if I look the same—because I feel happy. At least what I think happy feels like. Or what I can expect it to feel like after everything.

When we reach the elephant pen, a keeper is standing at the fence, talking to a group of people.

"Elephants." I hear the excitement in my voice as I smile at Torrin.

He frowns, but it's another pathetic attempt. "Elephants."

I hurry around the edge of the crowd and try to wedge in closer so I can hear what the keeper's saying. Torrin shadows my every step.

"Some of you might have heard of the practice of chaining an elephant from the time it's a baby. Like most everything relating to the training and exhibiting of animals, it's a controversial topic." The keeper leans down to pick up something from the ground. I can't see what it is. "I'm not going to talk about the controversy because it gets real ugly, real fast. We're talking the-lions-are-loose bloodbath ugly."

A soft chuckle rolls through the crowd gathered around.

"I'm just going to talk about the practice of baby elephant chaining and the reasons it's done. Simply put, it's done because it works. It's the only way a person my size can control something that size." The keeper's arm swings behind him toward the elephants.

When I see what's in his hand, I feel like someone's just stabbed me in the stomach.

"One of these chains we use on a baby, and one we use on big Brutus out there. Which one of these chains do you think goes on a baby elephant? This thick heavy one or this one that looks like paperclips strung together in comparison?" The keeper bounces the two chains in his hands.

The way they rattle makes me want to cover my ears. The way they move in his hands, almost like two iron snakes slithering, makes me want to close my eyes. I feel Torrin's hand on my shoulder, gently pulling me back, but I don't move.

The keeper points at a kid who shouts out the paperclip chain. Another kid says the same.

The keeper shakes his head at both and lifts the heavy chain. "This goes on the baby elephant." His hands switch, and the paperclip chain goes high. "This one's for big Brutus. You wanna know why?"

The crowd is looking around at each other with surprise. The kids are gaping at him.

"You see, a baby elephant's going to fight the chain like crazy the first time he's tied to it. He's going to cry and fight and make everyone and anyone think he's being attacked by a herd of hyenas. Baby elephant's going to fight. She's going to fight hard."

The keeper shakes the heavy chain again, and the knife-slashing sensation travels higher. Now it's stabbing into the hollow of my neck.

"So why does this chain go on junior and this one go on big daddy?" the keeper asks the crowd, still jingling those chains.

No one's saying anything, probably afraid to be wrong like the two kids before. I'm not afraid to speak up, because I know why.

"The baby elephant stops fighting." I don't realize it's me talking until I notice the keeper's gaze shift in my direction. "It learns it can't break the chain no matter how hard it fights, so it just . . ." When I pause, I feel Torrin move closer behind me. "It gives up trying to escape."

The keeper nods. "That's correct. It's called learned helplessness, and I would not suggest typing that into an internet search engine unless you want to spend the rest of your life in a chronically depressed state."

He's smiling, and so is the crowd, but I don't understand why. What about any of this is funny? How is taking an animal and fucking with its head to control it worth a smile?

"So by the time junior grows up into a five-ton mammoth that could move a semi if it wanted to, it's learned it's helpless. It doesn't fight this chain or this one because it's figured out that the chain is stronger than him." The keeper lets go of the chains and lifts two different things, one still giant in comparison to the other. "It's the same with the stakes they're chained to. Junior gets the one that looks like it's as heavy as Thor's hammer, and Dad gets the one that looks like a paper cutter in comparison."

My lungs are straining, and I feel the urge to run. To remind myself I'm free and no chain is trapping me.

"To make this more relatable, it would be like tying a length of Silly String to this guy's ankle and staking him to the ground with a toothpick." The keeper points at a guy who looks like he could be the leader of a motorcycle gang. "It would work too, but only if we'd beaten the fight out of him from the start with something a little more substantial." The keeper kicks at the chains at his feet.

When my gaze flickers to the elephants roaming behind him, I have this intense urge to rip apart the barrier stretching around their exhibit to free them. So they *know* they're free. So it's not a manipulation keeping them from realizing how powerful they are.

"It's cruel," spouts from my mouth before I know I'm thinking it.

Torrin's hand squeezes my shoulder. It's not a suggestive one to shut up. It's not one to pull me away. It's one to support me—to let me know he's here.

"Why's it cruel? It's the only way for humans and elephants to coexist in relatively close quarters." The keeper has warm eyes, but I learned ten years ago that warmth on the surface doesn't mean that what's deeper isn't encased in ice. I don't let it fool me. I won't let it fool me again.

"Elephants don't need to coexist with us. They don't ask to be around us. They don't want to." I move a little closer to the keeper. Torrin moves with me. "The reason they coexist with humans is because we've taken them from their homes and forced them into a life they'd never choose. They're here because someone took them from their lives in Africa or Asia or they took their parents or grandparents, because some asshole decided they wanted an elephant, and why the hell not?"

I notice a few parents take their kids by the hand and pull them away from the "crazy lady." I should stop. I don't know what I'm saying—it just feels like I have to say it.

"You can't just take something because you want it," I say. "You can't just fuck with its freedom then chain it up and fuck with its head too."

The crowd is quiet now. Really quiet. I've been shouting loudly enough that more of a crowd has gathered. As I scan the crowd, I see phones raised and what I guess are people snapping photos or videos.

It isn't until the keeper's eyes lower to my neck that I realize what's happened. The scarf has come loose in the midst of my fit. People are staring at the scar, recognition flickering in their eyes. With the way some of them are looking at my neck, I start to wonder if I have a real knife sticking out of it.

"I'm sorry, ma'am." The keeper sets the stakes down and kicks the chains back a ways. Recognition is on his face too. "I didn't mean to make it so personal."

More people stare—even the kids are looking at me like they know something's off. I feel like everyone knows who I am and what happened to me. The scar is like walking around with a sign listing my darkest, deepest secrets. I haven't seen the news or read the headlines, but I can imagine what has been blasted out there.

How many young girls in this area have wide purple scars winding around their necks?

From the phones that continue to rise toward me, I know not many.

"This isn't about me," I shout to the keeper as I back away. "This is about the goddamned elephants."

I turn to leave because I've seen enough of the zoo for one day. Phones pan with me as I hurry back up the same path we just walked. Torrin is beside me before I get more than a few steps away.

"I don't like the zoo anymore," I say, trying to ignore a few of the cameras still following me.

Torrin curls his nose. "Yeah. Zoos suck."

I catch one last look of the elephants before we reach the top of the pathway. I didn't get close enough to look in their eyes this time. If I had, I wonder if I'd still think I could see their souls. I doubt it—how could a soul survive when it had been strangled out by a length of chain?

The scarf is swinging at my sides, my neck drawing more attention as we fly to the zoo's entrance. Grabbing the scarf, I start to wind it back around my neck, tighter this time so it stays. When I'm about to wrap it around a third time, Torrin stops me. Taking the end of the scarf from me, he unwinds what I've just done. Then he lets it slide off the back of my neck and clutches it in his hand.

"You're better without it."

Ten

SINCE I CLEARLY don't like the zoo anymore, I let my mom drag me to the mall close by the house. Maybe I've gone all opposites on myself and what I used to loathe now I love.

I realize that's not the case the instant I step inside the mall in Bellevue. It's a Saturday after lunch, and I remember this place being crazy busy on a Tuesday morning. It feels like just as many people are milling about here as at the zoo a few days ago, but we're enclosed here. No fresh air to help me flush out the panic attack before it digs its claws into me.

"Anywhere you want to start?" Mom asks as we join the masses of shoppers zipping around like Christmas is seven hours away instead of seven months. "You'll need new everything, so we might want to start at one of the big anchor stores first."

I'm wearing another one of my old outfits. It's a shirt of a band that's not even around anymore, and my cut-offs are only staying up because I borrowed one of Mom's belts. I know I need new clothes, but I'm not in the mood to shop.

Shopping. Spending hours and hours skimming through, trying on, and purchasing things that will be dumped off at a thrift store next year was a practice I hadn't really understood as a teenager—it's even more extreme now.

I know it means a lot to my mom though, so I try to look interested. "Okay, sounds good."

She waits for me, but I can't remember the names of the big stores or in what direction they are. "Let's start at Nordstrom."

She starts down the hall, and I follow. I know she still feels uncomfortable around me. Sometimes I catch her looking at me like she can't figure out who invaded her daughter's body or how I can be exorcised. She isn't the only one who looks at me that way.

Torrin's the only one who still looks at and talks to me the way he used to. I'd rather have the old mom who would be ordering me to keep up and to wipe the sulk off my face than the one who keeps glancing back at me like she's waiting for me to blow.

As we pass a cell store, I pause to look inside. The phones have changed a lot since I had one. "I think I need a cell phone."

Mom backs up toward where I'm hovering at the entrance, and she glances inside. "Why do you think you need one?"

I shrug. "In case I want to call anyone."

"We've got a landline for that." She tries moving on,

but I don't move with her. She stops and waits.

"In case anyone wants to call me."

Recognition settles into her expression. "You mean in case Torrin wants to call you."

I shrug again. "Since Dad's been screening my calls, yeah, it would be nice to be able to talk to who I want to when I want to. I'm not a kid anymore, Mom."

When I say the "I'm not a kid" part, my mom's shoulders fall just enough to notice. She knows it's not quite the truth. Even I know it's not. I might be twenty-seven, but I still feel very much like the seventeen-year-old I was. I might as well have been cryogenically frozen because I feel like ten years have slipped by without including me.

"You know Torrin's a—"

"A priest?" I interrupt. "Yeah, kind of hard to miss."

"You might not have missed it, but do you understand what that means?"

Right then, I feel very much like a teenager having an argument with her mom about a boy in the middle of a mall. "That hopefully he likes wearing black? A lot?"

"Jade." I hear a fragment of the mom I remember. It urges me on.

"Mom, let it go. I know what I'm doing. We're friends." I cross my arms like she has. "Even if he wasn't a priest, it wouldn't matter because I'm not ready to jump into a relationship with anyone right now. Or ever."

I look away, but I'm too late. She didn't miss the look that flashed on my face when I decided to involuntarily gut myself in front of her.

"I just don't want to see you hurt," she says. "You've been through enough. Don't put yourself in a position to open yourself up to more."

"Torrin would never hurt me."

"Not intentionally, but him being back, being around so much . . . I wonder if he already has."

The idea of a cell phone withers. She's right, of course. I don't need a cell phone just so he can call me when he wants to. He's stopped by every day since I got home, and we can say whatever we need to then. I shouldn't need a private phone so he can reach me any hour of the day . . . or so I can reach him.

We haven't crossed a line, but I wonder if we'd know if we had.

I end the cell phone argument by continuing past the store. It takes a second for Mom to follow me, but when she comes up beside me, I can tell she's torn. I know she can see that whatever happy is in my world now is when Torrin's around. I know she doesn't miss the way my smiles are less fake when he's close. How I laugh when he's near. How the heaviness pressing me down seems to take a break when I'm with him.

She knows.

She also knows the way I used to feel about him. I couldn't tell my dad, but Mom was easier to talk to. She knows I'm playing with fire by spending so much time with him.

I know I am too.

But maybe I'm too selfish to stop it, or maybe I'm just too fucked up to know better.

Nordstrom is slammed when we stroll up to the first-floor entrance. A line of customers waiting for their coffees stretches into the hall. Every salesperson in the shoe department is bustling about, tending to a few customers at once. Women are dabbing on samples of lip gloss at the makeup counter, and men are perusing expensive watches behind the glass cases.

It's too much. Overstimulating sensory overload.

The smells of dozens of different perfumes almost knock me over. The roar of customers shopping isn't so dull. The overhead lights are more than a little too bright.

I feel like a strobe is flashing in my face; the light is that debilitating. I've avoided going out thanks to the news crews still camped out in front of our house. I managed a quick trip to the grocery store with my mom late one night, and I squeezed in a trip to my favorite drive-thru for lunch yesterday. But it's kind of hard to still love a restaurant known for its hamburgers when I'm done with meat.

"What department should we start in?" Mom moves for the up escalator. "Women's casual wear?"

I nod and pretend like I know what she's talking about. Women's casual wear? Sounds like a disease or something. I used to do most of my shopping at garage sales and concert merch tables.

When we weave through the people and get to the escalator, I balk. Not long enough for Mom to notice, but I do. Ten years. From the way I just had to run through how to step onto an escalator, it might as well have been a century.

When we reach the second floor, Mom gets off. I'm

thankful we don't have to climb on the one stretching to the third floor. She starts for a department with a lot of jeans and cotton shirts—*women's casual wear*—when I hear my name shouted from behind.

I flinch, half expecting it to be the swarm of reporters who've resorted to shouting my name whenever I drive by. So far I haven't been stalked out in public, but I know that won't last. Not with the interview deals I'm getting. Everyone in the world seems to need to know every last ugly detail of my captivity.

"Jade!" the voice calls again.

I turn around slowly to find a couple of girls my age powering my way, balancing on heels so high they might as well be stilts.

"Jade Childs, no frickin' way." The brown-haired one nudges the blond one when they stop in front of me.

Mom comes up beside me, but instead of glaring at them with skepticism like I am, she's smiling politely. "Candace. Morgan. How are you girls?"

Candace. Morgan. The names are familiar. I can't remember last names, but I remember us being friends. They don't look like anyone I remember, but a decade's gone by. I'm probably not recognizable either.

"Taking advantage of the shoe sale, so pretty darn amazing." Candace, the brown-haired one, holds up a couple of large bags.

Beside her, Morgan does the same.

"But enough about us. How are you?" Candace leans in and rests her hand on my wrist like we're best friends.

"I'm good." I slip to the side so her hand drops from

my wrist.

She and Morgan exchange a look. "Yeah?"

"Yeah."

Mom shifts.

"I'm so sorry about what happened. What a night-mare." Morgan sets her bags down and looks like she wants to hug me. I slide back some more. "When we heard you were found, god, we threw a celebration party."

"You threw a party?" It seems like a strange thing to do after what happened. I can't process it.

"Practically everyone from our class came. They're all so happy you're back, Jade. You know how much eve-ryone liked you."

I sweep my hair behind my ear. "Everyone came?"

I'm on repeat because I don't know what to say. I was missing for ten years, and people threw a party when I came back? I can't make it compute. I should be glad friends were happy I'm back, but it's been so long that so much of the old me is gone. I don't remember them.

"Of course. Well, everyone but the ones who moved away or, you know, died." Morgan bites her lip and looks to Candace for an interception.

"And Torrin—he didn't make it." Candace gives me a look I feel like I'm supposed to understand, but I can't translate it.

"He's a busy guy."

Morgan bobs her head while Candace shakes hers. "You've heard about him, right? Well, of course you have. I saw you two on the news when you came home from the hospital." She nudges Morgan, but I don't know what it means. "Can you believe that though? I mean, crap, I go to St. Marks." Her head shakes again. "Do you know how awkward it is to go to confession and talk about my dirty thoughts to the same guy who's responsible for them? Sheesh. That's one boy who grew up in all the right places."

She laughs a little, then Morgan stabs her elbow into Candace's side. Another look.

Candace's face drops. "Oh yeah, you guys were a pretty big thing in high school, right?"

If you consider agreeing to marry each other one day a pretty big thing, then yeah, we were a pretty big thing. I answer her with a shrug.

"That must be crazy weird for you then . . ."

"Not weird at all."

Mom clears her throat and looks behind us.

"Really?" Morgan asks.

"Well, I was kidnapped for ten years, and no one thought I was still alive to be found, and here I am." I lift my hands at my sides. "Torrin becoming a priest isn't so hard to wrap my head around."

I think Morgan and Candace are regretting their decision to come up to me almost as much as I am. They're looking behind them now too.

"You know, we should get together." Candace pulls a phone from her pocket. "Like soon. We'll spread the word so you can catch up with all of your old friends. Oh"—she waves her phone at me—"I've got a friend who is so single and so hot it should be illegal. He's got a 401(k) that would drop an heiress's panties, and he drives a 911. I should introduce you two."

I guess the way I'm breathing catches Candace's attention because she stops talking. She looks at my mom, who's looking at me with the same concerned expression.

"You know, whenever you're ready for it," Candace adds.

"*If* you ever are." Morgan elbows her friend, watching me like everyone else is.

I feel like someone's dropped a beach ball into my chest and is blowing it up. My lungs are straining, my ribs are stretching—everything hurts. My vision blurs, and I know I need to get away.

Talking about Torrin and parties and set-ups with a couple of friends from my past who feel more to me like ghosts than real people has shoved me to the tipping point. I need to find a quiet place where I can be alone, or I'm going to go off. Right here on the second floor of Nordstrom.

From the way Mom's looking at me, I think she knows. "Jade"—her hand rests on the outside of my arm—"do you want to leave?"

Morgan and Candace look from me to each other then stare at my neck now that I'm preoccupied. Candace swallows and steps back. Morgan blinks and looks like she might cry.

"I'll . . ."—the word sputters out—"I'll . . ." My head whips around, looking for an escape. "I'll be . . . right back."

I take off, rushing toward the end of the store where I can just make out the words *Women's Dressing Room.* It'll have to do because I can't keep going. Not right now. Every day since returning has been a challenge. Every hour, minute, and second have tested me. I've been gripping an anvil hanging over the edge of a cliff and trying to keep it from falling, and that rope is slipping through my hands.

I can only hold on for so long before I give out.

This is the moment I give out.

I lunge into the dressing room.

A woman standing at the mirror whips her head around and gives me a concerned look. "Are you okay?"

I nod as I stumble down the row of rooms. "Yeah," I get out before pushing through the empty room at the end.

After I get the door locked, I slide to the floor. It's carpeted and clean, but when I curl my body onto it, a smell assaults me. Bleach. It's pungent and vile and too much. The end of the rope slides through my hands, and the weight I'm holding falls. I fall with it.

Eleven

Ten Years Ago

"**S**ARA? ARE YOU feeling better yet?"

The voice cuts through my consciousness, rousing me. How long was I out this time? With the black I'm shrouded in, it's impossible to know.

How long have I been here? Where is *here?*

"Sara?" The familiar trio of knocks sounds outside the door. It's a thick door from the sounds of it. The knock doesn't echo; it thuds like it's being absorbed into the wood.

I'm on my side like always because I can't sleep on my back anymore. I don't feel safe enough to sleep so exposed—it's better to stay curled up, huddled up. I let my legs stretch a little, my arms out in front. Everything aches—like I'm one giant pulsing bruise.

"Are you awake, Sara?" Another knock. Like his knock, his voice is strong. At least strong enough that when I hear it, I immediately feel weak.

"How long have I been in here?" My voice strains when I speak. It sounds like I've been stumbling through the desert for days without water.

There's a case of bottled water shoved in here somewhere. There's a box of energy bars too. I haven't touched any of it though because I don't want to live if this is going to be my life. A dark space that's so small I can't lie down sideways in it. A bucket stuffed in the back corner for me to use as a toilet. A small hard mattress that smells so strongly of bleach I gag when I forget to breathe through my mouth.

If this is my life now, separated from my family and friends and *him* forever, I don't want it. I'd rather die now than live this for whatever is left of my life.

I know the numbers. Comes with being a cop's kid. They aren't good in my case. The first twenty-four hours after an abduction are critical, and if the person isn't found in forty-eight, the family had better just accept they'll be planning a funeral where a body may or may not be present.

I don't know how long I've been gone exactly, but long enough my nails have grown enough to notice. Long enough I've dug at the four walls keeping me caged, searching for some weak spot, for something to give me hope that I might be able to escape. There's nothing. This place feels like it was built for a wild animal instead of a seventeen-year-old girl.

There is no weak spot. I'm never going home.

"How long have I been in here?" I cry out again, but

it's so weak sounding I don't think my words make it past the heavy door. It's not cold in here, but I still shiver. I refuse to use the blankets and pillow. They're still folded at the foot of the bed.

"Seven days." It sounds like he's right outside, pressed up against the door.

A week. I'd guessed half that. I'm never going to see any of them again. Ever.

"What do you want?" I start to cry. I've cried a lot. With the lack of water, I don't know how I haven't already dehydrated myself into an early death.

"I just want you to feel better, Sara. With your mom taking you away from me like she did . . ." There's another pound on the door. Or maybe it's the wall. "It had to be upsetting for you, but you're home now. You're safe. We can be together again."

The mattress is wet below my face from the tears. They don't dull the bleach smell though. Actually, they make it stronger. "Then let me out of here. I can't get better if you keep me locked in here."

"Not yet, Sara. You're not ready."

I don't know his name, which makes him that much scarier. Referring to the man who kidnapped me as Him is worse than calling him Bob or Bill.

"But I promise the minute you are, I'll let you out, and we can get back to being happy again. We can get back to the way life used to be."

I blink like I'm trying to adjust my eyes to the dark, but it's no use. This is the kind of dark so void of light no amount of time or adjusting will make it possible to see.

I'm blind in here.

"Sara?" he calls after I'm quiet for a minute.

I can't reply because I'm crying harder now.

Other than the van, the map, the needle, and him, I don't remember anything until waking up on this mattress. It had taken a minute for my head to clear from whatever he'd injected me with, then the panic cleared the rest. The first thing I did was make sure I was clothed and that nothing felt . . . violated.

That was the first time I cried—when I realized I hadn't been hurt in *that* way. The next thing I did was scream. I screamed so much after waking up I went hoarse. I didn't stop screaming then either. When no one came, I inspected the room with my hands. After that, when still no one came, I curled back up onto the mattress and cried myself asleep.

"Let me go. Please." I've pleaded those same words so many times I think they're embedded in the walls. "Let me go home."

The floor groans as I picture him shifting outside the door. "Sara." There's a finality in his voice. A certainty. "You are home."

I grab the bucket and throw it at the door. It clangs against it and clatters to the floor. Even with a bucket of waste splattered across the room, all I can smell is bleach. It burns my nostrils every time I breathe.

"I'm not Sara!" I yell, but right then, after only seven days, I start to wonder if I am her. I don't feel like myself anymore.

It doesn't take long for everything we think we are,

no matter how deeply grounded, to be rooted up and cut away. It doesn't take long to lose yourself in such a way you almost find yourself hoping you'll never be found.

All it takes is one week.

Twelve

IT'S THE DAY of Earl Rae's funeral.

It's also the day my parents have planned to have a big get-together at one of the event centers overlooking the Sound. I wonder if they planned it that way on purpose or if it's mere coincidence.

Two weeks have gone by since I was found. My parents are making it something to celebrate. I'm going along for their sakes, but after two weeks, I should be doing better. I shouldn't still be floundering in everyday conversations or fretting over the thought of going out in public or failing to move forward.

I should be easing back into normal life instead of feeling like I'm being dragged behind a truck against my will. I should be looking forward to the party tonight—seeing family I never thought I'd see again, catching up with old friends—but I'm not.

I think I'm dreading it mostly. Dreading most of it at least.

I'm tucked into the back of Dad's Tahoe, and I feel

like a little kid driving to her first day of kindergarten. My
nerves are standing on end, and my stomach feels like
someone's using it as a stress ball. Squeeze, release.
Squeeze, release. Maybe that's part of the reason I haven't
had much of an appetite lately—because I don't want to
have to worry about throwing up from the endless stomach
spasms.

Mom turns around in her seat as we roll into the event
center's parking lot. She's smiling. Her dress is sparkling
from the streetlights and so are her eyes. "Are you excited?"

They've done so much for me. They've put so much
into this night. "Yeah, I am."

"It's going to be one hell of a night, that's for sure."
Dad's in a tux, which is a big deal. I guess the last time he
wore one was for his wedding.

"Now, sweetie, if anytime you feel . . ." She bites her
lips, her memory probably flashing over the incident at the
mall. "Like you need to be alone, just let me know, and
we'll find you a special place. We'll lock the women's
bathroom if we have to, okay?"

I look out the window. To her knowledge, I've only
had one of those "incidents," but I've actually had several
since. All of them were brought on by feeling overwhelmed. All of them ended with me passing out and having some flashback of my time with Earl Rae. Not all of
the flashbacks were unpleasant either—I think those were
more disturbing than the unpleasant flashbacks.

"Okay," I answer as I scan the parking lot. It's filled
with cars. I don't see a single space open, and this isn't

exactly a small event center.

"I'll let you girls off here and go park." Dad brakes right in front of the main doors and waits.

Mom throws her door open and slides out, excited. I linger in the backseat.

I'm wearing a dress Mom picked out for me after she went back to the mall alone. She was way more productive on her own than she would have been with me in tow, having an "incident" whenever I ran into someone from my past.

It's a long, strapless plum-colored dress with a thin satin belt. It's really lovely actually. I might have picked it out on my own if I'd been with her. It fits pretty well too —other than the chest area. Although that problem was solved by mom's creativity with a padded strapless bra.

She picked up a pair of flats and a pair of heels, and I obviously chose the flats. A party with a couple hundred people was not the time to make my reappearance in heels after a ten-year break.

Mom made an appointment to have my hair done too. She found someone to come to our house even. Earl Rae occasionally trimmed my hair since he didn't let me handle anything sharp after the mirror incident, but he couldn't cut a straight line no matter how many times he tried.

When the hairstylist was done, she'd taken off some length, cut a *straight* line, and styled my hair in a way she called "Hollywood glam." I called it "driving me nuts all night from being in my face," but it did look nice.

Now that I'm sitting here, minutes from stepping inside the party, I feel like the dress and the hair are an illusion. Kind of like taking a can of gold spray paint to a rotten tooth—the shiny coat doesn't change that what's beneath it is still decaying.

Mom opens my door when I don't open it. "Are you okay, Jade?"

I've heard that question so many times over the past two weeks my automatic response is conditioned into me. "Yeah. Just making sure I have everything."

As I slide out of the backseat, Mom holds up a thin silk scarf in the same color as my dress. She had it dyed to match and everything. "Did you decide on this, sweetheart?"

I stare at it hanging from her hand. I don't want to hide behind it, but I wonder if I should. Just because everyone inside this building has to know about the collar by now and has probably seen pictures of my scar doesn't mean they need to see it two feet in front of them.

It doesn't mean they don't have to either.

I think of the turquoise wrap Torrin got me. I think of the way he unwound it from me. I think of what he said to me.

"No, I'll go without."

Mom holds it for another second, seeing if I'll change my mind, before stuffing it into her purse. "It will be here if you change your mind."

Dad gives the horn a tap as he drives away, then we're walking inside. I hear the noise coming from the reception room right away. Mom told me there'd only be a hundred people or so, but it sounds more like a thousand.

It makes me freeze in the middle of the hallway.

"Jade?" Mom stops when she realizes I'm not beside her anymore. "Is this too much too fast? You don't have to do this. I'll explain to everyone—I know they'll understand." She grabs my hand and holds it like it's a flower that's petals are about to fall off. "We can try this again later. You don't have to do this."

The doors leading to the room are closed, but the noise keeps growing.

"I want to." I swallow. "I'll be okay."

"Jade . . ."

"Really, Mom, I'm good." When I move to unfreeze my feet, they come loose.

She exhales like she doesn't believe me, but she keeps moving with me.

"Everyone's not going to, like, yell surprise and throw confetti, are they?"

"No, absolutely not. I asked everyone just to keep doing whatever they're doing when you come in so you don't feel like the center of attention."

I catch the scent of Mom's perfume. It's the same one she's worn for as long as I can remember, and for some reason, it calms me.

"Is that okay?" she asks.

A rush of air comes from my mouth. "So okay."

The longer we walk, the longer the hallway seems to become. I feel like those double doors will always be fifty steps away no matter how long we walk.

"Have you given any more thought to the news interviews?"

My spine goes rigid. "I'm not ready."

"The cameras, the reporters, they're not going away until you tell your story. At least, I don't think they will."

"They'll lose interest eventually."

Mom sees right through my lie. "What some of those national networks are offering . . . it's substantial. It could set you up for the rest of your life."

I've heard the numbers. They've been in the seven-figure range. Instead of making the interviews more appealing, it makes them less. Almost like I'm ready to announce the exact price for whatever is left of my soul. "Mom, I don't even know what my life is right now. I'm not exactly worried about financial planning for whatever it is."

She wants to say more—her thoughts are that loud—but she keeps her words to herself and forces a smile. "Then let's not worry about any of that. Let's just enjoy tonight, okay?"

Somehow we've ended up in front of the ballroom doors. They're closed still, but the noise is almost deafening. It sounds like I've just stuck my head into a beehive.

"Ready?" Mom's hand drops to the handle of the door.

I take in a breath. It doesn't reach my lungs. "Ready."

As she opens the door, I wonder how much longer I'll have to lie about being ready. I'm starting to believe I'll always have to lie.

She opens the door slowly, noiselessly, like she knows I don't want a grand entrance but a secret one. She waves me inside with a careful smile. I focus on her face as I move inside because the buzz that had been coming from in here a moment ago is fading. Fast.

The secret entrance is turning into the other kind.

This is confirmed when I make myself look around the room. It's swollen with bodies, brimming with people dressed in nice clothes, holding their drinks as closely as they're holding their expressions.

I feel like everyone has noticed me. Some are doing a better job of hiding it, but everyone's stolen a glance. The noise continues to dull in volume.

Behind me, the door whispers closed as Mom steps up beside me. She waves at a few people who are motioning us over, but she stays at my side.

Smile, I tell myself. *Just smile.*

At least that's a start.

I don't recognize a single face in the sea of them rolling over me. Strangers are everywhere I look. The ones who hadn't been outright staring are now. It isn't my face they're staring at though.

My fingers curl together. I wish I'd taken the scarf from Mom.

I feel it grappling at me again—that feeling of spinning out of control. The sensation of losing my grip on the weight I'm hanging onto.

This was a bad idea. The worst. If I lose it right here, all of these people won't just have the external scars burned into their memories.

My breaths are coming harder and faster, but it isn't oxygen I'm taking in—it's something else. Something that cripples me instead of reviving me.

171

The sequins from cocktail dresses catch the overhead lights just right, bouncing lasers around the room. The smells coming from the food tables. The smells coming from the open bar. The heat pulsing over me from all of the bodies.

My vision blurs again, and just when the familiar flash of white starts to go off before I pass out, everything goes dark.

If it weren't for the shrieks firing around the room joined with my mom's gasp, I would assume I'd blacked out. I haven't though. The lights have just gone off.

I don't gasp or shriek or even shift though. This isn't dark. Not like I know it.

"What happened to the lights, for God's sake?" Mom's voice rings through the room, a note of nervousness in it.

I know why. She's worried this will be the straw that breaks my back. She doesn't realize I feel more comfortable now than I did when I stepped into the light just now.

I take a few steps inside the room, my breath returning, and someone reaches for my arm. "Let's leave them in the dark for another minute—what do you think?"

I hear the tipped smile in his voice. I feel the warmth in his fingers radiate up my arm. I smell the hint of the same shaving cream he's been using since his first shave the summer he turned sixteen. I feel my nerves unravel, my stomach coil, and everything else get pulled in his direction. Like I'm a million shavings of iron and he's a magnet, everything moves toward him.

"Are you responsible for this?" I whisper, turning toward him. It's dark, but I can make out his outline. Or maybe I've just memorized it enough to picture it.

"Why? Are you going to tell on me?"

When his hand slides away from my arm, I grab it. That isn't a conscious decision. It's something my subconscious dictates. "No, but I was going to thank you for it."

"And how are you going to thank me for it? I've made promises of celibacy, obedience, and to paraphrase, to abstain from anything of a fun nature." His voice is light as he braids his fingers through mine.

It's a small thing, but the sensation makes me teeter in place.

"I could always, you know, just thank you with words. The old-fashioned way." My voice is light too. It sounds strange to my ears, but it feels good. Right. "Thank you." I enunciate it slowly, which makes him laugh.

"Yooou're weeelcome," he replies.

That's when the lights fire back on. It takes me a few seconds to clear my vision, but when I do, he's staring down at me with something I don't recognize in his eyes. It's new. I want to ask him what it is, but I chicken out. I think I'm afraid of the answer.

"Okay, everyone. Crisis averted." Mom's voice echoes through the silent room. "Please just get back to enjoying the night. Thank you for coming."

He's still looking at me, and I'm still looking back, and now I know others are starting to look at us. He must realize it at the same time because he unwinds his hand free from mine.

"Probably don't need any more awkward questions

than you'll already get." His eyes scan the room as his hand slides into his pocket.

He's in black and white again, as he's always been in the past two weeks, but this isn't the same black-and-white outfit I'm used to. I step back just to make sure I'm not seeing things. And maybe I step back to get a better look at him.

"Are you wearing a tuxedo?" My heart picks up, and I know why. Seeing him like this, without his priest's collar, blurs the lines for me too much. It's easier to forget what he is and succumb to what I wish he was instead— mine again.

"I'm pretty sure that's what you call it." He glances down at himself. "At least that's what the guy at the rental place called it."

I glance at his neck. "You traded in your collar for a bow tie."

"Yeah," he says, yanking at the bow tie. "But it's still choking the hell out of me."

I smile at him yanking at the tie. It doesn't look as tight as his priest's collar. It doesn't look half as restraining. "You look good."

Actually, he looks better than good. He looks better than great. But I don't think I'm allowed to say that to a priest. Especially with the way people are tuning into our conversation, slowly creeping a little closer.

"No, *you* look good. I look like an eyesore next to you." His gaze skims down me, lingering in places I'm not sure a priest's eyes are supposed to linger.

My fingers curl into my palms. "Thank you for coming. I know you're busy and this probably isn't your thing, but I'm glad you're here."

"I'm glad I'm here. And you're wrong about this not being my thing." His eyes make their return trip to mine. "You're here."

The whole room feels like it's creeping in around us, listening, watching. I'm already a lightning rod because of what happened to me; I don't need to be one for being a priest's temptress.

"Jade, sweetie." Mom comes up beside Torrin and me, glancing around the room. "Your guests. Everyone's eager to say hello."

"Hi, Eleanor. Great party," Torrin says.

"Hello, Torrin. I'm pleased you could make it." Her voice isn't unkind, but it's stilted.

I know she doesn't want me getting hurt, but I've already been hurt. Being with him, in whatever way I am, makes me a little better each time. It's almost like every time I'm with him, another shattered piece comes back together.

"You wouldn't happen to know what happened to the lights, would you?" Mom asks him, an eyebrow arched.

Torrin's face goes flat. "I don't have a clue." He can't keep up the act though. A smile breaks as he winks. "It must have been a fluke."

"It must have been," Mom replies, looking at me. Her eyes soften from seeing me relaxed, smiling, not about to lose my shit all over the room. Leaning closer to Torrin, she pats his arm. "Thank you."

"For what?" Even his innocent face is guilty.

"Don't play innocent with me." She pats his arm one final time, waiting for me. "Father."

Torrin laughs a note and waves as Mom steers me away. I can't look away though. Not right away. Because he's in a tux, and he's staring at me the way I am at him, and he's trying to tell me something I think I'm starting to understand.

He makes himself look away first—like he knows I'm incapable of it.

Mom steers me through the room. I wave and smile at people when they do the same, but most I don't recognize. Other than some family members and a few close friends, everyone else is a blank.

"There's Sam and Patrick," Mom says when my sister and who I guess is her husband come through the door like they're not sure they're in the right place.

My dad shakes hands with Patrick and gives Sam a kiss on the cheek. That's my sister's husband. My *younger* sister's husband. They have a baby. They have impressive-sounding jobs. They've grown and evolved in the past decade while I haven't even managed to stay the same— I've wilted from the feel of it.

"You want to go say hi?" Mom catches me watching my sister, but I look away as soon as she brings it up.

They look happy. Relaxed. I don't want to change that by popping up and introducing myself to her husband as the sister who was kidnapped ten years ago.

"I think I'll mingle over here." I don't know most of the faces in the cluster of people closest by, but I'd rather face them than my sister.

Connor left last week for his Scottish adventure, and even though he offered to skip it, I encouraged him not to miss out just because I was back. Truthfully, I was relieved he was gone because it meant one less family member to have to pretend around. One last person to try to convince that I was okay.

Mom examines the group I'm moving toward. "Okay. Find me if you need anything. I'll stay close by."

She pats my arm and watches me as I keep going. She looks at me the same way as she did the day I started preschool—like she wanted to cry but was staying brave for me so I didn't.

When I'm a couple feet away from the group, the circle of people notices me coming and start to open up.

"Hey, Jade," one of the girls about my age says first. She's the only one not staring at my neck so obviously I can almost feel it burn. "I'm Paige Arlington. We were in choir together in high school."

I relax when I recognize her. The name, the association, it makes everything so much easier.

"Hey, Paige. Thanks for coming." I can't figure out where to put my arms. They feel strange at my sides. Weird behind my back. Wrong clasped in front of me. "Hey, everyone." I make eye contact with the others, not looking away until they stop gawking at my neck.

A variety of greetings come back at me. Everyone seems to shift at the same time. This is going so, so badly. I'm not just socially awkward now—I'm socially inept.

Someone wanders up to join the group, but this face I remember. Just not the name that goes with it. "Jade

Childs. You look just as great as ever."

He holds out his hand—I guess for me to shake. When I put my hand in his, he grasps it too firmly and shakes it too hard. He's probably using a perfectly acceptable touch, but it's crushing to me. I rub my hand when he releases it.

"Trent Covington. We were bio partners our sophomore year."

When he smiles at me, I remember. "You were on Torrin's soccer team." I snap my fingers. "You played goalie."

His smile falters but doesn't totally disappear. "Yeah, I played on the high school team, and actually, I played striker."

"Oh," I say, trying to remember. I can't. I wasn't exactly watching the other players on the field when I went to cheer at Torrin's games. "Yeah."

I glance over my shoulder, looking for an escape. I know these are my friends from school, and they seem like nice enough people, but I don't fit in. No one knows what to say to me—I don't know what to say to anyone.

I notice Torrin talking to another group of people we probably went to school with. He's smiling, and they're all laughing, and at least five conversations seem to be happening in that circle. No one's uncomfortable around him. And he's the priest.

His head turns, and he sees me watching him. His smile stretches. Just when he's about to get back to the conversation, he seems to notice something. His eyes slide away from me but land on someone close by. His smile vanishes.

"So, Jade . . ." Someone nudges me.

I flinch from the unexpected contact. It's Trent.

He's moved closer, and his smile's back. "It's been forever. How have you been?"

I don't really think much of his question, but the mouths of the people around me drop. Paige hisses something at Trent.

What he's said hits him. From the look on his face, it hits him like a hatchet to the back. "Oh my god. Sorry." He blows out a breath and brushes my arm. "Such a stupid question. Just ignore the idiot in the room."

I step back because I still haven't gotten used to people touching me.

"You want to hear a stupid question, Covington?" Torrin's voice breaks the silence. He's beside me like he's been here the whole time. Trent tips his head, but Torrin turns toward me. He lifts his elbow. "Wanna dance?"

"What?" I ask, able to fill my lungs again. "Really?"

Torrin's eyes lighten. "Really."

"There isn't any music." I wave around the room because not only is there no music, there's not really even a dance floor.

"Already taken care of." Torrin tips his head toward the front of the room where I see someone hooking up something that looks like it could play music. "The guy even has the song I requested."

"No one else is dancing."

"So? That doesn't mean we can't."

The guy with the machines up front flashes Torrin a

thumbs-up. Torrin returns the gesture.

"Costigan, dude"—Trent shifts closer—"you've got balls."

This time a couple others join Paige in hissing a warning at him.

Recognition flashes across Trent's face. "I mean, Father Costigan, dude. You've got . . . testicles."

I bite my cheek to keep from laughing, but the others don't. They just laugh. It's a nice sound. A real one. It takes me back to a time when I used to hang out with these people and watch movies and eat pizza. I relax a little more.

"Come on. Dance." I don't think Torrin even heard anything Trent said. "You promised to go to Sadie Hawkins, winter formal, and prom with me. We missed all three. I'm willing to exchange three dances for one song."

"Are priests allowed to dance?"

"I don't know—I think so. But Torrin Costigan's allowed to dance." He reaches out his hand like he's going to drop it onto my lower back. At the last second, he changes his mind and holds out his arm for me instead. He's not going to push me—he's letting me make the choice. "I'm not just a priest. There's more to me than that."

I take his arm because he's giving me the choice and I want to. I want to be with him in whatever way we're still allowed. "Kind of like I'm not just the missing girl?"

"Kind of like that," he replies.

Static breaks through the room right before a distantly familiar melody filters around us. Torrin leads me a few

180

feet away from the group but not far. Stepping around in front of me, one hand reaches for mine and the other slides around my back. It lowers until it's fitted into the small of my back. Then it presses deeper. My body slides against his, not quite so close that they're touching. But I'm so close I can feel the lapels of his jacket rubbing against my skin

The song plays, and people start to turn so they're facing us. I feel like everyone's been watching me all night anyway—at least now I'm doing something I want to do while they stare at me.

"Tell me this." I rest my free hand against his chest, slipping it just beneath his jacket. He still has on a vest and a dress shirt, but the motion feels intimate. "Did you ask me to dance because you wanted to or because you didn't like the way Trent was looking at me?"

Torrin's chest rises against mine. It falls a moment later. "Both."

He looks a little ashamed, but I don't. "Good."

"Trent Covington's had a thing for you since freshman year—I caught him talking about what he'd like to do to a certain part of your anatomy in the locker room after practice. Ten years later and I can still remember what he said—word for word."

I feel almost normal. So close I can feel it trying to cling to my skin. "Is that jealousy I detect in your voice?"

"No, it's loyalty. Which Covington doesn't know the first thing about." When I continue to look at him, saying nothing, he sighs. "And maybe a little bit of jealousy."

I focus on the shiny button of his dress shirt so he

doesn't notice my eyes lighten. "Good."

After that, we dance. Or I think this is what dancing is. It's been so long, but I know this is the same feeling I used to have when Torrin tucked me close to him while music played in the background. Sometimes he'd hum the tune in my ear. Sometimes he'd whisper something else. Sometimes he'd just tip his face against mine and breathe me in like he was trying to keep a part of me inside him forever.

I focus on the lyrics of the song because if I don't, I'm afraid I'm going to do something that I don't want a hundred people to witness.

"That's why you like the song, isn't it?" I say as we sway together. "Because we're lost souls?"

Torrin's hand tightens around mine. "No, we're not lost. We're right here."

He pauses to make sure I'm looking at him. I am. When I look at him like this, I know I'm here. I'm real and not some apparition that comes and goes.

"I chose this song because I used to listen to it day in and day out after . . ." He doesn't say anything else—he doesn't have to. "I thought that if I just listened to it enough, thought it enough, wanted it enough, the wishing you were here would become real. Now you're here. No more wishing. It's kind of cathartic, you know?"

My chests feels hollow when he says this because I know that even though we're dancing and reunited and still looking at each other the way we used to, we can never really belong to each other again. Something is digging out my insides, one shovelful at a time, because I'm in his arms but I've lost him.

I distract myself from the hollow feeling by touching his bow tie. "So why are you wearing a tux?"

"Remember what I said? Nothing kills a party like a priest showing up."

When my fingers pull away from his bow tie, it's a little crooked. I hadn't meant to twist it around. I'd just wanted to touch it. "Yeah, but just because you're not dressed like one doesn't mean you aren't one."

The song's winding to an end, but Torrin's hold is tightening. At least that's what it feels like. It's so gradual I'm not sure. "And just because I am one doesn't mean that's all I am."

"I know."

He blinks. "Do you?"

Pink Floyd's guitar is still playing, strumming to its end, when I see a large figure stride up behind Torrin. I know who it is, but I'm not ready. I'm not ready to let go. I'm not ready to go face more of the inevitable.

Accepting Torrin is lost to me in the way I want him is enough inevitability for one night.

Torrin must sense him there too because his mouth floats just outside my ear. "And maybe I'm wearing what I am because tonight because I don't want to remember who I am." His hands hold me closer right before they loosen. "Maybe tonight, I want to forget."

Maybe tonight and every night forward, I want to forget too. Forget it all. Except for this. Except for him. He's not supposed to be the one I tether myself to, but it doesn't change that he's the one I already have. He's not supposed to be the one . . . but he always has been The One.

I don't know what to do what that knowledge and the acceptance that he's a priest. I'm so damaged all I remember about love is how it's spelled.

"Jade." Dad's voice cuts through the final note of the song, slicing it in half. "You've got more than one guest here this evening. And most of them are starting to stare."

Torrin glances around the room, and his throat bobs.

I don't look, because I already know everyone's staring. I've had a lot of experience with that lately. "I don't care, Dad. We're just dancing."

I don't know if Torrin requested another song or not, but another one streams into the room.

"You and Torrin, you two could never just do anything." Dad motions between us like that confirms everything. "He might be who he is now, and you are who you are, but you're both fools if you think you can 'just be' anything." Dad must see my jaw setting because he angles toward Torrin. "You need to let her go, Torrin. She's going through enough without adding this to the headlines."

Dad's eyes move to Torrin's bow tie, but I know what he's seeing there instead. What I should see first and always whenever I look at him too.

"Dad . . ." I don't know what else to say.

"No, he's right." Torrin doesn't break eye contact with my dad for a second. "Besides, I got my dance. I can't keep you all to myself."

When his hand falls away from my back and unwinds from my hand, that hollowness opens up a little more.

"I wish you could," I whisper across the space separating us.

Torrin backs up—but just a step. "And I spent ten years wishing you were here. I got mine. Maybe one day . . . someday, you'll get yours too."

Thirteen

MY VOICE IS straining, my skin is burning, and my body aches. As much as I don't want to tell my parents this party was a bad idea, I'm about five more reintroductions and awkward embraces away from telling them.

It's too much. Too many people. Too many questions. Too many smiles of pity. Too many strangers touching me and talking to me and acting like I haven't missed the past decade of life.

I've met Patrick, who was a little warmer than Sam, but that doesn't say a lot. I've talked to every family member, most every old friend, and at least half of my parents' acquaintances and work friends. This would be a lot for anyone—to be at the center of this kind of attention. Up until two weeks ago, I'd spent years with one person— a person who talked without really speaking.

I'm proud of myself for doing so well tonight, but I know better than to push my limits. I don't want this day to end up with me passed out in a small room and flashing back to one of my worst memories.

I've just managed to pry myself away from a couple of our old neighbors to find one of my parents and tell them I need to leave when a conversation catches my attention as I pass the dessert table. They're work buddies of my dad's, and they're shaking their heads at each other.

"Can you imagine if that was your daughter? I don't know what I'd do," the one close to my dad's age says to the others. I can't remember his name, though I know I was told it when we were introduced.

"You know exactly what you'd do, and then Tom and I would have to arrest you, and you'd spend the rest of your life rotting with the same criminals you put away."

"How would that be a crime, for Christ's sake? I mean, come on, putting a guy like that out of his misery? Although if it was my daughter, I would have beat a lot more misery into that son of a bitch before putting him out of it, if you know what I mean."

The two men around him bob their heads.

"I know they're saying he never touched her like that, but he might as well have for as much as he fucked her up. That is not the same Jade. That's not Jade at all."

Chills spill down my back, and I know I should keep moving. I don't need to hear anything else.

"I wish that sick fucker was right here right now because let me tell you what." One of the others sets down his plate and points at the ceiling. "I'd string him up by his ankles and let everyone in this room take a swing. I'd let Jade take as many as she wanted until it was his guts spilling out instead of Butterfingers and bubblegum."

The other guys are still nodding, and I know I should keep going. Pretend I didn't hear any of it.

"I wouldn't want one." My voice doesn't sound as small as I'd thought it would.

The three officers twist around to find me standing in front of them. I see regret. I see shame. I see more pity.

"I wouldn't take a single swing."

"I'm sorry, Jade. We didn't mean for you to hear any of that. Just forget about it. We're a couple of old-school cops with a little too much whiskey in them right now," the one who suggested the stringing up says. He's fair-skinned, but he's reddening in embarrassment.

"He wasn't a bad man."

The three of them look at each other.

"He took a young girl. From her family. From her life. He took her for ten years and did terrible things to her," one of the others says, glancing at my neck. "That isn't just a bad man—that's the devil himself."

My throat is tightening with emotion. I've managed to not think about Earl Rae tonight, but now that I am, I can't stop thinking about how today was his funeral. Today was the day his body was laid to rest at Holy Names Cemetery, and all of these people are thinking the worst kinds of things about him. These three are talking about wanting to kill him all over again.

It's the day of his funeral, for Christ's sake, and I'm at a party, talking and smiling and pretending like I belong here.

I back away from the trio of men, eyeing the door. "He wasn't a bad man," I repeat, slipping farther away.

They don't argue with me this time. Instead they drop their heads and stare into their empty drinks.

I keep backing toward the door, managing to slip by friends and family and acquaintances. They don't see me. Or maybe they do and are just pretending not to for my sake. When I reach the doors, I slip through them undetected. Not even my mom, who hasn't seemed to look away from me for more than five seconds, sees me. I don't see Torrin anymore, but I guess he's still here. I want to invite him to leave with me, but I don't because somewhere inside, I know my dad's right—Torrin and I have never been able to "just" do anything.

Besides, for what I have planned for tonight, it's better if I'm alone. No one else understands. They all have opposite views from mine on this.

On my way out of the building, I skim through the coat closet to find the one I know Dad brought in for me. It's summer, but I still get cold. Especially when it gets dark. I find the dark jacket Mom picked out for me and slide into it. I check the pocket to make sure the twenty I slipped in there earlier is still there, and I keep going.

No one's in the hall as I leave. No one's outside the doors when I escape. No one's around to watch me disappear.

I'm glad for it.

I rode the bus a few times with Torrin when we sneaked into the city, but I'm nervous as I wander toward the bus stop a block down from the event center. It's late. It's dark. And I feel like a mewing white kitten that's just been dropped into a cage of owls. It's the first time I've

189

been on a dark sidewalk alone since . . . and every car that passes makes me flinch.

I tie my jacket around me tighter and wait for the bus. I don't have to wait long thankfully. When the giant machine whines up to the curb, its doors pop open.

"Will this take me by Holy Names Cemetery?" I ask the driver from the curb.

She looks down at me, in my long gown and afraid to climb the steps of the bus, and waves me on. "It will take you close. You'll have to walk a few blocks if you don't mind walking."

I exhale and climb on board. "I don't mind walking." I pay for the ride and slide into the first empty seat. The bus is mostly empty, and the ride goes fast.

After making a few stops, the driver twists back in her seat. "Hun, this is your stop. Holy Names is three or four blocks down Ash here."

I pop up and make my way off the bus. "Thank you."

"Be careful, okay? It's not safe for a woman to be out walking alone by herself at night."

I nod and smile at her, wondering what she'd say if I told her I was off to Holy Names to visit the grave of the very person who'd abducted me a decade ago.

The bus doors whine closed behind me, it screeches away from the curb, and then it's quiet. I double-check the street sign hanging above to make sure this is Ash, then I start walking.

I feel bad I didn't tell my parents or someone who could have told them because they don't need me going missing on them again. I'd just been in such a hurry to leave, and I knew they'd never have let me out those doors if they knew where I was going.

I wish I had a phone. At least I could call them to let them know I'm safe and fine and will be home later tonight. That is if I can find another bus that will somehow take me all the way back to Sammamish.

I sigh as I continue down the sidewalk. I haven't thought out any of this. All I'd been focused on was getting to the cemetery. The before and after and repercussions hadn't even flickered in my mind.

I keep going because I can't turn back.

The cemetery gates are locked, but it's only to keep cars out because I can slip right through the metal gates. Other than a few lights glowing from a couple of buildings, it's dark, and no one else is around.

I don't know where Earl Rae's buried—I only know the cemetery because of the article I read in the paper my dad left on the arm of his recliner. My parents have been careful to keep the television off during the prime news hours and make sure the daily paper is never in plain view, so yesterday's paper I found was a fluke. Or maybe it was meant to be.

I wander up and down the driveway for a while, examining the expanse of grass and graves for a patch of earth that looks freshly disrupted. I'm almost to the end of the cemetery when I notice a mound where the earth hasn't settled. Finding it takes me longer than I'd thought it would, making me thankful for the jacket I grabbed. I take a breath, hold it in, and weave my way toward it. This plot's tucked in the far back corner, so close to the fence's barrier that weeds coming from the other side have started to creep in.

When I'm close enough, I read the letters stamped onto the gravestone. I've found it. I've found him.

My chest moves faster as my legs feel like they're turning to stone. My pace slows. Taking the last few steps is next to impossible while dragging this kind of weight.

His tomb stares up at me. I can see him staring at me from beneath the ground. All at once, I feel everything I ever felt during those ten years with him. It drops me to my knees.

The earth is cold, damp. It soaks through my dress like my skin is lapping it up. His name is stamped across the gravestone in impersonal letters, the dates of his birth and death below. There's nothing else. Not even a scroll etched into the corners of it. No title, no scripture verse, no warmth.

When I lower my shaking hand to touch it, it's colder than the soft ground my knees are sinking into. So cold. So hard. So empty.

I don't want this to be my last memory of him. I don't want to remember him like this because if I do, how can I move on? I want to remember the person who celebrated my birthday every year with balloons and yellow roses . . . even if it wasn't Jade's birthday but Sara's. I want to remember the person who didn't do to me the things everyone assumes he did. I want to remember the soul who wasn't evil . . . just lost.

If anyone can empathize with a lost soul, it should be me.

The stone doesn't warm no matter how long I keep my hand pressed to it. Instead of accepting my warmth and radiating it back, it seems to consume it—to extinguish it. I feel the cold creep up my arm and tangle around my elbow.

Cold. Hard. Empty.

It's not just the stone that fits that description.

Today was his funeral. No one came. I know because there are no flowers. There are no footsteps pressed into the earth except for mine. No one came. No one left him flowers.

He didn't deserve to be put to rest like this—not even with what he did.

I hadn't noticed the person come up behind me, but I know he's there. I know because the cold blasting from in front of me wanes.

"What are you doing here, Jade?" Torrin exhales like he's been holding his breath for weeks.

I don't look back. "There aren't any flowers. No one left him any flowers." My back shakes from the sob I'm holding in. I cried in Earl Rae's presence so many times that I don't want this to be his last memory of me either.

Torrin doesn't say anything when he moves toward the fence line. He just kneels and picks through some of the weeds, plucking whatever slightly resembles a flower. I watch him, and I wonder if it hits him the same way—at this moment, he and I and Earl Rae are together. We're sharing the same space. All of those years of being separated . . . it's strange how this feels, watching him pull weeds that look like flowers for me to place on the grave

193

of the man who took me from him.

Torrin comes back once he's collected a small handful and holds them out for me. His jaw is tight, and his shoulders are tense. He won't look at the grave. He won't come close to it.

"How did you find me?" I take the bouquet of weeds and let my fingertips brush his before pulling away.

"I followed the trail of breadcrumbs you left." His voice is strained like he's being choked.

"I didn't leave any." No notes. No calls. No nothing.

"Not the visible kind maybe." He stares off in the other direction and shrugs. "And after what happened, I'm kind of hypersensitive to you suddenly disappearing."

I'm kind of hypersensitive to certain things too.

"Everyone's calling him a monster. A bad man. An evil one."

I clasp the weeds. There are a few small white flowers bursting from the ends of some, a couple dandelions sticking out. I lower the bouquet to the stone and position it above his name. I notice Torrin turn around completely.

"But he wasn't like that. He wasn't," I add when I hear him exhale sharply.

"What was he then?"

I don't recognize his voice. I've never heard it like this before.

"Sad. Confused. Lost." I pull my hand away and settle it back over my legs. "He kept me alive. He took care of me."

"After kidnapping you," he growls. The words seem to echo through the silent cemetery.

"He wasn't a bad person. He was sick. He needed help . . . but he wasn't the evil person everyone thinks he was." I twist my neck just enough so I can see him but not so far I can't see the gravestone.

"His medical records might read like an encyclopedia for mental illness, but he wasn't sick enough to not realize that swallowing a bullet when his house was surrounded by cops was a better option than spending the rest of his life in jail." He stops like he shouldn't say anymore, but he does. "Not sick enough to not have the sense to stalk you, meticulously plan your abduction, and keep you hidden for ten years. If that isn't evil, I must not know the definition."

I reach over my shoulder, unfolding my hand toward him. "I've forgiven him. You should too."

"I'll never forgive him." Even as he says this, he backs up and finds my hand with his.

Our backs stay to one another, but our hands connect us. The cold damp creeping up my legs vanishes. The stonelike heaviness crumbles.

"You're a priest," I say softly. "Aren't you supposed to be all about the forgiveness thing?"

His fingers grip mine harder. Almost so hard it hurts. "Forgiveness is in God's nature. Not man's. Not mine."

We're quiet after that. We don't move. Our hands stay connected, and he stays still, silent, letting the night wash over us.

I feel like it's time to leave—that nothing else can be achieved here tonight—but as I start to rise, something Torrin said hits me. "How do you know that he planned it?"

When Torrin stays quiet, I twist around until I'm angled toward him. He doesn't want to have this conversation. I can tell because his face is creased from the internal battle waging inside him.

He turns a little my way, his eyes shifting to our conjoined hands. "Because I've talked to the detectives working the case."

The same detectives who've wanted to talk to me for days. The same ones I've spent days avoiding and coming up with excuses for why I couldn't talk with them yet.

"Why did they want to talk with you?"

Torrin rolls his fingers in my hand—his knuckles pop. "Because I'm the one who ultimately led them to re-investigating Earl Rae Jackson."

I feel my forehead crease. "*Re*-investigating? As in they investigated him before?"

Torrin's head drops like he's been balancing a boulder on his neck for years. "I made a list, right after you went missing, of all the people I could think of that you'd come in contact with. All of them." His eyes narrow into the night. "Right down to the cashier at the gas station we used to buy our Slurpees from every day after school."

The ground moves beneath me. My world shifts as I go back in time to a period when I'd never been happier. I travel back to the afternoons spent with Torrin when we'd stopped for giant Slurpees after school to fuel up for what we had planned for later—when we told our parents we were studying. I remember the sweetness of the blueberry flavor that was our favorite, remember the way it would freeze my stomach and brain at the same time. The way the foam cup felt rubbing against the pads of my fingers. How Torrin would smile at me when I tried to pay, and instead he slipped a couple dollar bills from his wallet to the cashier before I could. I remember . . . *him.*

When I inhale, I feel like I've been drowning. I suck at the air until I feel my lungs about to burst.

"Oh my god," I breathe, doubling over because it hurts. Everything.

I never would have remembered Earl Rae's face from the gas station—I could barely remember anything from that life—but now that I do, I know I'll never forget it.

It's one memory I wish I could purge.

"The cops talked with Earl Rae after you went missing, but since he didn't have any priors and didn't fit the damn profile, they didn't take it any further."

I sway in place. Torrin's hand keeps me steady. "So how did they finally find him?" That voice isn't mine. It doesn't sound anything like mine.

For a second, Torrin leans away from me. Then he kneels beside me, but we're still not facing each other. He's aimed one way. I'm aimed the other.

"I remembered something a little while ago. Something he said to you one day after we paid for our Slurpee." Torrin blinks into the darkness. His jawbone pops through his skin. "He said you looked just like his daughter." He pauses to take a breath.

I feel like the breath was just pulled right out of my lungs.

"At the time, it didn't seem like a big deal, and it wasn't like I knew he'd lost his daughter, but for some reason, that night, I just knew it was him." When he exhales, his breath fogs the air. It's summer—it shouldn't be cold enough to steam the air with a breath. "I called the cops, told them what I remembered, and that's how they found you."

My eyes close, the eyelids too heavy to hold open anymore. I feel a tear slide down my face. Only one. But I know there are more. They never dry up.

"You're the reason I was found," I whisper.

Torrin's shoulders stiffen right before they fall. "No, I'm the reason you weren't found sooner. If I had just remembered that earlier . . . before . . ."

He leaves the words unsaid, but his face tells me the rest when it turns over his shoulder. I see it because my head's tipped over mine.

"Our lives could have been different?" My eyes stay on his as my palm presses deeper into his. "This could be more?"

He looks at our hands before his eyes sweep over my back facing him. "Yes."

I have to look away. It hurts too much. Seeing what my future could have been only to realize it never will be makes everything inside me feel like it's atrophying. Withering. Dying slowly.

I can't look at Torrin, so I look at the only place I have left. "I miss him, Torrin." I choke on the words, but they keep coming. "I'm not supposed to miss him. I can't tell anyone I miss him either . . . but I do. How fucked up am I?"

I have to break away from his hold because I need my

hands to cover my face. I don't like crying like this. Like I'm too weak to control my emotions—too weak to control my body. If I cover my face, no one has to see just how weak I really am.

"I miss the man who kidnapped me for ten goddamn years. What in the hell am I supposed to do with that?" My body's convulsing in rhythm to my sobs. I'm such a mess—the sobs only scrape the surface of that mess.

I feel the warmth of his body huddle close before his arms rope around me, holding me. Keeping me together. He's holding onto me so tightly I couldn't fall apart if I wanted to. His face lowers to my ear.

"Whatever you need to," he says in the voice I remember. "It's okay to feel whatever you're feeling. And it's okay to miss and mourn whoever you choose." His arms tighten again when a tremor slides down my back. "No one has the manual for a situation like this, so don't let anyone tell you how to feel. No one." He tucks his head into my neck and sighs. I can't tell if it's a sigh of frustration or contentedness.

With the way my vision is blurred from the tears, the bouquet looks more weed than flower now. "He was a good man, Torrin. Sick . . . but good."

His fingers curl deeper into my arms. "It's your right to believe what you think about him, and it's mine to believe how I feel about him."

"How do you feel about him?"

Torrin inhales against my neck, then he rises. He finally looks at the gravestone in front of me. His eyes narrow at it, and I see things flash in them I hadn't known existed inside of Torrin Costigan. I see things I hadn't known existed in any man.

"That hell has no inner circle bad enough for a man like Earl Rae Jackson."

Then Torrin turns his back on the grave, but before he walks away, he holds out his hand and waits. He's not going to let me fall behind.

Fourteen

FROM MY BEDROOM, I hear Mom arguing on the phone with someone. It has to be Dad because she only uses that tone on him. I don't have to listen in to wonder what they're arguing about. It's me.

I'm the source of tension in the house—the source of tension in the whole world it feels like sometimes.

I'm the houseguest who just won't go away. They'll never say anything, but the air is so thick with strain I think I've died of suffocation a hundred times. I keep being resurrected though. Back into the same life I don't belong in and have to be expelled from a few hours later again.

Mom's in the kitchen, trying to keep quiet, so I wander into the living room when I come downstairs. I haven't gotten used to the skinny jeans Mom picked up for me yet—they feel like they're cutting off the circulation to my ankles—but that's the only style she bought. I guess bootleg isn't as popular anymore.

Dad keeps the daily paper tucked into the middle

drawer of the antique desk pushed up against the window facing the front door, and I find myself being pulled in that direction. Call it morbid curiosity, but I can't help it. I think part of me's still hoping "The Childs Child Abduction" will pass eventually. The only way to know for sure is to check the headlines.

When I slide open the drawer and pull out the paper, I don't have to unfold it to know nothing has passed yet. They haven't gotten bored by me staying sealed inside my parents' house or sneaking out through the alley tucked down in the backseat of Dad's Tahoe.

My hands brace against the edge of the desk for support because on the front page of the local paper are two photos; blown up so large they're blurry. The first one is of Torrin rushing me to my front door after leaving the hospital. He's in his priest outfit and managing to block me almost entirely from the photographer's angle. The second photo isn't quite as blurry and was taken last night at the party. Torrin's in his tux, and I'm in my dress, and it was taken when we were dancing. Not just when we were dancing though—when we were looking at each other and smiling. I don't remember being that close to him. I don't remember my hand disappearing that far beneath his jacket. I don't remember his hand being that low on my back.

We look like two people in love. We look like newlyweds dancing their first dance at their wedding. We look like . . . nothing like we should with him being who he is and me being who I am.

The first thing that hits me is that someone at the party had to have taken that picture and sold it. A friend, a family member, an acquaintance. The betrayal cuts through me like a hot knife.

The next thing I feel is anger. Red, volatile anger that starts in my chest and spills though the rest of my body.

Then I read the headline:

Father Costigan or Father Charming?

That's it. Nothing else. Just those five words stamped in thick black letters as big as my pinkie finger.

I shouldn't read the article. I should stuff the paper back in the drawer and forget I ever saw it. No good will come from going deeper down this rabbit hole. I know that, but I let myself fall in.

I skim the article, absorbing sentences, all of them making my intestines feel like a tangled, knotted mess. They know about Torrin's and my relationship in high school. I guess it wouldn't have been that hard to learn about since everyone at our high school, on this street, who was in the same movie theatre where we spent more time kissing than watching, would remember.

It goes on to talk about Torrin after I disappeared. His trouble in school. A couple run-ins with the law that were only charged as misdemeanors given his "special circumstances"—those being his girlfriend getting abducted minutes after being with him. How he barely graduated high school, how he organized search parties, candlelight vigils, national and local television interviews to keep my picture in the public's face.

Then the article talks about him going to college, then seminary after that as the explosive Torrin Costigan transformed into the respected Father Costigan of St. Marks.

How he's a favorite in the Seattle Catholic community. How he spends endless hours volunteering in the community, bringing bags of burgers to street kids and helping the elderly measure out their medications into pillboxes. There's a quote from one of the members of St. Marks who claims Torrin does what four people couldn't accomplish.

Then there are a couple of anonymous quotes from guests at the party last night. One person talks about how cozy Torrin and I seemed most of the night, and the other . . . it makes me crumple the paper. The other friend, family member, or acquaintance told the reporter how they'd watched me sneak out of the party early without saying good-bye. How Torrin had followed me in the same clandestine way a few minutes later. No conclusions are stated, but it's so obvious what's being implied that I feel my nails digging into the wood desk.

This will put him in a bad situation. This won't blow over. People will read it, they'll talk to other people, and on Sunday, everyone sitting in those pews will stare at him wondering . . . judging.

They're going after the people around me—the ones closest to me. They can't get to me because I won't let them, so they're swinging their meat hooks into the closest alternatives.

My head lifts, and I glare out the window. They're still here. All of them. Metal barriers have been set up and flaggers have been stationed outside twenty-four-seven to guide traffic through the maze of trucks and cameras and life-suckers.

Almost two weeks, and they won't go away. They won't take a hint. They won't respect my privacy. They won't leave. Not until they've gotten what they want—however they can get it.

Including crucifying the person I care about most to his own cross if necessary.

I'm still glaring out the window, feeling like I'm about to detonate, when a series of honks pops off outside the barricade. The beeps turn into a blare when the driver isn't allowed through.

I can just make out Sam's dark blue sedan being swarmed by reporters who are "supposed" to let her, or anyone else trying to get into our driveway, pass. They're not though. Why would they? She's Jade Childs's sister. Jade Childs isn't around for them to dissect her life into bloody pieces, so why not just dissect everyone else around her?

In some places, they're five deep around Sam's car, and she's still blasting the horn, but I can see her through the windshield of her car. She's scared. She's holding that brave face I've seen a lot since returning, but it's a façade. When reporters knock on her windows, tapping their microphones against them, she starts to cry. Her forehead lowers to the steering wheel, and the horn stops.

I'm running through the living room, and when I reach the front door, Mom's roaming out of the kitchen, phone still tucked to her ear.

"What's going on out there?" she asks me.

My hand curls around the door handle. Then I yank it open. "Stay here."

Before her eyes finish widening, I step outside.

At first, no one notices. They'll all too busy harassing my sister.

She's still leaning over the steering wheel, her body shaking. My disappearance ruined this family once. I'd never have guessed me being found would ruin them again. If I had known the lives of everyone I loved would be destroyed a second time, I wouldn't have spent so much time wishing to be found.

"Leave her alone!" I shout, but my voice doesn't carry above the roar. I jog down the steps and storm across the lawn.

Now they're starting to notice. What feels like hundreds of cameras and people whip my way. There's a hush for one moment, then the noise starts back up as questions spill across the front yard at me.

"Get away from her!" I try waving away the stragglers still hovering around Sam's car. When that doesn't work, I shove them. "Get away. Just leave her the hell alone."

When one of the guys I push away trips and lands on the grass, there's another hush of silence. I look up to see them all staring at me, cameras rolling like I'm a spectacle and nothing else.

"This is what you want, right?" I lift my arms and shout. "This is what you've been waiting for? To confirm just how messed up I am now?"

I spin and wave at the man I just knocked on his ass. Flashes fire around me. I feel like with each one, a little of my soul is taken.

"To see just how positively fucked up I'll be the rest of my life? To see what ten years of being held against my will has done? To see this?" I shake my hair behind my back and draw a line with my finger across my neck.

Photos fire faster. The street has become a giant flashing strobe.

"My family's been through enough! The people I care about have suffered enough." I think about the article on Torrin. Lava replaces the blood in my veins. "Can't you see that?!"

That's when I drop to the ground because I can't hold myself up anymore. Adrenaline got me out the door, but now that I've burned through that, there's nothing left to keep me going.

"I've been through enough." I cup my face in my hands. "Just leave us alone."

The noise blasts through me, encapsulating me at the same time. Questions fire at me, but I've given all I have to give. I don't have anything left.

The front door's not far, but it feels like I'll have to cross an ocean to reach it. I can't stand. I don't think I can crawl. I'm stuck. Every flash going off catches another shot of me losing myself on the front lawn of the house I grew up in.

I wonder if there's an inner circle in hell reserved for reporters too. After my experience with them, I think there must be.

When I feel a couple of hands reach for me, I startle.

It's my mom, and she's smiling at me with strength in her expression. "Come on, Jade. Let's go."

As she starts to help me up, another pair of hands reaches for me from the other side. It's Sam. She's not crying anymore.

"I can't get up," I say when I test my legs. If I had muscles in them a minute ago, they're gone now.

"I know," Sam says, guiding me up with my mom. I drape an arm around each of their shoulders as they turn our backs to the cameras and guide me toward the house. "We'll help you."

Fifteen

S INCE I BROKE my silence with the media, I decide to do the same with the police. The detectives working my case have been patient, and unlike the home-wrecking media, I think their reasons for wanting to know what happened to me are legitimate.

The detectives agreed to meet at my house, and even though they said I could have whomever I wanted present during the interview, I've decided to do this on my own. My decision practically sends Dad into cardiac arrest. I guess that to him, it feels like I've just benched the captain of the team when the championship game is going into sudden death overtime.

Torrin would have been here if I'd asked, but I didn't ask. I couldn't ask. Not with everything I've already done to him. After the article in the newspaper a few days ago, I've tried to build a little distance between us. I don't want to do that—we've had ten years of "distance"—but I have to. It's what's best for him.

I know he was confused when I said I was too tired to

go out the other day or when I wouldn't come to the phone when Mom told me he was on the line, but confusion can fade—a ruined reputation can't.

Mom set up the farm table in the kitchen with mugs and a coffee pot. She even baked cookies and lit a candle like she was trying to make the interview a little easier on me. I appreciate her efforts even though I know the only way the interview will be easier on me is if it never happens.

I know the detectives are here when the noise from outside rumbles to a roar. The damn vampires do the same thing when the delivery driver shows up. After my display in the front yard, they've gotten a taste for blood that won't be satisfied until they've drained me of every last drop.

I don't feel far away from that last drop.

Dad greets them at the door, and I hear footsteps echo closer. I've taken the seat at the table closest to the door because I want to be able to escape if I need to. I need to know I'm not trapped.

I've got on an oversized cowl-neck sweater, even though it's summer, because of the scar. I caught a glimpse of one of the photos taken that day on the lawn, and it made my scar look different than what I saw in the mirror.

I didn't know how large and ugly it was until I saw it in a photo.

I asked Mom to pick up a few tops that would cover it, and she did. She picked up a few colorful scarves too.

"Miss Childs, good to meet you," a woman in a charcoal suit says as she and who I guess is her partner approaches.

Dad lingers in the doorway for a moment before leaving with a sigh.

"I'm Detective Reyes, and this is Detective Burnside. Thank you for taking the time to talk with us." She holds out her hand for me to shake, then something flickers on her face.

She's about to lower her hand when I grab it. I shake it gently. Even though touching others has gotten easier, it still burns a little. Kind of like an arm waking up after sleeping on it all night.

"I'm sorry it took me so long to do this." I reach for the pot of coffee and pour some into all of our cups. Mom left cream and sugar out, but none of us take any. "Thanks for your patience."

Detective Reyes is clearly taking the lead in the interview since, other than smiling at me and sliding into a chair across from me, Burnside hasn't said a thing. I wonder if that's because the department thought putting a female on the case would make it easier on the victim. I wonder if everyone sees me as being so damaged I won't trust another man again.

Maybe they're right. I don't know.

Burnside pulls a recorder out of his jacket and sets it on the table. I stare at the thing I'm about to spill my soul out to, and I wonder if when I'm done, I'll feel better or worse. I think I know.

"First off, how are you doing?" Reyes takes the lead with the questions as I'd guessed she would. Burnside's probably just here as a formality.

"I'm okay," I say on autopilot. My expression even knows the way to form so I seem convincing. "Each day gets a little easier."

When Reyes nods at me, I get the impression she knows my secret though. She knows, but she doesn't say anything.

"We'd like to ask you some questions. I realize some of them might be uncomfortable for you, so just take as much time as you need, okay? We cleared our schedules for the rest of the day, so we've got nowhere to rush off to. Take as long as you need."

The thought of spending the rest of the day with these detectives, answering questions about those ten years, makes the room sway. I have to grip the edge of my chair to stay in it. I take a breath and nod. I'm not ready, but that doesn't seem to matter to anyone anymore.

"The night you were taken, how did Jackson get you into his van?" Reyes folds her hands on the table and waits.

No one's taken a drink of his or her coffee. No one's sneaked a cookie from the plate in the middle of the table.

"He said he was lost. Had a map and was trying to find Driscoll Street." I swallow and try to remember without reliving the scene. "When I got close enough, he injected me with something. I don't know what, but it made me foggy right away, and then my body kind of gave out, and after that . . . I don't know how long I was blacked out."

"When you woke up, where were you?"

I try to figure out how to keep my voice as emotionless as Reyes's. "In a dark closet. I didn't know it was a closet at first, or that it was inside his house, but that's where I woke up. I don't know if it was hours or days later. I'm guessing days."

The essence of the panic I awoke with floats up from the place where I've tried to bury it. My breaths quicken.

"And how long did he keep you in the closet?"

"I don't know."

"What would you guess?" Reyes presses.

I want to tell her what dark like that does to a person. How direction and time and everything are lost and totally meaningless. "I don't know."

"Weeks? Months?" Reyes pauses. "Years?"

I don't know, so I go with answer B. "Months, I think."

"And what did you do during this time?"

Besides survive? "I screamed a lot at first, thinking someone might hear me. Then I moved on to crying. Then I gave up on that and mostly just slept."

"And what did Jackson do during this time you were in the closet?"

I know what she's asking. I thought this had been clear and confirmed by the hospital tests, but apparently no one can believe that I spent ten years with the man who kidnapped me and wasn't molested in some way.

"Nothing. I mean, he talked to me. Brought in fresh water and food and a fresh bucket, but that was all the contact I had with him at first."

"What did he talk about?"

I stare at the recorder. A little red light flashes on it, and I watch that until it puts me into a trance. "He called me Sara. He referred to me as his daughter. He talked about memories of them going to the park, the time he taught her to swim. He said that he wasn't going to let anyone take me away from him again. He promised he'd keep me safe."

"And did you say anything back?"

I blink, focusing on the red light again. "At first I tried to convince him that I wasn't his daughter and to let me go, but after a while, that dark closet just kinda broke me. By the end, I would have said anything, been anyone, just to get out of it."

Burnside shifts in his chair.

"When he finally let you out, what happened then?" Reyes continues.

Even though she doesn't have a notepad in front of her, I can tell she's crossing off questions one at a time.

"Um . . ." I rub my neck and tug at the neck of the sweater. "He chained me up. At first the chain was only long enough to move around a bedroom, but as time went by, he kept adding a little more length until I could move around most of the first floor."

"Did he ever take the collar off of you?" Reyes glances at my neck, but her eyes don't linger there.

"No. Never. I slept in it, showered in it. It never came off."

"So you never had a chance to escape? To get away from him?" Reyes's index finger taps the table like she's knocking at something.

"Never."

Her finger stops tapping. "So you weren't aware that when we found you, the end of chain wasn't tied up to anything?"

My throat goes dry, but I know I've heard her wrong. "What?"

Burnside and Reyes exchange a look.

Reyes leans in closer. "The other end of the chain you were tied to wasn't connected to anything. It was just sitting on the basement floor. There was a padlock attached to one of the links, but we have no idea when Jackson unlocked it." Reyes pauses, looking at me. "Do you?"

The ground feels like it's crumbling beneath my chair. "I'm sorry. I don't think I heard you right." I shake my head, trying to clear it. "Did you just say I wasn't chained to anything when you found me?"

That can't be what she said. I know I heard her wrong. There's no way he took off the lock keeping me there so I could get away. There's no way he would have chanced me getting away . . . unless he knew that I'd accepted the chain and would never try to fight it . . .

God, I'm the baby elephant. Actually, I'm the adult elephant whose will to fight's been crushed.

Whatever's left of my soul detaches and dissipates into the dark.

"When we found you, no, the chain wasn't attached to anything. You weren't tied to anything that would have forced you to stay there." Reyes exhales, and I can tell from the way her expression falters that this next question will be a hard one. "Did Jackson ever leave the house?"

I nod, knowing where she's going.

"Why didn't you try to escape, Jade? Why didn't you try to get away?" For the first time, I hear emotion in Reyes's voice.

My head is spinning, and I feel like I've just been thrown in that closet again. All sense of time and direction and meaning drain from me. I'm floating in a black vacuum.

"I didn't know . . . I didn't try. I just stopped trying after a while and gave up." My voice is shaking, but I'm not crying. I think this is what shock feels like.

"So you don't think Jackson freed your chain because he was letting you go?" Reyes asks.

My head lowers. "No, he did it because he knew he'd broken me."

Sixteen

Ten Years Ago

I'VE HEARD IT said that love makes us weak. It makes us weak because our survival instincts, along with our reasoning, become dulled. We first consider every move through the filter of that love. In a way, what we love makes us better people, more intuitive and less impulsive.

In another way, it makes us worse. It turns us into an immoral, corrupt being that knows no bounds when it comes to protecting what it loves.

I've come to accept that what we love makes us weak. I've learned something else on my own though, ever since becoming a prisoner of this black room—what we love is what kills us too.

I want to die. My will to survive has been extinguished. My hope of being found has been consumed by this black world. Even my anger has been tempered into something so dull I can't feel its heat boil in my veins anymore.

I've been missing for weeks. Maybe months. Hopefully not years, but I know that along with hope, I've lost all sense of time. The chance of finding a missing person after one week is one in one hundred. The chance of finding a missing child in my situation after the same time is one in one thousand.

Every day that ticks by, those odds get worse. Every second that ticks past feels like another nail pounded into my coffin. I'm dead to the world. I'm practically dead to myself.

A few sleeps ago, I woke up and couldn't remember my name. It passed in a few moments, but in that span of grappling for my name, I came to realize that I'm slowly breaking away. Piece by piece is falling into a black abyss I'll never be able to collect them from. They're gone forever.

Nothing can be plastered into those crumbled places either. Nothing. So when the last of me crumbles away, I'll just be gone. Too empty to even become a ghost.

Gone. That's what I feel like.

Dead. That's what I wish I could be.

I haven't screamed in dozens of sleeps—that's how I now measure time, in sleeps—because screaming doesn't do anything but hurt me. I've stopped kicking at the walls in hopes someone will hear because hope was the first thing to wither. I don't claw at the walls anymore, looking for a weak spot, because I know the only weak thing in this black world is me.

What I love has made me weak.

It's what I'm holding on to that's responsible for wishing myself dead. If it weren't for the life I had that I'm still clinging to, this wouldn't be such a stark contrast. If it weren't for everything and everyone I loved back in that life, I wouldn't feel like I've been dropped into the worst place on earth.

Maybe if I don't cling to that life so hard . . . maybe if I don't hold onto those people I loved . . . maybe if I don't still grasp how crazy I loved him, this will be easier. Maybe if I build a wall between the two worlds, I can find some shadow of a new life.

Maybe if I saw at that life and them and him until I've severed the connection, I can move on . . . to whatever life this is.

I cry again when I think that because I know I have to do it. It's the only chance I have of being let out of this place that's gnawing at the very marrow of my soul. I need out of here before I become one with the black, and I'll never be able to accept this life while I'm holding on to the old one.

I curl up more tightly on the mattress. My muscles feel kind of dead from underuse, and my body feels the same. At the same time it feels softer, it feels bonier. I can count my ribs now, and I can't lie on one side for too long or my hipbone starts to ache. My body, along with what it encases, is withering away.

I don't have long—at least, I don't think so. I've started sipping at the water now, and I've nibbled on the bars, but if it isn't the lack of water and food that does me in, there's no shortage of backups. For all I know, he's planning to kill me. I *know* if I had access to something lethal, I've been in dark enough places that I'd do it. Lack of sunshine, lack of movement, lack of human interaction . . . I'm not sure if those can kill me, but they feel like they can.

"Sara." That name. That voice. That trio of knocks on that thick door.

He's wearing me down. He's trying to break me down. Once he does that and I roll over, I'll get something as a kind of reward. I know that. Yet another pro-con of growing up around cops.

I don't know what that reward will be, but more will come if I continue to bend to his will. He demands. I submit. Reward. I know the whole point of bending is to get someone to their breaking point because once they're broken, a person can build them back however they want.

I know he wants to break me. I know he wants to build me back into Sara, his daughter. I know that's why he took me because if he did it for the typical reason men abduct young girls, that would have already been revealed. In that way, I don't have to fear him, but at this point, bending to breaking and becoming Sara seems just as terrifying.

All I've got left of myself is my name and the images of the life I had. If I become Sara, all of that goes. If I bend, then I'll break, and a knife will run across the throat of that whole life.

"Sara, are you asleep? We need to talk sometime. You can't stay in there forever." Three more knocks.

The dark seems to circle around me tighter until it

feels like a python coiled from my ankles to my chin. I wake up feeling like this all the time. Like I'm being suffocated. I wake up feeling like I'm dying, gasping for breath, and it isn't until I've managed to catch my breath and remember where I am that I wish the dark would just finish the job already. Just suffocate me and be done with it.

The dark constricts more tightly around me, and when I choke out loud, I realize why I feel like something's choking the breath out of me—I'm picturing him. In my mind, I'm holding on to the picture of him on the sidewalk with his hands in his pockets, staring at me like we had forever.

We did have forever. For all of thirty seconds before someone stole it because we were both fools to believe in the promise of forever. The only promise is that there is no promise. Forever can be destroyed as easily as a blade of grass can be trampled. Forever is fragile. Forever is fleeting. Forever is finite.

Forever is gone.

When I clear the image of him from my mind, I feel the black recede. When I bury the image in the dusty, dark attic of my memory, I feel the black almost disappear completely.

"Sara? Just talk to me. We can work this out. Everything can go back to the way things used to be, I know it."

His voice doesn't sound as evil as it used to. Without travelling through the film of panic, I think I've translated his tone more accurately—it's sadness I hear. After everything, I'm better equipped to identify it.

I haven't spoken to him in days, maybe weeks. I gave up shouting at him and screaming for answers. I gave up demanding to be let go and threatening that he'd be found and locked away for good.

I gave up.

I guess I was finally ready to give up the rest.

"Yeah?" My voice is hoarse from underuse. It's strange how it can become the same after hours of screaming, but I guess silence is its own kind of scream. "I'm awake."

I feel another piece of me crumbling away into that void, but it doesn't stop me. I'm going to fall apart either way—I might as well do it with the chance of finally getting out of this hell like he's been promising from the beginning. I'll earn my freedom . . . by imprisoning the old me.

Outside the door, he is quiet. When I hear him clear his throat, it sounds like he has to dislodge something from it.

"I've missed you so much." He clears his throat again. "I'm sorry I had to put you in there, Sara, but I couldn't have you getting away from me again. I know you were confused when you left with your mom. I'm not angry. I'm just happy you're back."

I feel tears well in my eyes, but I force them to seep back into wherever they came from. Jade was crying, but she was gone. Or about to be.

"Me too." My hollow voice echoes in the small space. Already I don't recognize it.

"I'm going to open the door and let you out, but you

have to promise you're not going to try running away again. You have to promise that if I let you out, you won't try to escape."

I hear the key clicking into the lock, but it hasn't turned over yet. He's waiting.

When I close my eyes, it's dark. It used to feel the opposite. That was part of the reason why I slept so much. Now though, it's darker when I close my eyes. "I promise. I won't run."

I couldn't run if I wanted to. Those muscles have been turned into mush from the feel of them.

He's still waiting. I know what for, but in order to say it, I have to build that wall between lives a little higher. I have to make it a little thicker.

"I promise"—the word tastes bitter in my mouth—"Dad."

He sighs, then the key turns. He's come in before to change my bucket and drop off fresh supplies, but he's always ordered me to tuck into the corner and close my eyes. He isn't demanding that right now.

Is this my reward? All of it or part of it? The chance to catch a glimpse of light—to see something other than black—makes my body rock with a sob. Light. After being held captive by weeks of dark, the slightest flicker of it would light up my whole world.

When the door opens, I'm blinded by light. I have to cover my eyes because it's daytime for the first time when that door's been opened, and I feel like the sun's blasting five feet in front of me. I never knew light could be just as blinding as its counterpart, but I've been learning lots of lessons lately.

Even though I can't see it, I feel it. It's subtle warmth. It attaches to my skin until I can almost feel it seeping deeper.

The rush of fresh air hits me next. This I'm used to, and it hits me as powerfully as ever. I don't realize how putrid my world is until I realize what the outside world smells like. I don't realize how dead I smell until I catch a whiff of life.

I sigh as the fresh air clears out the stale, then I notice the light slicing inside dim some.

"Is that better?"

It's the first time he's spoken to me without the door between us. His voice is familiar in that "distant dream" kind of way, but I can't say from where or if it's just familiar because every wire in my brain has become crossed and frayed.

"Yeah." I shield my eyes and attempt to blink them open. It's still blinding, but I can't close my eyes to the light again. After being robbed of it for so long, I can't look away just because it's too painful.

I hear him step closer, but my eyes are having a hard time adjusting. I can see bright white light and a dark shadow, but that's all. There's no detail. No color.

"Everything's going to be different now, Sara. You'll see."

Hearing his voice like this reminds me of the night he took me. I want to slink away from him, but I make myself stay where I am.

When I hear a sharp, rattling sound, I shiver. It

sounds cold. Unfriendly.

"This is for your own good, Sara. I know you didn't want to leave, but teenagers can be impulsive." The rattling moves closer. "This will keep you from giving in to those impulses."

When I feel my hair lift, I flinch back. I haven't been touched in weeks, and his touch is strange and almost awkward feeling. Giving my hair a sharp tug, he pulls me back.

When I cry out, he sighs but doesn't say anything else. Now that he isn't blocking most of the light streaming into the little room, it's blinding me again. Even when I close my eyes, I still see strobes flashing.

"What are you doing?" My voice quivers, and my body is close to following.

He's still quiet, but when I feel something cold and hard ring around my neck, I panic. I fight against him and it, but I'm as weak as I knew I would be . . . and weaker.

The fight bubbles out of me after a few seconds, then my body goes limp, seeming to sink into that heavy ring being locked around my neck. I don't even have the strength to lift my hands to inspect what's there, but I already know. It's not a necklace. It's not a noose.

It's a collar. A metal one that feels at least an inch wide and so heavy I'm not sure I'll ever be able to rise with it on. A chain dangles from it, and to what it's attached, I don't know. All I know is that I'm stuck. The door to this dark room has been removed, but it's only been opened into a darker world.

I hear him move away once everything's been fitted

into place. I think I'm going to throw up. I think I wish that door had never been opened. I think feeling free to move about a small space on my own is better than being collared like a wild animal.

"I promised I wouldn't run away." I slump against the wall behind me and realize I can't bend anymore.

"And I promised that I'd never let you leave again." He moves out of the room. "This way, we'll both be able to keep our promises."

When I curl back onto the mattress, the chain rattles. The collar cuts into the side of my neck, and I know I'll never be able to sleep with it on. At least when I slept before, I could escape this world and trespass in the other.

I can't bend anymore. I'm already broken.

Seventeen

I HAVEN'T LEFT my room in two days. I haven't left the house in seven.

My parents don't know what to do. I don't know either.

Ever since the meeting with the detectives and finding out about the end of my chain being locked to absolutely nothing, my sense of reality, my perception of freedom . . . it's all changing.

The closer I get to accepting I was tied to nothing—free to go whenever I figured that out—the more confined I feel. The smaller my sense of safety shrinks. The longer I think about it, the more scared I become. How am I supposed to know what's real and what isn't when nothing is as it seems?

How am I supposed to be free of the past when I hadn't known what freedom felt like the moment Earl Rae slid that padlock free?

I don't want to leave the house. I don't want to leave my room.

Here there are no cameras or uncomfortable questions or people to stare at me. I'm safe.

At least I think I am. I'm not sure if I remember the way safe feels anymore.

"Jade?" My mom's muffled voice comes from out-side of my door. "You need to come out, sweetheart."

"I'm not ready." I curl lower into the rocking chair and draw the stuffed elephant tighter to my chest.

"You can't stay in there by yourself. It's not healthy."

I double-check the lock on the door. It's still turned over. "I spent months in a dark closet, crying on an old mattress and shitting in a metal bucket. Don't tell me what is and isn't healthy."

"Jade!" Dad's voice booms followed by a hard pounding. "Come out. Enough of this. Now."

I don't say anything. I just keep rocking, staring at the same patch of carpet I've spent all morning watching. I'm pretty sure it's where Torrin kissed me for the first time. I keep trying to conjure up the image, but I can't get a firm enough grip on it. The moment it starts to surface, some-thing pulls it back down.

All I can remember is that we were laughing about something and then, the next second, we were kissing. I don't remember what he was wearing or where my hands settled on him, but I remember his hands weaving into my hair and pulling me toward him, holding me close.

I remember these shadows like the girl in them is someone else because she's so different from the one slumped in this rocking chair that they can't be the same. I replay the shards of the memory like I'm jealous of the seventeen-year-old version of this girl and think about how I'd trade my life for hers in an instant . . . then I kill that wish. I don't want her happiness to come to an end any sooner than it already did.

I might have been that girl, but there's too much poison in me now. It killed her off, and she can never come back. I'm stuck with this. Me. Whoever that is.

"Don't make me kick this door in, Jade, because so help me God, I will do it." My dad's voice quivers as he pounds on the door again. It seems to shake the whole room.

"Just do it then. Go ahead. You wouldn't be the first person to take away my freedom."

The pounding stops, and I think I hear Mom cry, but I cover my ears because I'm so tired of tears. I'm so tired of knowing I'm responsible for them. I've heard so many, late at night when they think I'm asleep, that I've started wishing my family had found me dead. At least they'd have had some measure of peace once my body was laid to rest.

At least they could move on. But now, alive, I'm dragging them under with me.

I'm still covering my ears when I hear more knocking, but this kind is different. It isn't the same thud of knuckles on wood—it's lighter. Clearer sounding. I lower my hands and look in the direction it's coming from—my window.

When he sees he's caught my attention, he stops tapping at the glass and waves. When he smiles, my chest seizes. I haven't seen Torrin in days. Seeing him now, even through a sheet of glass, makes me feel like everything's going to be okay. I feel like that for a few seconds.

Then I notice his priest's collar, then my neck burns with phantom pain, and I realize the sheet of glass separating us isn't the smallest thing keeping us apart.

When I stay in the chair, he lifts his hands like he's waiting for me to say something. Or do something.

Torrin and I used to climb the roofs to each other's bedrooms so much as kids that my dad had threatened to grow thorn bushes on this side of the house when we became teenagers. He planted them the day we went on our first "date" to the pizza parlor on Lake Washington. Except he didn't realize the climbing rose bush he'd planted was a thornless variety. It didn't keep Torrin from climbing up here, and when they were in bloom, he always snagged a rose on his way up. So yeah, Dad's plan had totally backfired.

How nice it must be to wind up with roses when you were expecting thorns.

After a minute, Torrin shrugs and takes a seat. He doesn't turn away though—he just keeps looking at me through the pane of glass.

I don't last more than a minute before shoving out of the rocking chair and moving toward the window. After unlocking it, I lift it. When I step back so he can climb in, he doesn't move.

"Can I come in?" he asks.

He isn't ordering. He isn't demanding. He isn't forcing. He's asking.

"You can come in," I reply.

When he climbs inside, the air moves in my room like the heaviness of it is escaping out the window. He leaves the window open and stands in front of me. The last time Torrin and I were in my bedroom together behind a locked door, he laid me down on my bed and kissed me until I felt that spot where this world recedes and the curtain to the other side starts to lift.

He glances around my room for a moment. I wonder if he's thinking the same thing. I wonder if he knows the exact spot where we had our first kiss, cross-legged and laughing on the floor.

"So I noticed you've been avoiding the world lately." He backs into the closet doors and leans into them. My bed's in the opposite corner.

"The world can just kiss my ass." I settle the stuffed elephant back onto the rocking chair.

Torrin notices it, something flickering in his eyes. "Do you want to talk about it?"

My exhale comes out in a huff. "No.

"Good." He claps and continues. "So let's move on to the reason I scaled your roof." He holds my eyes, not letting them wander away from him. "Why have you been avoiding me?"

I wander my room, not sure where to go now that he's here. I'm not sure where I fit now. I'm not sure where I fit in his life.

"You know why," I say quietly. "Could have saved yourself the scaling."

"I want to hear you tell me why."

"Why?"

"So I can change your mind." His hands slide into his front pockets, and the sunlight catches on his dad's watch and casts golden beams through the room. It lights up like someone just lit a million candles at once. "I can't do that unless I know exactly why you don't want to see me."

"Because I don't want to drag you into my mess of a world any more than I already have. Because I don't want to smear you through the mud on the media's march to burying me. Because I don't want to hurt you—again—and because I want to protect you."

"I can protect myself from them."

I shake my head and cover my chest with my hand. "To protect you from *me*."

Torrin's jaw hardens. He works it loose the moment after. "I don't need protection from you."

"Everyone needs protection from me. There's something dark in me now, Torrin, and I can't get it out. It's growing, spreading, and I don't want it to infect the people I love."

He pushes off the closet doors and crosses the room before I know he's coming. "There is nothing dark in you, Jade. Nothing." He backs me into the wall and stares at me, unblinking. "There is light and good in you. There always has been. There always will be."

"That's gone. He took it from me."

"No, he didn't." Torrin's hand slams into the wall beside my head. "It's still there. You had to bury it to keep it safe, but it's still there. You'll find it. I know it."

I want to believe him, but that doesn't make it true. "You can't find what isn't there, Torrin."

232

"Dammit, stop talking like that," he says, his jaw tightening. "It's there. I know it."

"I've tried. I can't find it." Even as I say it, I start to feel differently. It's because of him being so close, saying what he is in the way he is. He's the tether that keeps me from floating away.

His eyes lower to mine. "I'll help you find it."

I feel my heart again. My lungs. Everything else. I feel them waking up after a week. "What makes you so sure you can find it?"

"Because when I look in your eyes, I still see it." His other hand fits against the wall. "Because when I'm close to you like this, I can still feel it." He leans a little closer, and I feel something too. "It's there, Jade. It's not gone. He took ten years of your life—*ten years*." The corners of his eyes crease as an emotion fires in his eyes. "Don't hand him the rest of it by believing that kind of shit."

I'm so surprised by his sudden outburst I'm kind of shocked right out of whatever grey patch I've been hovering in. The constraints around my chest start to loosen. "You just said shit. Again."

His brow cocks. "So?"

"You're a priest. Again."

The corner of his mouth twitches. He leans in and winks. "I'm not a very good one, remember? I forget the small stuff all the time."

His hands are stationed around my head, his face aimed right in front of mine. I feel . . . *alive*. "Like cussing?"

"Like cussing." His shoulder lifts. "And other things."

"What other things?"

He leans in even closer, until I can see the flecks of pewter in his light eyes. Then he shoves away from the wall. "You'll know them when you see them."

My palms are stuck to the wall, and when I peel them away, they make a sound. It's nice to feel alive. To feel something . . . for someone. Even if it's just sweaty palms caused from an intense stare.

"So now that we've cleared up all that, you have no reason to avoid me anymore." Torrin's fingers brush across my vanity where my dried corsages used to be.

"Nothing's cleared up. I won't let everyone think you're some kind of immoral person because there are pictures of us dancing and someone said you followed me out of a party."

His eyes drop to the spots on the wall my hands were just splayed across. His head tips, and I notice two slightly darker impressions from my clammy hands. He doesn't say anything. But that kinda says more than any words could.

He does a slow spin. "I'm a priest. Everyone already looks at me and thinks the worst. I don't care what anyone thinks anyway. I care what you think. What you want."

"I can't have what I want."

"Maybe you can't. Maybe you can. But first you have to decide what you want."

I don't know what to do again. Where to hold my arms. Alone. In my bedroom. With Torrin. It messes with my mind. "I like spending time with you. I *want* to spend time with you—"

"I like being with you too." He stops in front of my nightstand, his brows coming together like he's trying to figure out what's missing. *Him*. He's missing. The photos of us that used to sit there. "So what else is there left to talk about?"

"Just this little thing known as the international media. You. Me. Headlines trying to draw an illicit connection between us. Just those things and a few hundred others." I decide to settle on the bottom corner of my bed. Seems like a safe spot . . . without seeming like I'm looking for one.

Torrin makes a face. "Their objective is to sell papers, advertising time, not the truth. People know that. Let them write whatever the hell they want about me. I don't care."

My eyes cut to him. "Well, I do."

He walks to the end of the bed and stares at the same spot on the carpet I was concentrating on. He comes close to smiling, then he scrubs his face. "Earl Rae kept you chained up for ten years. He took a decade. How much longer are you going to let him keep you chained away from doing the things you want to do and being with the people you want to be with?"

His question hits me in the gut like he's swinging a bat. I lean forward and comb my fingers through my hair. "I don't know, Torrin. I don't know. I miss the strong girl I used to be. The one who wouldn't let anything slow her down or get in her way." My fingers curl into my hair. "God, I miss her."

I feel the mattress move when he sits on the opposite end of it. He's leaning forward like I am, still concentrating on that spot. "She's still there. You just have to find her."

I bite my lip and slowly nod.

"So you've been locked inside for a week. Barely went out the weeks before that. Were missing from the world for ten years." The mattress whines when he shifts. "Is there anything you've really missed? I'm talking 'you have one day to live—where do you spend it?'"

He doesn't ask me who I'm going to spend it with, and I'm grateful because I don't need to complicate things between us. They're already too complicated.

"The beach," I say. "I miss the beach."

Torrin's head turns my way. "Our beach?"

I nod. "That one."

He's quiet for a minute—his thoughts are loud though. "Well, you miss the beach. I'll have to figure out a way to get you to the beach."

Eighteen

I TRIED LEAVING my room last night after Torrin left. I tried until my forehead was sweating and my hands were shaking. I tried for a solid hour, working up the courage and mentally preparing myself.

I never made it out the door. I got as far as my hand on the doorknob, but I couldn't manage the next part. My hand couldn't twist the handle. My fingers couldn't pull the door open.

No one had locked me in the room. I'd locked myself in . . . and I couldn't free myself. I felt as powerless as I had on the end of that chain. The one I could have just picked up and walked out the front door with.

The same thing is happening, but this time, I know I'm free to go. This time, the only thing holding me back is myself.

I've heard footsteps moving up and down the hall all morning, but no one has banged on my door or tried to beg or order me out. I kind of wish someone would though because, like that day when I dropped to my knees on the lawn in front of hundreds of cameras, I can't do the next part alone. I need help to get out from behind this door, and I've forgotten how to ask for it.

After years of asking, hoping, and waiting for it, help is just as much a fairy tale as happily ever after.

I've just stepped out of the bathroom adjoining my room, towel-drying my hair, when I hear that knock. It doesn't sound like any of the others I've heard so far.

"Jade?"

I stop dabbing the towel through my hair.

"So I know you're in there since, you know, you re-fuse to leave your room." He pauses. "Are you going to talk to me, or should I climb the roof again?"

"What is it, Torrin?" I sail the towel back into the bathroom and tug on the sweater I pulled out of the closet.

"I want to talk to you."

"You *are* talking to me."

He sighs. "I want to talk to *you*, not your door."

I move toward the door. "What do you want to talk about?"

"Actually, I want to show you something. Talking isn't required if you're sick of talking to me."

I don't smile, but I want to. I can feel it beneath the surface, trying to push through toward the light. "Fine. What do you want to *show* me?"

"It's a surprise."

"Is this your way of trying to get me to leave my room?"

"No, you don't have to go far. Just down the hall and two doors to the left. That's it."

238

My feet pad across the carpet, moving closer to the door. "What's the surprise?"

"You know the definition of surprise, right?"

I lean into the wall the door's on, staring at it. "I can't do it, Torrin. I tried . . . I can't get the door open."

The handle jars a little when I guess he puts his hand on it. "I'll help you."

I bite my lip and try to keep the panic from rolling to a boil. It's crazy what three days of isolation will do to a person. It's crazy how the world outside of these four walls can seem so scary and unreachable.

It's crazy that after finally earning my freedom, I seem to have checked it back in.

"You can do this, Jade. You're strong. Stronger than your biggest, ugliest fear. Ten times stronger than that."

I don't believe it, but the confidence in his voice gets my hand to the handle. This is as far as I made it earlier, and already my hand is trembling. I wonder if Torrin can feel from the other side how scared I am.

"Ready?" His voice rolls through the crack in the door.

"I think so."

I manage to twist the handle a little, and I feel Torrin twisting it at the same time. The knob turns all the way over, but when he starts to push it open, the door stays in place.

"It's locked. You can't open it like that. I can't help you open it if it's locked."

The handle's slippery from my hand, and I don't dare let go because I'm not sure my hand could find its way back. So I lift my other hand and guide it toward the lock. This hand's quivering too, but before it grows into shakes, I manage to turn the lock over in a quick motion.

"There." My voice is high with strain. "It's unlocked."

"Then open the door, Jade."

My heart is firing, and I'm not sure I can, but then I feel my hand twisting and my fingers pulling and then . . . the door opens. Something inside me is ready to be free.

Torrin's hand is still wrapped around the handle when the door swings into my room. He doesn't let go until the door's open all the way.

He's smiling and looking at me the way he used to. Like ten years of separation weren't real. "Welcome back to the world."

I brace myself in the doorjamb and look up and down the hall. Nothing's different, but I feel like I'm seeing it differently. Like the house isn't some reflection of my past but maybe a shadow of my future.

"Well, at least back to the hallway." I smile back and take my first step out of the bedroom.

Torrin backs up to give me some space and waits. "Ready for your surprise?"

"I didn't just ward off a panic attack for nothing."

He waves down the hall. "Good. Then close your eyes and let's get going."

"Wait. No one said anything about closing my eyes."

"Why do I feel like you're still failing to understand the definition of a surprise?"

"Why do I feel like you're still failing to take no for

an answer to anything?" I sigh and close my eyes.

"Promise they're closed?"

I feel his hand whipping right in front of my eyes, checking. "Promise."

I hear some rustling. I have no idea what's making it, but it's coming from Torrin's direction.

"Is this going to be anything like the last surprise you walked me to with my eyes closed?" I ask.

More rustling. "If you're referring to the disaster known as The Night I Tried to Cook Dinner for You, then no. Hopefully nothing like that." His voice is muffled for a few words, but it clears.

"What are you talking about? That was the best over-cooked chicken and undercooked pasta I'd ever had."

"Yeah, chicken marsala might have been a bit ambitious for a guy who hadn't mastered the toasting of bread yet."

My laugh chimes down the hall. It feels so good I just don't want it to stop. I don't want to stop smiling and laughing, because maybe, one day, they'll outweigh the tears and sadness and I'll remember what it feels like to just live . . . instead of feeling like I'm practicing for life.

Torrin comes up behind me and holds the side of my arm. I'm expecting his other hand to wrap around my other arm when his hand slides over my eyes.

"You peek," he says like he's defending himself.

I don't argue, because he's right. Even now, I can feel my eyelashes fluttering against his hand as I fight to keep my eyes closed.

When I feel him move, I move with him. He stays

close, his hands on me, guiding me. Even though by my vision's measure, it's dark, it doesn't seep in the way I'm used to. It can't find the door to let itself in.

We move down the hall, and it's not long before we're rolling to a stop. I hear a door open, Torrin guides me a couple more steps forward, then his hands drop away. He doesn't tell me I can open my eyes, but I open them anyway. I have to glance behind me to make sure we're still in the same hall and didn't take some wrong turn into a wormhole.

I think this room used to be Sam's, but it doesn't look like it. At all.

Torrin shoulders up beside me and motions at the room. "You missed the beach. I brought you the beach."

My eyes haven't taken in a quarter of the room before my hand finds his. Tying my fingers through his warm hand, I give it a squeeze of thanks. He replies with a longer squeeze.

I try to take in the rest of the room, but there's too much to see. Too much I don't want to miss. Heat lamps are positioned around the room, radiating down at us, and a couple of fans are spinning at a low setting, creating a warm breeze that rolls over my body in a familiar way. If I close my eyes, I could be standing on the beach on a warm summer day.

The room's been emptied of all guest room furniture, and replacing it is one of those hard plastic kiddie pools filled with water that's been dyed blue. A beige tarp's been laid out behind the pool, taking up most of the room, and it's covered in what looks like sand. Real sand. Buckets of it. I have to move closer to see if it's real or just some mirage.

I skim my bare foot through it and discover it's the real stuff. It's warm on top and everything from the heat lamps.

Brightly colored buckets and shovels are stationed around the sand, and there's even a small floating kite that's been tied to one of the fans. The sound of waves crashing and seagulls chortling echoes around the room.

It's the beach. Two doors down from my room.

"Did you do this?" I wander farther in, closing my eyes at the way the sand feels on my feet. The way it gives when I walk, leaving footprints behind to remind me I was there.

He hovers behind, letting me explore on my own. "Your family helped too. All of them."

That would explain all of the footsteps I kept hearing. "Everyone?"

"Well, your dad helped by not throwing me out of the house like I know he wanted to."

I twist around in the sand, burying my feet in a little deeper. I'm surprised when I see him because when he helped open my door, he was in the black-and-white priest outfit I'm used to seeing him in. He isn't anymore.

So I can guess what the rustling sounds were caused by. "Did you seriously just strip in the hallway?" I motion at his swim trunks and faded hoodie he's thrown on.

"Why? Should I not have?"

"Not if you don't want everyone to think there's a naked priest running around the top floor."

Torrin lifts his eyes to the ceiling and closes the door. "What do you want to do first?"

There's a picnic basket and blanket spread out in one corner of the room, but I take a seat where I am, lifting my face to the pretend sun, and smile. "This."

With my eyes closed, it feels so much like the beach I'm half-anticipating a cool wave to break around my ankles.

"So I've noticed you've taken to wearing sweaters in the summer—ones that cover your neck . . ."

"You know what's great about going to the beach?" I pause a beat. "How relaxing it is."

"So does that mean you don't want to talk about your sudden addiction to high-necked sweaters?"

I elbow him when he settles into the sand beside me. "No, it means I was hoping to not have to, but now you've brought it up . . ."

"That doesn't mean you have to talk about it if you don't want to."

I don't realize I'm rubbing my neck until Torrin's eyes drop to it. "It's just this big, ugly reminder to everyone that I was weak—that I was powerless."

Torrin's brows come together like he's trying to figure out if I'm being serious. "I look at that scar, and I see strength. I see a person who survived ten years in a situation most would have crumbled under in less than a month. I see a survivor." He stares at the pool in front of us like it's the Pacific. "That scar doesn't prove you're weak, Jade. It proves the opposite."

I lie back and stretch out, wiggling my feet and hands

into the sand. I close my eyes because if I tell him what I think I'm about to, I don't want to see what he looks like when he finds out. I cover my eyes with my forearm like I'm shielding them from the sun, but really I'm shielding them so he can't see them squeeze closed tighter. "I wasn't chained to anything, Torrin."

He's quiet for a minute. "What do you mean?"

I haven't told anyone—not even my parents. I'd planned to never tell anyone either, but right now, I have to tell Torrin. "The other end, it wasn't locked to anything. I was . . . free. I just didn't know it."

Torrin's quiet. "How—"

"The detectives I met with last week told me."

"How long?"

"I don't know. No one ever will either. I was free. I should have known it. I should have felt it or been able to tell, but I didn't. I could have left. I could have gotten back to my life. I could have . . ." I know we can both fill in what I don't say. "He'd broken me though. My will, my spirit, my soul, whatever you call it. All of it. He broke it."

I feel him lie down beside me before his hand digs under the sand to find mine. He pulls it to the surface. "You can't keep beating yourself up for that. You can't let it keep you locked in your room for the rest of your life."

My fingers feel limp compared to his, but he rubs my fingers, warming them, bringing them back to life. "That's not why I've locked myself away."

"Why then?"

I don't want to reflect on that question, because I'm scared of the answer. I'm scared where thinking about it will lead me. I'm not ready. But . . . "What if I had found out I wasn't chained to anything, Torrin? That I was free to go out that front door one day?"

"I don't know."

"I don't know either. That's the problem."

He scoots closer until his arm is running down mine. His body's warmer than the warm breeze blowing over us. "Well, nothing like an afternoon at the beach to relax and reflect, right?"

"Yeah, but it doesn't smell the same," I say, wondering if I can just delay the inevitable forever. I think it would be better than confronting the realization that I might never have carried that chain out of the front door if I had found it was bound to nothing.

Torrin lifts our hands and drops them on his chest. He's not letting me bury mine again. "Well, you know where to find that when you're ready."

Nineteen

I'M READY. OR at least I think I'm ready. Or I am for sure pretending to be ready.

Either way, we've loaded the Tahoe and are parking at the public beach access, and Dad's shutting off the engine. It's my first time outside in two weeks, and I've been on the cusp of a meltdown ever since we backed out of the garage.

The media's still camped out, as abundant and vicious as ever, but Dad got his windows tinted super dark a few days ago. That, and a blanket tossed over me sprawled out in the back, meant a successful escape without a caravan of news trucks following us.

"Hey, you've got this." Torrin gives my hand a quick squeeze before moving it away because my dad has spent as much time checking the rearview mirror as he has the windshield. "I'll be right here the whole time." When Dad exhales loudly, Torrin adds, "We'll all be right here." When Dad turns around in his seat, Torrin tacks on, "The whole time."

I bite my lip and bob my head, but I'm losing it on the inside. Not even Torrin's injection of confidence can penetrate my skin this time. It doesn't get inside and spread like I'm used to.

When I'd worked up the nerve to go to the real beach, I'd only planned on including Torrin. But when my parents found out, I knew they were hurt that the plan didn't include them. So I invited them. And they invited Sam and her family.

So my first outing outside the house in two weeks is a family affair. I'd wanted to only include Torrin so that if I lost it—like I felt close to—my family wouldn't have to witness it happening. Again.

"I'll grab the cooler and chairs and find us a spot." Dad checks me through his sunglasses then lifts a brow at Torrin before crawling out the door.

"Okay, so, sweetheart, you put on that special sunscreen I gave you, right?" It's Mom's turn to twist around in her seat and inspect me.

I answer her with a nod.

"And you've got the glasses and hat?"

I nod again.

"I brought the sunshade, so why don't you just wait here while your dad gets it set up?"

I exhale at this suggestion. Lately, she's been treating me like a preemie in the neonatal unit who has to be protected inside a clear plastic box.

"I know you put on your swimsuit, but you should probably stay covered up today just to be safe. Your skin hasn't been exposed to sun in years. I don't know if it'll

248

burn or blister, but let's be safe just in case." I sigh, but she keeps going. From the looks of the mental checklist she's crossing off, she's just getting started. "Oh, and the ocean. I know I used to not be able to get you out of the water, but it's been a long time since you've swam. You should start in a pool first . . . not with the currents and tides and everything."

This time I groan as I reach for the door handle. I need to get out of this car and away from my mom's endless stream of concerns. "I'm made of flesh, Mom, not porcelain. Give me a little more credit."

I swing my legs out the door, and the sticky ocean breeze coats them instantly. The smell hits me next, and it's everything I remember. Briny—like seawood's drying in the sunshine—and a little sweet.

"Torrin . . ." Mom says as I start for the beach.

"She'll be fine, Eleanor."

The waves are breaking, and the breeze is blowing, and the sun's ducking in and out of the clouds, and the seagulls are screaming—and I can't imagine anywhere else I'd want to be than right here. With him. With them.

Torrin lopes up to me when I'm halfway to the ocean's edge. He's loaded down with bags and chairs and boards, but he's moving as fast as I am—like neither of us can wait to go play. Dad pauses from working on the sunshade when he sees us coming. He even breaks form and smiles in Torrin's general direction when he sees the one on my face.

"Great day for the beach, isn't it?" Dad says, wrestling with one of the shade's poles.

I nod, but great doesn't begin to sum it up. This is something else.

Torrin drops his load and helps my dad with the shade. Torrin's wearing the same boardshorts and sweat-shirt from our afternoon at the guest bedroom beach. I smile when I watch him. With the wind toying with his hair and the flip-flops on, he looks like the Torrin I fell in love with. The fifteen-year-old version is inside the man before me.

It makes my stomach feel funny. Like something's dancing around inside it.

"Look who made it!" Mom's voice carries from be-hind me.

When I turn to look, I see Sam and Patrick and . . . I cover my mouth with my hand. I've never seen her before, but I know I'm seeing my niece for the first time ever. Not a photo of her but the real, live her.

Sam's holding her, and when she notices me looking all overwhelmed and speechless, she smiles and makes her way over. Patrick is even more weighted down with beach junk than Torrin was. I can barely make out his face from beneath all of it.

Mom stays back a bit, letting Sam and me have a mi-nute. I haven't really talked to Sam since the day I went nuclear on the reporters swarming her car, but she doesn't look at me like we're on opposite teams anymore. She stops in front of me and looks at her daughter bouncing in her arms. She looks a lot like Sam did as a baby except she's got brown eyes. I suppose one part of her dad had to make it into the genetic pool.

"This is Maisy." Sam bounces her a few times, which makes her giggle and screech. Then she nuzzles her nose against her daughter. "This is Aunt Jade."

A ball pops into my throat out of nowhere. Off to the side, Mom has to turn around as she wipes at her eyes. I know this is a big deal—Sam feeling comfortable enough to bring her daughter around me. I know that this is Sam's way of accepting me back into the family, and when all I want to say is thank you, all I can do is wrestle with that ball.

Maisy stops bouncing and tips her head at me like she's trying to figure out who this Aunt Jade person is. Then she giggles again and reaches out so far for me Sam has to tighten her hold so she doesn't fall out of Sam's arms.

"Um," I say as she continues to wave her little arms at me, "is it okay?"

Sam looks at her daughter, and when she shallows, I'm pretty sure that same ball's in her throat. "Of course it's okay." Her voice is tight when she hands Maisy to me. "You're her family."

I freeze once Maisy's in my arms. She's heavier than I'd guessed, and wigglier. She bounces against me like she's giving me a hint. I'm so worried about dropping her or hurting her or anything else bad that can happen to a little baby I stay frozen a moment longer.

"It's okay, Jade." Sam touches my arm. "You won't hurt her."

I swallow and let go of the ball. "You want to bounce?"

Maisy blinks her brown eyes and makes a funny noise with her mouth. Sounds like a fart. It makes me laugh, and when I bounce her against me, she laughs with me.

"You're a silly girl. You really must be my niece." I keep bouncing her, and from the look on her face, I don't think she'll ever get tired of this.

When I turn a little so she can see the ocean, I see him.

Torrin's watching me with an intensity that pulls my breath straight up out of my lungs. I want to look away because I think I know what's going through his mind—in another life, under other circumstances, the baby laughing in my arms could have been ours.

When I smile at him, for the first time I'm met by something that looks almost like pain on his face. He turns away and wanders down to the water.

Twenty

NOW THAT I'M outdoors, in the open, I can't imagine crawling back inside my room and locking myself away from the world.

I've always loved the beach. Even the beaches up north that don't know sunshine and blue skies the way the ones in the south do. The ones that are rocky and blustery and spend most days shrouded in gray.

I think, after everything, I love the beach even more now. And I love this day, with these people, shaping these memories.

We're just about finished with the veggie burgers my dad grilled on his little charcoal grill when Mom gets that look on her face. I've seen it aimed my way a lot since coming home.

"Have you looked at the GED test dates and thought about registering for one yet?"

I lower the burger I've actually managed to eat half of. I think it's the ocean air making me hungry, but there's nothing like the pressure of picking-up-where-I-left-off to curb an appetite. "No, actually I haven't."

Torrin's beside me on the beach blanket, and he sets down his plate.

"When do you think you might get around to doing that?" Mom plays with the cap of her water bottle.

"Once I figure out how to be in public without passing out, melting down, or blowing up. Once I figure out how to quiet my head enough to think about literature and algebra. Once I find a tutor who can catch me up on everything I missed and everything I've probably forgotten."

Mom waves at me. "Oh, Jade, you were an honors student. You'll have no problem passing the GED."

"Yeah, I was an honor's student in high school. Ten years ago." I tip the brim of the big hat Mom insisted I wear lower down on my forehead.

Torrin leans back and casually spreads his arms wide so one's behind me. I don't lean into it because I know I can't with my family scattered around us, but I feel its support.

"You're a smart girl."

I look at her without blinking. "No, Mom, I'm not. Smart girls don't get fooled into walking right up to strange men in vans. Smart girls don't stay trapped in a house when . . ." The words lodge in my throat, creating a barricade. They still don't know. But Torrin does.

"You need to start moving on, sweetie. You can't stay trapped in your room, breaking out for occasional visits to the beach. It isn't healthy."

Her voice isn't unkind, and I know she's saying it because she wants the best for me, but she can't understand.

She can't comprehend how trivial a GED and college degree seem to me when I'm struggling to roll out of bed each morning. Why should I care about what I'm going to do with my life if I can't muster up the will to live more moments than not?

"Why? Why isn't it healthy?" Torrin's voice cuts into the conversation as he leans forward to look at my mom. His arm stays planted behind me. "My god, Eleanor, do you realize what your daughter went through? She didn't wander off at the mall and get lost for a few minutes—she was kidnapped. By a sick, sick person. Who kept her chained up and made her pretend to be his daughter." His voice is growing, and I'm glad Sam and Patrick are letting Maisy kick at the waves so they don't have to witness this. "There is no protocol for this. There is no right or wrong way to behave after something like that. So why don't you stop telling her what she should be doing and what she should be feeling and just listen to what she's telling you?" Torrin settles his hands on his hips, grasping to collect his emotions.

Dad stays quiet in his chair, chewing on what's left of his hamburger. That means he's with Torrin. He'd never come out and say it—I still see his fists form when Torrin comes within a body-length of me—but his silence is support enough.

Mom continues to twist the cap of her water bottle, but she stays quiet.

Torrin suddenly pulls his sweatshirt over his head and drops it into my lap. He's shirtless, and when he marches toward the water, I'm glad Mom insisted I wear dark glasses. No one can see the way I'm looking at him. I'm thankful for them when he looks over his shoulder and his eyes find me so *he* doesn't see the way I'm looking at him.

His dark hair bouncing with his pace, his back familiar and foreign at the same time, his eyes trying to tell me the same thing I've ignored up to this moment.

I don't realize I'm standing until I slip the hat from my head and drop it on the blanket. My sunglasses follow, then I shrug out of the long cotton dress.

"Where are you going?" Mom's voice is worried as I step out of the dress onto the sand.

"For a swim."

"Jade . . ."

The sun. The ocean. The current. It's all a danger to her, and I know that feeling. But today, I'm not letting it keep me from the things I want to do and the people I want to be with.

Torrin's already disappeared into the waves before I make it to the dark line where the wet sand starts and the dry sand ends. I feel strange in my old swimsuit. It kind of sags around my butt and puckers where I used to have this great part of the female anatomy known as boobs, but it still fits. Mostly.

When I reach the edge of the water, the first wave that crashes around my ankles sends ice into my veins. The Pacific at this latitude is so cold that most people prefer to watch it from the beach rather than swim in it.

I give myself a moment to adjust, then I walk out a little farther. Torrin's making his way back now that he's noticed me. His expression has cleared, but his eyes are still clouded by something. I think I know what it is since he doesn't seem to have an issue with looking at me the way I was looking at him behind my dark glasses.

I want to shift in place and cover myself, but I don't. If he wants to check me out like I'm still the seventeen-year-old who spilled out of her suit instead of swimming in it like I am now, I'm going to let him.

"I always loved that suit." His arms stroke through the water.

"Yeah, I remember."

He gets that look on his face like he's remembering too.

"I feel like an eight-year-old in it now." When I glance down at myself, all I see are flat planes and bony joints.

Torrin shakes his head, swimming closer. His wet hair plasters across his forehead. "You look good. Believe me."

I clear my throat, and this time, I do shift. "I look like a deflated balloon. All limp and saggy and sad looking."

Torrin makes a face and squirts a stream of ocean water at me. "You are fluent in the language of crazy, you know that?"

"I'm not the only one."

He huffs, swimming closer as a wave catches him. "Whatever. You're still the most beautiful girl I've ever seen."

I shift again, then he stands up in the waist-deep water. Seeing his back from a distance had been enough to make whatever had gone into hibernation in that region below my stomach stir. Seeing him so close, facing me, ocean water falling down the lines and ridges that had just been developing the last time I touched them fans that stirring feeling inside. The softness of boyhood has been ironed out by the harder, rougher planes of manhood.

"You're checking me out, aren't you?" He grins, and I swear he intentionally makes his stomach muscles tighten beneath the skin.

"I am *not* checking you out. I'm just examining. Making sure you don't have any jellyfish or sharks hanging off of you."

His smile spreads. "Whatever. You're totally checking me out, but that's okay because I'm totally checking you out."

I wade out a little deeper because I need more of my body hidden. That flicker of a spark has grown into something that's spreading. "Are people in your profession allowed to 'check out' others?"

Torrin's shoulder lifts. Water rolls off the triangle carved into the top of his shoulders and trickles down his chest. "Not sure. That's another one of those gray areas I'm happy to leave open to interpretation."

I step out deeper until the waves are crashing across the bottoms of my thighs. My legs from my knees down have gone numb. "Thanks for sticking up for me back there."

"I was just saying what you were too nice to."

I wade out a little farther until the water's breaking across my stomach. We're in the same spot in the water, but I keep some space between us because I have to. I don't trust myself to be too close with the way my body's responding to his right now.

I feel something swirl at my ankle, then it grabs me. I'm sucked under instantly as the undercurrent slams me to the ocean bottom and tumbles me around. It's happened before, so I don't panic. I know that once it's done with me, it will let me go. Once it's twirled me around a few times, it will leave me alone.

I can feel it starting to lose momentum when two arms brace around me and break me free. When we pop through the surface, Torrin spins me around, terror drawing up his expression.

"Are you okay?" He holds me with one hand, inspecting me with the other like he's going to find an elbow or organ missing.

I'm totally wet. I feel ocean water draining out of my ears and nose. My hair feels like a cyclone just had its way with it, and I know my skin's red and blotchy from the sand exfoliation treatment I just received free of charge.

I laugh. This is what alive feels like. I remember.

It's adrenaline pulsing so hard in my veins they feel about to burst. It's feelings that twist my stomach into knots. It's feeling so cold my body goes numb and so attracted to someone my body feels the opposite of numb.

This is it. Living. I can almost feel the blood warm in my veins as it starts to run again.

"Why are you laughing?" Torrin's face flashes with relief when he sees I'm okay, but he doesn't let go of me.

On the beach, my parents slowly make their way back to the beach blankets once they've seen I'm okay.

259

"That was fun." I rub my stomach because it hurts. From the laughter. I'd forgotten stomachs could hurt from laughing.

"Fun? Not my idea of fun."

I wipe the water from my face and find just as much sand pasted to it. "What's your idea of fun then?"

Torrin's still shaking his head when he suddenly shouts, "This!"

He pulls me under the water with him. He lets me go right away, but I don't want him to. I don't want him to ever let go.

I splash him when he resurfaces a few feet away. "Did you just dunk me?"

He splashes back. "I just did."

"You've heard of payback, right?" I move a little closer, ignoring the way I can feel my parents watching us from the beach.

"I've heard of it. Not really a big fan though."

When I lunge at him and try to knock him under, he's clearly bracing for it because all I do is smash into him. My wet body against his, our arms tangled together, our faces too close to not be aware of where each other's mouths are . . .

"What's this payback thing again?" He's practically gloating, so I come at it from a different angle.

My eyes drop to his mouth and stay there until his lips part from his breaths coming faster. When my hand curves against the side of his face, sweeping down the line of his jaw, I feel his chest moving hard against mine. His arms tangle more tightly behind me because I'm slipping through them. When that doesn't work, he hoists me higher, and his arms form a net beneath my backside.

I need to clear my head before I can't remember what I'm doing.

My eyes lift to his and hold there. When he blinks, a drop of water rolls off his eyelashes. My hand slides lower until my thumb is touching the corner of his mouth.

"Torrin?" I whisper, my mouth lowering.

"Yeah?" His voice is rough, coming from low in his throat.

I move my mouth just outside his ear. "This . . . is . . ."—I burst free of his hold and slide his legs out from beneath him with my foot—"payback!"

He goes down with a surprised shout and an explosive splash. I'm laughing again, and so is he when he pops his head above the water.

"Well played, Childs."

"Thank you very much," I say with a bow, hoping he can't see right through me the way I feel he can sometimes.

If he does, he'll know. He'll know I would have rather kissed him. I would rather still be kissing him. He'll know that while I'm content to put most of the past behind me, there's one part I want to pack and bring with me to the future.

Him.

I think he might see it though because I think I might see it in him too.

The sun catches his eyes just right when he looks at me. "You always had a way of taking the ground right out from beneath me."

Twenty-One

I GO OUT on my own the next day. I'm hoping that courage is like a muscle—the more you work it, the stronger it becomes. Yesterday, the beach. Today, the library.

Mom drops me off, but her car stays parked at the library, engine running, for five minutes after I go inside. I've been watching. I asked her to bring me to the library because it seems unthreatening and, other than a potential paper cut, safe. What I really want to do is go on a walk. For hours. For miles. I want to walk until my legs can't go any farther.

I don't just want to walk though. I want to walk alone. To think. To process. To clear my head and try to figure out some stuff. I knew there was no way she would agree to just drop me off at some corner and let me weave around the city though, so an afternoon at the library it is.

I'm wearing a ball cap, and I've braided my hair back so hopefully no one will recognize me. If they do and the reporters find out . . . I'm stuck. I can only escape as fast as my legs will take me.

The risk is worth the reward though.

When I realize Mom isn't going to pull away the moment after I enter the library, I kill some time wandering around the lobby. Once Mom's car finally leaves the parking lot, I decide to wait another minute just in case.

I take a last spin around the lobby, and an elderly man walks in, reading a paper. It catches my attention because of the big headline and photos taking up the whole front page. As the man rounds into the library, he drops the paper in the recycle bin and keeps going. I rush over and snatch it out of the bin. I shake the front page open, and I feel something pull a plug in my stomach as everything inside seems to drain away.

Father Torrin's Torrid Love Affair

There's one photo of us, and it's from yesterday. How someone found us or recognized us or whatever ill fate had a hand in it, I don't know, but somehow they managed to get just the right shot of us in the water where it looks like our lips are almost touching. We're in the ocean up to our thighs; my legs are wound around him; his arms are tied below my backside.

My eyes are open. His are closed.

He thought I was going to kiss him. He really believed I was. But that's not what makes me have to lean into the wall to hold myself up—it's that he was ready to kiss me back. He would have if I'd moved just a little closer.

What am I supposed to make out of that? A moment of weakness? He'd never seemed so sure of himself as he did yesterday.

I slide the cell phone Mom picked up for me a few days ago from my pocket, find the last number in my memory, and hit Call.

He answers in the middle of the second ring. "Jade?"

I should have taken a minute to catch my breath before calling him because I can't reply for a minute.

"What's wrong?"

I lean my head into the wall and suck in a deep breath. "Where are you?"

"At St. Al's Hospital."

I don't know where it is, but I know how to find it on my phone. "Wait there."

"I'm about to perform a last rites in twenty minutes."

I shove off the wall, clutching the paper in my other hand as I hurry for the door. "I'll wait. Just stay there, okay?"

He's quiet for a second. "Okay."

I hit End and shove through the doors, trying to pull up the location of St. Al's Hospital on my phone. I'm catching up on technology—slowly. It shows St. Al's is a mile away. Driving distance is ten minutes thanks to traffic. Walking distance is fifteen.

I take the walking option since I set out to walk anyway and there isn't a taxi or bus stop in sight. Following the directions, I clip off turn after turn, cruising along at almost but not quite a jog. My body still gets tired from exertion, but it's adapting to everyday life again. It's getting stronger.

When an ambulance flies by me, I know I'm getting

close, and I follow its sirens to the top of the hill. The climb feels like it's going to make my heart explode even though I'm *barely* walking. By the time I make it to the top and am in front of the hospital, I've almost been reduced to a crawl.

Taking a second to let my lungs relax, I follow the signs to the main entrance and brake to a stop when I realize I have no idea *where* in this megaplex of a hospital Torrin is.

"Can I help you, miss?" a woman at the reception desk asks when I stay frozen just inside the doors.

"Torrin Costigan?" I say, guessing it's a long shot she'd know where one person is in this place.

"Patient?" she replies, typing something into her computer. Her eyes squint at the screen, and she shakes her head.

"No, he's a visitor . . ." Then I realize I'm probably one of the few people who still calls him Torrin. "Father Costigan?" I tuck the paper tighter into my armpit.

"Oh, sure." She pushes back from her computer and slides off her reader glasses. "He's up on the fifth floor with Mrs. Delaney."

When she waves toward the elevators, I start moving. "Thank you."

I'm antsy waiting for one of them to open, and when one finally does, I jump inside before anyone has a chance to climb off. I punch the five button a dozen times, but it doesn't make the doors close any faster.

What am I in such a hurry to find out? Why do I need to see him so badly?

Is it to let him know about the article . . . the picture? Or is to confront him about the kiss that could have been?

I'm not sure, and I guess I won't be until I'm standing in front of him. It makes me want to get there even sooner. I run—*run*—off of the elevator before the doors finish opening. A nurse at a pill cart twists around when she hears my sneakers squeak across the tile.

"Mrs. Delaney's room?" I ask.

She lifts her tablet to check.

"Father Costigan?"

Her eyes lift away from the tablet. "Room 542."

I hurry down the hall, feeling like it's the last room in this never-ending tunnel. Actually, it is. I skid to a stop when I come to the end of the hall. The door to 542 is partly closed, but I hear him inside. I can see him too.

I can't see Mrs. Delaney because he's blocking her, but I can see her weathered hand swimming in his. The skin looks thin, frail . . . cold. I'm not Catholic, but I know enough from the times I went with Torrin to his church. I know what the last rites are. I know the woman whose hand he's holding is dying. Soon.

He finishes his recitation, crosses himself, and then he's quiet. He doesn't say good-bye and turn to leave now that it's done. He doesn't pat her hand before setting it on the bed. He stays. He keeps holding her hand.

I know the woman's crying. I can hear her, and I can tell by the way Torrin's jaw grinds together. He's never been able to handle a woman crying well. But he lets her cry, staying still beside her the entire time. Her hand stays solidly in his the whole time.

Mrs. Delaney sniffs, and her thin fingers curl around Torrin's hand. "You're a bright light in this dark world, Father." Her voice carries out of the room, then she slips her hand from his. "Thank you."

He moves for the door, but before he goes, he rests his hand on the foot of her bed. "Be at peace."

"Now"—she exhales like all of the pain and fear has been emptied from her—"I am."

He smiles, but his jaw's still straining, then he heads for the door. I creep back a ways because I don't want him to know I was listening in. I don't want him to know that what I just witnessed might have been the most beautiful thing I've ever seen.

He doesn't look surprised to see me when he steps into the hall, but he doesn't say anything until he closes the door.

"What's the matter?" he asks in a hushed voice. I can tell sound carries up and down these halls like the scent of disinfectant.

For a minute, I'd forgotten. I'd been too hypnotized by what just happened in that room. "Have you seen the paper today?"

I begin to pull it out from under my arm when he stops me. His fingers curl into my arm, and I think about the kiss that could have been.

He takes in a breath through his nose. "I've seen it."

I hadn't been expecting that answer. "You have?"

"The one with a picture the size of a soccer ball of the two of us? Yeah, I have."

"And you're not concerned?" I let the paper fall open

in front of him.

He doesn't look at it. "About 'Father Torrin's Torrid Love Affair'? No, considering it's a lie, I'm not concerned."

I turn the paper around to make sure I didn't see the picture wrong the first time. Nope, still looks like if things aren't, they're about to get plenty 'torrid.' And why the hell are they referring to him as Father Torrin when even I know you call a priest by his last name? I know why though—torrid and Costigan don't pack the same punch. "And what about the picture? This doesn't worry you?"

I shake the paper in his face, but he still won't look. "It's a picture. It doesn't tell the whole story. It can't show what came before and what came after. If people are going to let a perfectly timed photo and a fancy headline form their opinions for them, that's not my problem." His forehead creases when he looks at me. "Are you worried?"

"Very."

Now his removed expression shifts. Concern takes its place. "This is going to make things worse for you, isn't it? They're going to send more reporters to your front door. You won't be able to sneak out without them following you . . . speaking of . . ." He motions at me. "What *are* you doing here? By yourself?" He scans the hall, probably looking for my parents.

"Forget about that right now. I'm here—we don't need to talk about how I got here." I drop the paper at my side. "I'm not worried about how this affects me. I'm worried about how this affects you."

"How will this possibly affect me when it's trash and

lies?"

"Because you were about to kiss me"—I wave at him like that explains it all—"and you're a priest."

I notice one of the nurses down the hall turn her head toward us. Torrin does too. Taking my arm, he leads me into an empty waiting room.

"You were about to kiss me too," he says, moving in front of me, "knowing exactly what I am."

I could deny it. I could argue. I don't because he's right. "I shouldn't have. You're right, I do know what you are." My eyes lower to his neck. "I shouldn't have."

"Want to try that again? With a little conviction this time maybe?"

The way he says it, the way he closes the space between us, makes me back up because there it is—the urge. The longing. The pull. The attraction. It's still there. A decade later, and it hasn't diminished. It hasn't stayed the same.

It's grown.

"Why are you doing this, Torrin? What are you even saying right now?" I squeeze my eyes shut because I can't look away from him when he's looking at me like that. "You are a goddamn priest. You made your choice."

"You were gone, Jade. I made the only choice I had left." His voice rolls over me. He's upset.

I don't want him to be upset because of me anymore. I don't want to be that in his life.

"You're not just a priest. You're a good one. A really good one." I think of the woman in that room and how he made her last moments on this planet better. "You're doing this for a reason. Don't throw it all away."

"And what if I'm willing to? Give it all up? Throw it all away?"

My eyes flash open. "Then I'd tell you you're a damn fool."

He moves toward me, matching my every step as I back away. "And what if I don't care what you say because when you look at me, you're telling me something different every time?"

"I wouldn't let you. I *won't* let you do it."

His phone vibrates in his pocket. He exhales when he pulls it out and checks the screen.

"They're calling about us, aren't they?"

He pockets the phone. "'They' being my governing bishop and the church elders? Probably."

"What are you going to tell them?"

"The truth."

"And what is that?" I say, glad we're in the privacy of the waiting room because my voice is getting louder. "The truth?"

Torrin's eyes narrow. "You know it. You're just not ready to admit it."

I hear the phone vibrate in his pocket again. He can only ignore them for so long. I feel desperate, trying to think of anything I can say to him to get him to change his mind.

Though I'm not sure I want him to change his mind, because he's right—I do know the truth. But he's also right about me not being ready to admit it.

"Why did you become a priest?"

He tips his head. "I already told you why."

"Yeah, because I was gone and maybe never coming back and you wanted to help people. You could have done a hundred different things if you wanted to help people. Why else?"

His jawbone pops through his skin. He glares out the window for a minute, then he falls into the chair behind him. He leans forward and glares at the floor. "After you went missing, I changed. A lot. I was consumed with trying to find you, and that led me down a lot of roads I never should have wandered down. One of those roads took me to a serious beating that almost killed me." His shoulder lifts. "I wanted to die. That night under the Ship Canal Bridge, when I confronted some bad people who I'd heard might know something about your disappearance, I wanted to just leave this world for good. I thought that if nothing else, maybe you'd be waiting for me on the other side."

I hadn't been expecting this story. I hadn't been expecting to hear about the time he almost died because he hadn't been able to let me go. I drop into the chair across from him.

"Someone found me though. Someone who'd been out delivering sandwiches to the homeless. He helped me up, drove me home, and listened to my story. The whole drive, he didn't say anything. He just listened. He was the first person to do that, you know? Listen. Everyone else had been throwing so much 'you'll be okay with a little time' or 'she's in a better place' at me I was ready to break the nose of the next person who said it." Torrin clasps his hands in front of him, popping his knuckles as he rolls them together. "After he dropped me off back at home, he told me that if I wanted to ever talk again, I could find him at St. Mark's. He was the priest there."

That's when he glances at me. The look on his face makes me want to crawl into the chair beside him and hold him.

"I went back. A bunch of times. I talked. He listened. Until finally one day, I was done talking. It was the same day he finally offered me some kind of advice or reassurance." His phone buzzes in his pocket again, but I don't think he hears it. "He told me that I wouldn't be any help to you if I got myself killed. He told me that as long as there was still hope, not to give up on it. He told me that when I felt like an absolute failure and that I was getting nowhere, to repeat a certain quote to myself."

I tip my head and wait.

Torrin exhales, his face bound by emotions I'm not sure I know the names of. "'Try again. Fail again. Fail better.'"

I repeat the words to myself. I imagine a young, desperate Torrin repeating them to himself. I wonder if those words could help get me through my dark period, if they could pull me up when the weight of a thousand failures was holding me down. "Who said that?"

"I don't know. Someone brilliant." Torrin stares at his hands, his brows drawn together. "Because it worked. It's what got me through a decade of dead-ends and cold trails. I just kept failing better until I ultimately remembered something that would lead the police to the man who took you."

273

I have this priest and those words to thank for my freedom. It kind of knocks the wind out of me, and I sink deeper into the chair. "If you never gave up hope, why did you go to seminary? If you still felt like I'd be found, why did you become this?" I gently motion at him, my eyes lingering on his collar.

He takes a moment to answer. He's still studying his hands like they're not his but someone else's. "Because holding on to *that* kind of hope—that there was still a chance for you and me?—made me too desperate. It was counterproductive. The tighter I held on to you, the further away you seemed to slip." His hands curl into fists before he looks at me. "Once I committed to this, I was able to approach your case from an unbiased, almost objective perspective. Once I gave up that selfish part of wanting you back, I could think clearly. If I hadn't become this . . . I'm not sure you'd be sitting across from me now."

"So you sacrificed your whole life for me?" I work my tongue into my cheek, overwhelmed. With guilt, appreciation, and unworthiness.

He leans across the distance between us, refusing to tame his stare. I feel my heart beating in my throat. "I'd sacrifice this life and every life I have coming for you."

I have to close my eyes. "I'm so sorry, Torrin. God, I'm sorry. I didn't want you to give up ten years of your life for me. I didn't want you to give up whatever could have come after before you became this . . ."

He stretches closer. His eyes refuse to blink. "You were my first. And you were my last." His words echo in the small space. "A man could have a thousand different partners and settle down with an amazing woman, and I'd still hold the bragging rights. Don't feel sorry for me for that. I'm not."

Everything I want is in front of me, but I can't have it. It's the carrot dangled in front of me—just out of reach, never to be realized. Life is so goddamn unfair.

"I'm sorry," I say again because what else is there to say? He's given so much, and I have so little left to give.

"I'm not sorry. Never." The air stirs when he pulls back. "Besides . . . *this* is not a death sentence. This is not an executioner's swing. I knew exactly what I was doing when I started down this path, and I went into it with both eyes open and with reasons other than just hoping to fail better at finding you." When he smiles, it's a sad one.

"What reasons?" I ask, glancing toward the doorway. I need to leave, but I'm not sure I know how.

Torrin rolls his fingers, and his knuckles snap one after the other. "Father Sullivan was my light in the darkest time of my life. I was hoping that maybe I might be able to be the same for someone else one day."

I clasp my hands together when I feel them reaching for him. "You *are* that. To that woman inside that room, you are." I lean back to look at him. He's still hunched over. "You were that to me. You *are* that to me."

When he glances up, I see it in his eyes again. That look takes me back in time to a dark sidewalk, to a certain question, and an answer in the form of a kiss.

Before he can say anything, I continue. I can't risk him opening his mouth and changing my mind. "You became this for a lot of reasons. Good reasons. Remember those when you feel that conflict. Remember how great you are at this. Remember how many more dark places you can shine light on."

"When I feel conflict, it isn't those things I remember, Jade." He holds his hand out for me to take. I want to. Everything inside me is being pulled to it. "I remember *you.*"

His hand hangs there for another minute, then his fingers curl into his palm, and he draws it back. He runs his finger beneath his collar like it's choking him.

"I don't get it. How you can be so good at this"—I wave at him sitting there in his black and white—"and not feel conflicted when it comes to us."

"There's conflict in me." His eyes lift to meet mine. "So much I feel like it could eat me alive if I let it. I love what I do. I believe in what I do. I know I took vows, but I made a promise to you first. If I'm forced to make a choice, it will be you. Every time." He exhales, and his eyes lower. "It will be you."

I feel as close as I ever have to taking his hand and asking him to make that choice. I feel my resolve weaken, and I know the longer I stay, the worse it will become.

When his phone goes off again, I say, "I'll give you some privacy."

Standing up to walk away, I feel conflict of my own ripping me apart. I want him back. I want what we had back. Everything, not just the friendship and adventures. I want to pretend we can pick up where we left off and that the question he asked me that last night can become a reality.

I also want him to have as peaceful a life as he can from now on. I don't want him to give up everything for me, because he's already done it once. I've already had the love of a man who gave me everything—I have no right to expect it a second time.

To ask him to give it all up so we can be together would be such a selfish act that I think it could rip us apart anyway. He's sacrificed enough.

"Jade—" He turns in his seat, watching me leave.

I keep going, but each step gets harder. Each one rips off another chunk of my heart. "Just let me go, Torrin."

A sigh drifts from the waiting room. "I don't know how."

Twenty-Two

IT ISN'T GRIEF I feel when I pass through the cemetery gates this time—it's rage. The kind that feels like it's about to spill out of me in waves.

After leaving Torrin at the hospital and saying what I did, I'd fought the urge to turn around and go back—to tell him what I want to . . . but what I know I can't.

Once the bus stops at that same bus stop and I get out, my mind shifts. It isn't Torrin I'm thinking about now.

There are actual cars and people around today but not many, and instead of crawling through the gates like last time, I pass through them. As I storm down the same roads and paths, I feel hot instead of cold. It's another sunny day, and I'm wearing another sweater that conceals my neck, but it isn't anything on the outside that's heating me—it's coming from the inside.

A furnace has been installed inside me, and it's pumping heat throughout my body. The closer I get to the gravestone, the hotter I feel.

Jogging the last bit toward it, I have to bite my lip

from shouting what I need to say right here. This time, I'm glad he's been buried out here because I can scream all I want and probably no one will hear.

This time, I don't kneel at his grave. This time, I don't cry silent tears. This time, I don't feel confusion. This time, the only thing I miss are the ten years that have been stolen from me.

"It's me, Earl Rae." My voice quivers with its anger as I step onto the cement gravestone. I glare at it. "Remember that girl you decided to take one night and play make-believe was your daughter? *That* girl?"

I see Torrin's face fall in that fifth-floor waiting room. I see him reach for me and me unable to reach back. I see his smile and hear his question and envision the way my life could have been.

Then I see red.

"You took my life from me, you sick, pathetic bastard. You didn't ask. You didn't care. You just took it. That was my life. *Mine.* It was a great life that you took away because you were a bad person. An evil man."

I don't wipe the tears away, because unlike the others, these are derived from anger. They don't hurt as much as the other kind. They actually feel pretty damn good.

"I loved him. He loved me. And you took that from us. You took it, and I can never get it back because you twisted and twisted me until I'm not sure I even remember what love is. How it feels. How it looks. I can't remember . . ."

When a splash of sadness soaks its way inside me, I grind the dried weeds still resting above his name with the toe of my shoe.

"He still loves me, and I still love him, but I'm a fraction of what I used to be. That's all I've got left to love back with, and it's not enough. He deserves it all, and all I've got left are scraps." I surge with anger that rolls down from my head. I hope it soaks into the ground and somewhere, in that inner circle, Earl Rae's hell gets a little hotter. "I hate you. I hate you so, so much. I hate you more than any person has ever hated someone else."

I don't know if anyone hears me. I don't know if anyone sees me. I don't care.

"You want to know why your daughter probably ran away with her mom, you sick, sick fuck? Because she couldn't wait to get away from you. You want to know why she stayed away? Because she never wanted to see you again. Because look at your gravestone, Earl Rae—no one cares." I kick the dried weeds away until they've disappeared into the grass. "You are a bad man, and no one mourns a bad person. You are a sick man, and no one loves a sick person."

My throat constricts when I shout the last part, and I start kicking the gravestone. With the heel of my sneaker, with the toe of it, any part of it I can smash against it. "I wish you hadn't taken the chicken-shit way out. I wish you hadn't because that was my right. You took my life; it's only fair I get to take yours. Except I wouldn't have used a gun and made it quick. I would have used my hands. Around your neck. Until the life drained out of you the way it has out of me." I'm jumping now, like I can break the cement in half if I just don't stop. "I want to kill you!

Again . . . and again . . . and again."

I pause for a minute, panting. I'm staring at the gravestone like I'm waiting for him to say something back. I'm waiting for an explanation or an apology or something that will give me some peace as to why my life was ripped away.

There's nothing. Only silence.

There'll never be an explanation. Never an apology. Never absolution.

And without any of that, how is peace possible?

"I hate you, Earl Rae, you hear me? I hate you." I glare at the gravestone, picturing the innocent look on his face that night I disappeared. How could someone so evil master such innocence?

"Burn in hell." I wipe the sweat from my forehead and pull at the collar of my sweater because I'm stifling from the heat coursing through me. "I'm burning in my own."

Twenty-Three

WHEN I SNEAK into the backyard hours later, it's dark, and more houses are dark than light. My parents' house is one of the few with lights still on, burning brightly inside.

I've missed dozens of calls from them. I've missed just as many from Torrin, whom they probably called after being unable to reach me, assuming I'd be with him. I don't want them to worry. I don't want to cause them any more pain, but it seems inevitable. Even when I try not to, I still find some way to hurt them. Like I did Torrin today when all I wanted to do was protect him.

Like when I didn't answer my parents' calls because I didn't want them to hear me as I'd been earlier—I didn't want them to discover just how damaged their daughter is now.

In my desire to protect them, I still hurt them.

It's inevitable. I've accepted that now.

I've absorbed a decade of isolation and despair. I am swimming in it, and I can't just find the right place to squeeze and wring every drop of it away. I might be able to find a way to drain a couple of drops here and there, but it will take time.

It might take as long to be free of it as it took accruing it.

I might *never* be free of it.

My thoughts have been dark for most of the day, and I'm hoping that I'll be able to slip up to my room undetected and get a night's rest before confronting my parents. I've barely turned the key over in the back door before I hear their muffled footsteps rushing in my direction.

By the time I'm inside and locking the door, they're both here. Mom's face is puffy, and her eyes are red. She starts crying again. The wear from the day doesn't show on Dad so obviously, but it can be found in the finer details: the way his hair isn't so perfectly laid, his wrinkled slacks, the creases at the corners of his eyes.

"Thank god." Mom's voice shakes. "Thank god you're safe."

"I'm okay, Mom. I'm fine." I lift my hands and step inside like I'm surrendering.

"Where have you been? The library—you weren't there when I went back." Her hand braces around the top of a kitchen chair as fresh tears fall down her face. "Why didn't you answer any of our calls? Did you lose your phone?"

I slide the phone from my pocket. It's shut off. "I didn't lose it."

"Why, Jade?" Mom sniffs. "Why didn't you answer?"

"Because I didn't know what to say."

"I just wanted to know you were safe. That you were okay."

I lift a shoulder and stay by the door. "I didn't know what to say."

"Torrin said you were at the hospital today, that you two had a difficult talk. Is that what this is about?" Dad's voice seems like a roar compared to Mom's and mine.

"This is about everything. What happened. What's *happening*. Torrin. You guys. The media. Earl Rae Jackson." My parents recoil when I speak his name. "This is about everything."

Dad pops off a little huff. I take it as a contradiction to everything I just said, and it fans the anger I wrestled into submission earlier.

"Oh, and you can stop worrying about Torrin and me, Dad, since I know the idea of us being together has always pissed you off. That's over. All of it. Should make you happy."

Dad's forehead creases. "Happy? Do you think any of this makes me happy?"

I spread my arms and shout, "How do you think it makes me feel?" My vision blurs, but I blink it clear. "I lost everything. And even though I'm back now, I've still lost everything. I'm a twenty-seven-year-old with a high school junior education. I'm a woman in a girl's body." I pinch the billowing sweater hanging off from me. "I'm an adult living in her parents' house who has to depend on them for practically everything. I love a man I can't love. I want a life I can't have."

Dad reaches for Mom's hand because she's crying

harder now.

"None of this makes me happy," I whisper.

"And you think any of this makes us happy? Seeing you like this?" Dad motions at me, his jaw locking up for a moment. "Do you think it's easy having you home after ten years and knowing you were so close that whole time? Knowing I'm a damn chief of police and couldn't find my own daughter in the very same state she was abducted in?" Now it's Mom reaching for Dad because he's the one who looks close to tears. "I couldn't find you, Jade. I should have been able to, and I didn't. I had the resources and the manpower and the experience . . . I should have been able to find you. And I'm sorry. I'm sorry I failed you."

I want to cross the kitchen and throw my arms around him, but I stay where I am. I'm too close to crying, and I don't want them to have to watch me shed another single tear. I don't want them to feel any more pain or guilt or regret than I know they already do.

"Dad, please don't. You didn't fail me. Please don't blame yourself." I have to look away because I can't watch my parents like this any longer. "The man who took me's to blame. Not the people left behind who tried to find me."

Dad moves a little closer, but he lets me have my space. "The person who got taken isn't to blame either, Jade," he says in as gentle a voice as he is capable. "You promise to keep that in mind, and I'll promise to take what you just said to heart."

I nod after a minute—not because I'm agreeing but because I'm too exhausted to argue.

"We're trying here, Jade. We know this is hard on

you, but it's not easy for us." Dad shifts and opens his mouth like there's more to say, but nothing else comes.

"I know. You guys are doing such a great job, I swear. It's me. I feel like every morning I'm climbing a mountain, but when I look behind me at the end of the day, I'm still in the same spot. I try to move on, to get better, but I get nowhere." I'm staring at my hands the way Torrin was earlier—like I don't recognize them anymore. "I think it's because I'm still hanging on to my old life. Trying to get back to that. If I have any chance of getting better, I need to create a new life as the person I am now." My brain is finally working, managing to get the ideas put together and the words out in a cohesive way.

"And how do you do that, sweetheart?" Mom's putting on the brave face, but I know she'd still be crying if I wasn't standing in front of her.

"I don't know exactly, but if I want to make a new life for myself, I need to move out and find my own place."

Mom's eyes widen while Dad swallows.

"Coming back to this house, my bedroom . . . it's too hard to move on when all I see is my old life here."

"You just came back, Jade. You've never lived on your own," she says.

"I've been on my own for ten years. I can do this."

"Not right away. Give yourself some time to ease back into the world." Mom glances around the kitchen like the walls are collapsing around her.

"The longer I stay here, the more time I'm wasting."

"What about the GED? College?"

286

"I don't know yet." I shake my head. "I just know that I can't figure any of that out until I'm on my own, able to make my own decisions as the person I am now."

Dad clears his throat. "When are you thinking you'd like to start looking for your own place, Jade?"

Mom glances at him like she's heard him wrong.

"As soon as possible," I answer.

Dad nods. "Okay. Tomorrow we'll start looking."

Mom's eyes close, but she doesn't argue. I think she knows I need this. She's just not ready to admit it out loud.

"Thank you," I breathe.

"And next time your mom and I call you over and over, would you please answer? After what happened to you . . . you can't just go and not answer when we don't know where you are." Dad has to look away. "Please?"

"I won't," I promise, feeling guilt gurgle up my throat. "I'm sorry."

As I make my way through the kitchen to go upstairs, Dad's head turns. "And you should call Torrin back."

I stop. That's the first time Dad has ever suggested I call Torrin back. "I should?"

"He's been put on temporary suspension." Dad's hand settles on his hip. "He could probably use a good friend to talk to right now."

My tongue works into my cheek. Even when I try to make things right, everything just kind of goes wrong. "They suspended him?"

"Yeah. Temporarily, at least. He's on some sort of probation."

"Because of me?"

The room is silent for a moment, then Dad sighs.

I guess it wasn't really a question. Of course it's because of me. Of course his life is falling apart because of me. Of course he's going to suffer because of me. Of course he's going to lose everything because of me all over again.

My shoulders tremble from what I'm feeling. When I try to keep moving, my feet are stuck in place.

"Are you okay?" Mom's small voice rolls over me.

I bite my lip, but the honest answer finally wells up from deep inside. "No, I'm not."

Twenty-Four

PAGE ONE OF my new life is ready to be written. I have no idea how to start.

Fear has a way of crippling me, making it impossible for me to think or put one foot forward.

I wasn't scared earlier. When everyone was here helping me get moved in, I didn't feel fear digging its claws into me the way I feel it now. I didn't even feel it right after I walked my parents and Sam's family to the door to say good night.

They were the ones fighting the fear bug then, lingering at the front door, reminding me to call if I needed anything at any hour, confirming they'd be back over after breakfast to finish unpacking. The look on Mom's face had convinced me she was going to spend the night camped out on my front stoop, but she left. After Dad practically dragged her away.

The fear doesn't hit me until I start turning off the lights, one by one, around my little apartment. The fear doesn't find me until darkness casts its veil around me and welcomes me into it.

I focus on my breathing and tell myself I'm safe and there's nothing to be scared of, but it doesn't help. The fear only gets worse with every light that switches off.

The apartment is still in Sammamish, in a gated community. My parents even had a security system installed, and Dad pulled me aside before they left to tell me he'd stationed canisters of pepper spray at my front door, back door, kitchen window, nightstand, and in my purse. He'd also propped one of his old bats in the corner of my bedroom. I know he's just trying to make me feel safe—they all are—but the security system and pepper spray and gates make the world seem more scary, not less.

The apartment is about a thousand square feet, but as it gets darker, it shrinks. First down to half its size, then a quarter, until it's become a small, dark closet I feel trapped inside of.

My hands tremble as I walk through my new room toward my bed. I've set the alarm, double-checked the locks, made sure the stove is off, and turned off the lights. This is what adults do when they go to bed. They don't break out in a cold sweat and feel like a scream's crawling up their throat with every dark second that passes.

This is being an adult. The first day in my new life. I knew it would be hard . . . I can handle it. This night will be the hardest. Tomorrow will be easier, and each one after will follow the same trend until I can flip off the lights, crawl into bed, and fall right asleep. Until one day, the dark won't hold sway over me.

My heartbeat is the only thing disturbing the silence.

When I sit on the edge of the bed, I tell myself to lie down and crawl under the covers. I can't. The dark isn't as thick as the kind I've known, but the little bit of light cutting through the drawn shades is drawing patterns on my walls, sketching images I'm reading too much into.

When I close my eyes, the dark's still there.

My heart picks up speed, and my breath follows.

A crashing sound erupts from right outside my room. It's so loud that when I spin around, I expect to find a smashed piano that has dropped from the sky in front of my rocking chair.

But my room's the same. Nothing's different.

I hear another crash; this one seems even louder. If it's not inside my room, it has to be right outside my room. From the sound of it, just outside my window or the back door coming off the miniscule laundry room.

Someone's trying to break in. Someone knows I'm here and is coming to take me. For another decade or forever this time. He's here, and this time, I'm not getting out.

I grab my phone from my nightstand, fly across the room, and duck into the closet. After throwing the doors closed, I slide back until I find the corner. I can't tell if the crashing noise I hear is an echoing in my head or real. So I cover my ears and close my eyes, but it's still there. It can't be real. I couldn't hear that sound with my ears covered like this—it would be duller, not so sharp, like it's clapping right between my ears.

I tell myself this, over and over again, but it doesn't chase away the fear. Fear stays fitted around me like a suit of armor, heavy and impenetrable.

I lift the phone and focus on its light. I want to call my parents. I want to beg them to come get me and keep me safe. I want to ask them to lock me in a cell that no one has the key to. I want to ask them to hide me from the world for the rest of my life so I don't have to feel like this.

Right now, I'd exchange uncertain freedom for a safe cage. I wouldn't think twice about it.

That's why I know I can't call them. I can't let them know I'm so terrified I just want to crawl into Mom's lap and let her rock away my fears. I can't let them know I feel so exposed that I want to slip under their blankets and fall asleep between them.

I can't let them know I feel the same way they do, because then I'll never get better. I'll continue to stagnate on my best days and decay on my worst.

I can't get better by giving in to my fear—I can only get better by facing it.

When I hit the call button, it isn't the number to my parents. It's not even the one to Sam's cell. It's the number I still have in the number one spot.

Even though I haven't called it in two weeks. Even though I should probably delete it. Even though . . . he's still in the number one spot.

My hands are still shaking as the phone rings, but they're not quaking as they had been.

The phone rings twice, then three times, and when it hits a fourth, I worry he's not going to answer. I worry he's never going to answer again because I've done enough damage and he's had enough.

I'm anticipating his voicemail when he answers. He's quiet.

"Torrin?" I let out a long breath, trying to exhale the pent-up fear. "Torrin?"

He's quiet for another minute, then I hear his sigh. "I'm here, Jade. What is it?"

He sounds tired. Since it's almost eleven, he was probably asleep. It's not just tired I hear in his voice though; it's something stronger. Exhaustion? Fatigue? Something not brought on just by lack of or need for sleep.

"I'm sorry to call you so late . . . after not talking to you for a while—"

"You're sorry for ignoring my calls for the past two weeks? Is that what you're saying?"

I hear more noises, but these are different than the crashing ones that sent me flying into the closet. These ones sound like they're right above me, like something's trying to crawl through the ceiling to get me.

"I'm sorry for that and everything else." My voice is breaking from the fear.

"What's the matter?" His voice is a note higher, more urgent sounding now. "Jade, what is it?"

"I just moved into my new place and . . ." I don't know what to say. I'm scared? I feel alone? I need someone here with me? I don't know what to say or what I can say. "I know it's really late . . ."

"Yeah, you mentioned that already. Can we move past that it's really late to the reason you called me?" Worry is playing with his voice, breaking it over words like my own.

"I just . . . it's probably nothing . . . but I keep hearing these noises . . ." I feel like a child running into her parents' bedroom during a thunderstorm. I'm about to ask him if he'll come over when I hear something in his background. Movement.

"Where are you?" More noise in the background.

"The Bluff Apartments. I'm unit 2B."

"I'm coming." I hear what sounds like a door slam shut. "I can be there in ten minutes."

I try to ignore the noises coming from above me, but I can't. The more I ignore them, the louder they seem to become. "There's a gate. The code is . . ."

I scan my memory for it. Four numbers. Dad wrote them down for me and stuck them to my fridge and tucked them in my purse, but I'd have to leave the closet to get to them. I can't move. I feel as trapped in this closet as I did in the one Earl Rae kept me in.

"The code is . . ."—I try again—"2477 . . . or maybe it's 2677. One of those. I think."

I hear what sounds like the door of his old truck whining open. "I'm coming."

The line goes dead, but I keep the phone propped to my ear and replay his voice in my head. *I'm coming. I'm coming. I'm coming.* I repeat it over and over. It isn't the first time I've repeated these words to myself, picturing Torrin's face as he says it. *I'm coming. I'm coming. I'm coming.*

I don't stop until I hear a pounding on my door followed by the doorbell.

I crawl through the closet, shove the doors open, and run for the front door that's being pounded on. I run like something's chasing me and whoever's on the other side of that door is that only one who can save me.

"Jade?" Torrin hollers, still pounding.

"Coming." I know he can't hear me because even I can't hear me; that's how small my voice is.

Another pounding—this one seems to rattle the hinges. "Are you in there?"

I slide to a stop in front of the door and just barely manage to remember to disarm the security system before opening the door. It takes me a few tries to enter the right code, and now he's really pounding on the door. I'd say something to let him know I'm here and okay, but my voice has disappeared. Finally done with the alarm, I twist back to the door and my fingers fight with the deadbolt. When I finally pull the door open, I feel like I'm about to rattle apart from adrenaline and anxiety.

"I'm here," I pant, feeling my fear start to shed away just from seeing his face.

"What took you so long?" Torrin's forehead creases as he examines my dark apartment.

"I was in the bedroom."

He continues to search around me. "Did you lock yourself in the closet or something? Because I was about to break down the door if it took you five more seconds to get here."

"Um, yeah, actually, I did kind of lock myself in the closet."

He stops searching the room and looks at me. The

hard lines fade from his expression. "I'm sorry, I didn't mean . . ."

"No, it's okay." I shake my head. "It's okay. I just . . . after hearing those noises, being alone in a new place, my first night." I close my mouth when I realize I'm speaking a run-on list of fragmented thoughts. "I was scared, and all I could think to do was call you."

"Because I was the closest one?"

I step aside and pull the door open wider for him. "Because you know how to chase the fear away."

Because you're my tether. The one who can pull me back from the dark places and lead me forward into the bright places again. Because you keep me connected to the person I used to be but stay at my side as I navigate the world this new person's landed in. That's what I really want to say, but like most of what I want to say to Torrin, it never actually gets said.

He stares at the doorway with his brows drawn together like he's working out a problem with no obvious solution. When he steps inside finally, the dark shifts, feeling more benign than threatening now that he's here. My whole body relaxes.

"Where did you hear the sounds?"

I point down the hall. "In my bedroom. At first I heard it right outside my window, but then I heard things from above too."

After closing the door and locking it back up, I turn around to find him stationed in front of me, his back facing me, still checking the apartment like he's ready for anything.

"Wait here. I'll be right back." Torrin moves down the hall and rounds into my room.

I stay by the door, listening, waiting. I don't hear the noises anymore, and I wonder if I did hear them again, would I crawl into a closet like I had or barely notice them now that he's here? From my room, I hear the shades moving and the closet doors whining. I hear some rustling and sliding, then I hear nothing.

"Torrin?"

His figure floats out of my room. As he comes down the hall, he stops to flip on a light. "Why's it so dark in here?"

"I was going to bed. I thought I was supposed to turn off all the lights."

He flips on a lamp just inside the living room. "You're not *supposed* to do anything unless you want to. For someone who doesn't seem like a big fan of the dark, I wouldn't expect her apartment to be pitch-black on her first night on her own." Torrin leans into the kitchen to flip on the lights in there too and stops when he notices me lingering by the door.

"You're wearing my old soccer shirt." His eyes drop to the worn shirt I threw on to sleep in.

I glance down and stretch it out at the sides. "Well, you scored the winning goal at the state championship that year. Someone ought to wear it proudly." Then I cross my arms, feeling like this shirt is somehow an extension of my soul and I'm bearing it for him to see.

"Proudly as in wearing it to bed? Where people snore and drool and wake up with morning breath?"

I lift a brow and feel relieved he's acting normal, giving me a hard time and all. "Exactly."

He looks away for a second, but his eyes find their way back to me. "I checked around your room and outside your window. There are some big recycle bins behind your room, so someone could have been dumping their bottles or something and made that noise. You've also got people living above you, and with the way apartments are built, a person could be tiptoeing up there and it would sound like a hippo had moved in." Torrin points at the ceiling. "I can't find anything else, but I can hang around for a while. You know, just in case you hear it again. So you know for sure."

Recycle bins. Upstairs neighbors. Everyday noises of apartment life that had practically put me in some kind of PTSD state. I feel embarrassed and silly and immature and a bunch of other things.

"Thanks for checking." I shift. "And sorry. I'll try not to wake you up in the middle of the night the next time my neighbor flushes the toilet."

Torrin smiles. It's a different one than I'm used to. It looks more forced than natural. "It's okay. And I wasn't asleep anyway. This was actually a welcome distraction."

"A distraction from what?"

He shrugs. "My thoughts."

I don't know what to do with him here—inside my own place. Do I invite him in for something to drink? Would we have that in the kitchen? The living room? Not that I can move anyway because his eyes are pinning me to the door.

"I heard about them suspending you." I swallow. I never made that call my dad recommended. I didn't because I knew if I did, I couldn't just say I was sorry like I'm going to try to now. "You don't deserve that. I'm sorry."

"*They* didn't do that. I did that to myself. I requested the suspension." He wanders into the living room, and I follow him. He turns on another lamp.

"Why?"

His back stays to me when he stops. "I needed time to think . . . thus, the thoughts keeping me awake tonight."

My living room, like the rest of the house, contains a mishmash of furniture. An old sofa from Sam's place. An overstuffed chair and coffee table from my parents' basement. A couple of side tables from a yard sale and a houseplant from the nursery in town. It has no theme or cohesion at all, but I like it. Nothing here belongs together, so I guess there's one characteristic it all shares.

Torrin's taking in the room. I think he likes it too.

"Sorry I interrupted them—your thoughts. Do you want to, you know, talk?" I curl my leg beneath me as I sit on the couch.

Torrin glances over his shoulder. "Do you?"

The way he asks, I know he's not thinking about his summer plans or what day of the week's his favorite. "Should I?"

"I don't know." He turns around to face me, and in the light, I can see how tired he looks. I was right though, it's not just tired—it's exhaustion. Like someone's wrung him dry and is still holding on. "You've definitely been the highlight of my thoughts—a little firsthand knowledge would be helpful."

"I don't know, Torrin . . ." I say, summing up every answer to every unanswered question that hangs between us.

"Tell you what—you help me with that firsthand knowledge thing, and I'll help you unpack." He tips his chin at the stack of boxes stuffed in the corner.

I check the retro clock stationed on the coffee table. "It's almost midnight."

"Are you actually planning on going to bed tonight?" He looks at me like he knows better.

He does. Sleep is out of the question after being scared into a closet by some footsteps and recyclables.

"Because I've been trying for two weeks, and I've officially lost my knack for it," he adds.

I exhale, and his eyes trace the shadows below my eyes. "I've lost my knack for it too."

"So unpacking it is?" He's already moving toward the boxes. He heaves the top one from the pile.

"Thought dissection it is," I mutter and rise to help him unpack . . . and with the other thing.

"You got your own place." Torrin carries the box over to a side table and sets it down. "I like it."

I grab the box cutter to rip it open, and Torrin doesn't jump back when I pop out the blade. "I thought it was time to get my own place and figure out whoever this new Jade is and let go of the one I was clinging to." I slice through the tape and open the box. It's a few vases Mom wrapped up for me to use for decoration or for flowers.

"I get it." Torrin unwraps the first vase from its pile of newspaper. "Dumping the dead weight, right? Getting rid of the baggage?"

I feel something else inside the box that isn't a vase but is wrapped up with the rest. I pull it out and unfold the paper. Then I hold it up for him. "Not all of it."

His hands stop working the newspaper free when he sees the picture. It's one of the photos of the two of us I found stuffed in my parents' attic. I "unstuffed" them and packed them all to bring here with me.

In this one, Torrin and I are at Westport Beach. He's up to his knees in the ocean, and I'm on his shoulders. I'm looking down at him, and he's staring up at me, and we're both somewhere between a grin and a laugh. Our hair's messy from the salt and wind, and our skin's showing the faintest of pink from a sunscreen-less day at the beach.

"Why are you showing me this?" He sits on the arm of the couch, staring at the photo.

I pull out another one and unwrap it. I hold this one out for him to see. It's an old dance picture of us—cheesy pose, background, and everything. "To show you I'm hanging on to some things from that life. Some of it I'm bringing with me."

I set down the cheesy dance photo and reach into the box to unwrap the next one. When I pull it out, Torrin's hand reaches for my wrist, and he pulls me to him.

He doesn't stop tugging me closer until my leg bumps against his. He takes the photo from me and sets it down. "What part of us are you bringing with you? Just the memories? Or is there room for anything else?"

"Torrin, don't." I close my eyes and imagine that armor again, but this time, it's keeping him out.

His hand around my wrist tightens. "Why not?"

Why? The question that I'd give just about anything to have answered.

When I feel his other hand start to move around my side, my eyes snap open. "This? I can't bring this with me." I break away and wave a finger between us. "That part's over between us. It has to be."

Torrin rises from the couch arm and moves toward me. His light eyes watch me like he knows I'm lying, and in them, I see him calling my bluff. "It's not over, and you know it."

"No, I don't." I back around the side of the coffee table.

He matches my every step. I step back; he steps forward. I move away; he moves in.

"Yes, you do because you know it will *never* be over." When I trip over the chair leg, he grabs my arm to keep me from falling. He lets me keep moving though. He doesn't stop following. "Time, circumstance, tragedy—nothing can change that. You and me, there isn't an over for us."

"There has to be." This time I catch myself when I trip over a table leg. "This, it's killing me, Torrin. I can't keep doing it."

I don't notice the picture rocking on the end of the table. I don't see it teeter to the edge after I knock into it. I don't miss it crash to the ground and shatter.

It's the one of us at the beach. My favorite one.

I stare at the broken pieces and feel like I'm looking at myself if I were made of glass. A hundred sharp, broken pieces that will never be right again even if I could glue them back together. It'll never reflect what's hiding below the way it used to.

"What do you want from me, Jade?" Torrin kneels beside the broken picture and reaches for the frame. A piece of glass snags his skin, and his thumb starts to bleed. He doesn't even notice—he just keeps putting the pieces back in place, one at a time. Patiently. Methodically. "One minute I think I know, and the next I don't have a damn clue. So what *exactly* do you want from me?"

I keep backing out of the living room. "I don't know."

"Well, do you think you can figure it out? It would sure make my life easier."

When he looks up, he notices how far I've gotten from him. He stands and puts the frame and its shattered pieces back on the table.

"Do you think this is easy for me?" I cry, motioning at him because doesn't he get it? He's everything—*everything*—and I've just got nothing left to give. "Any of it? Having these feelings, knowing I'm not supposed to?"

"Will you stop with the supposed to?" He powers across the room and stops in front of me when I'm bracing for him to crash into me. His eyes are burning. "What do you want? Not what you think you're supposed to want. Not what everyone's trying to tell you you should want. What do *you* want?"

I look at him and think about that question. What do I want? I keep looking at him. I don't think of the person I am or the one he is. I don't think about what happened to me or what he is. I don't think about the possibility of it or the practicality of it or consequences and repercussions.

I think about his question—what do *I* want?

It's a simple question and an easy answer but a complicated reality. I

"You," I say, followed by a shrug. "Just you."

His mouth starts to open like he was all prepared to argue back, but then what I said sets in. He doesn't say anything. He just stands there, seeming to measure the space between us. His knuckles pop as he glances at the door. *God, what did I say? What am I doing?*

"Just forget it. I don't know what I'm saying." I cross my arms and move for the door to open it. Leaving would be easier on him if I act like I'm the one suggesting it. "You should just go."

When I don't hear him move, I turn around.

He's staring at the space between us with an expression that makes it seem like he's fighting something. "Did you mean that?"

I let go of the breath I'm holding and start to pull the door open. "Yes."

Torrin powers toward the door, and just when I think he's about to disappear through it, he slams it shut. His body slides in front of mine, and his chest slowly presses me into the door. "Then I'm not going anywhere."

My hands splay against the door when I feel the heat of his body mixing with the warmth of mine. "Are you sure?"

His strong hand grips the side of my neck, and he

aligns his eyes with mine. "I've been sure about you since I was fifteen years old. And I'll be sure about you for the rest of my life."

His eyes lower to my mouth, and when he sees the speed of my breath, one corner of his mouth twitches. His other hand slides up my leg and slips just beneath his old shirt. His fingers curl into the skin of my hipbone, then his face moves closer to mine. I stop breathing when his mouth moves toward mine. Before he kisses me, his fingers slide up my neck until two of them press into the space below my jaw.

My pulse beats against the pads of his fingers, and my breath gets away from me again.

When he kisses me, I don't know what to do at first. It's been ten years since I kissed Torrin Costigan, but with the way he's kissing me now, holding me so tight between him and the door that I can't fall apart, it makes a decade going without seem worth it.

It's the first kiss of a decade. The kiss of the decade. Maybe the kiss of my life.

It doesn't take him long to melt my lips, and as I start to kiss him back—my hands winding around his neck to pull him closer—I feel something inside me melting. I'm not sure what it is, but I think it might be resolve.

He tastes like I remember. He feels like I remember. He sounds like I remember. He still makes that low groan in his chest when I tie my fingers into his hair. His hands still dig in deeper when I trace my tongue down his. He's familiar . . . and he's different.

I don't remember the strength he possesses now. The

way I feel safe and protected and like nothing could get to me when he's close. I don't remember the scrape of his stubble being so sharp against my cheek. I don't remember the rough growl that vibrates against me when I run my fingers down his chest.

I do remember some of this, and I don't recall the rest. After tonight, I know I'll remember it all.

My fingers find the hem of his Henley and tug it up his body. He steps back just enough to let me finish pulling it off, then his mouth is on me again with an urgency that's new. He hasn't kissed me in ten years. It's the kind of urgency of trying to make up for that time.

When I put my hands on his bare chest, I roam his shoulders first, then I take my exploration down the peaks of his chest and end on the planes of his stomach. My fingers skim along the waist of his jeans, slowing where his zipper is. Another rumble vibrates against me. When he fits his hips a little tighter against mine, his fingers still on my pulse curl in a little deeper. I feel his smile even as we kiss.

As he pulls back again, his hands work my shirt up my body. Slowly. Like he's giving me the chance to stop if I need to. I look at him and lift my arms above my head.

His old shirt flutters in front of my face, and I feel a cool rush of air break across my bare skin, but it only lasts a moment. Before the shirt hits the floor, Torrin's body is pressing into mine again. His warm body against mine, his chest hard against mine . . . I think I've found whatever kind of healing I need if I can just stay like this forever. If we could stay like this, I'd be fine.

But I know we can't—this moment is fleeting—so I kiss him again.

When he lifts me up and curls my legs around him, he stares at me. His lips are parted from his breath, and his eyes are alive. I see something hanging from his neck I hadn't noticed at first. Seeing the man wearing the ring I gave the boy ten years ago makes my chest ache.

"You still have it." I let the gold chain slide through my fingers before I reach the ring resting against his chest. Time hasn't tarnished it like it tends to do. Age hasn't worn at the intricate grooves of the design. Wear hasn't rendered it useless.

It looks the same as it did the night I gave it to him.

His hand curls around the ring and my hand as he carries me into the bedroom. "It's staying on my neck or going around your finger."

Twenty-Five

I NEVER KNEW broken could feel so whole.

That's the first thing I think as I feel myself starting to wake up. Part of it is the anesthetic of sleep talking, but part of it is me. The shattered me.

Torrin's arm is caged around me, and his body is tucked beside mine, curled around me from head to toe. His leg is tucked through mine, and his slow breath fogs the side of my neck. I can faintly make out his heart beating against my back, and I can make out other parts pressed up against me below his chest.

I want to fall back asleep and freeze this moment. I don't want to finish waking up. I want to stay in this world between asleep and awake and feel whole for the rest of my life. But I can't. I know the moment, like the intact feeling, is ephemeral.

It will pass. It has to. But that doesn't keep me from enjoying it while it's happening.

He shifts in his sleep, somehow managing to roll closer. Now I can feel his zipper running against my spine.

We're still clothed. Mostly. Restraint was something both of us seemed to have a tankful of last night when it came to crossing that final threshold. Torrin knew I wasn't ready . . . and I knew that while he was definitely ready, it wasn't the right time. Not yet. My head might have been swimming with the things his body was doing to mine but not so much it drowned out the acknowledgement of what he was.

When he carried me into my room last night, before lowering me onto my bed, he'd stopped. I thought he'd just reminded himself of what he was and given himself a mental cold shower, but he kissed my forehead and whispered something in my ear.

You're not falling into bed with a priest. You're climbing into it with me.

I think it was important for me to hear that. I know it was important to him that I believed that. And I did . . . but that didn't change that he is what he is, just like I am who I am.

In each of our own ways, we're unavailable.

This still feels right though. So right nothing feels wrong, not even if the Vatican is calling or the media is parading through my apartment.

When his body stirs against mine again, I know he's waking up. Torrin's always been a heavy sleeper—he goes through a process before he can wake up. I think sometimes his consciousness thinks he belongs more in the dream world than the real one.

I want to get some breakfast ready for him this morning, and I need to find something to put on because if he wakes up and we're still like this, getting back to what we spent most of the night doing is inevitable. We wouldn't be able to stop it, just like a person who rolls a rock to the edge of a cliff can't stop it from falling. We'll get trapped on this carousel ride of touching and kissing. I know I'm incapable of stepping off it when I'm with him, and I think he is too. So I need to find a shirt.

Holding my breath, I shimmy down the mattress, kicking the sheets off of me as I move. His arms tighten for a moment—like he can feel me escaping—but when I freeze, they relax. I keep shimmying and sliding. Untucking my head from beneath his arm's the hardest because I have to lift it a little, and it feels like it weighs fifty pounds.

When my legs are swinging over the side of the mattress, I glance back at him. He's still asleep. Still wrapped around my phantom shell, hanging on like the nothing around him is all the substance he needs.

I hold my breath and rise so slowly even the mattress doesn't make a noise. I have lots of practice with this from before, when Torrin would sneak into my room late at night via my roof and we'd make out until my alarm was a few minutes from going off. We both know how to move around a mattress without making a sound.

I pad across my bedroom and tuck behind the half-open door. In the hall, I grab his soccer shirt from the floor and pull it on. The lights are still on. Almost all of them. It's roughly seven in the morning, and the sun's streaming through all of the windows, but my whole apartment is glowing from the inside out now too. Thanks to Torrin.

I won't crawl into bed with the lights out again for a while. I don't care what adults are "supposed" to do. Most of them don't know the dark the way I do.

It isn't just the absence of light—it's the executioner of it.

The kitchen's white cupboards are gleaming in the morning light, and I go to the other window in front of the dining table to let in more light. Mom picked up some basic groceries for me yesterday, but I don't know what she grabbed. Since I still have to remind myself to eat, I didn't check the fridge or cupboards last night.

What does a girl make for the guy in her bed the next morning?

I lean into the kitchen counter and think about that. If we were still seventeen, I would sneak a can of soda from the fridge and a box of whatever sugary cereal is in the cupboard. But what would twenty-seven-year-old Torrin want? What does he eat for breakfast now? What does he drink?

I don't know.

Leaning into that kitchen counter, I never would have expected the realization that I don't know what he eats for breakfast anymore to hit me like it does. I still know him—the man he is at the core of it all—but I don't know what goes beyond that. At least not much of it.

Like what he eats. What he does in his spare time. What color his toothbrush is. Who his friends are. If he visits his dad's grave every month. If he still changes his own oil or what candy bar he'd pick from a vending machine. I know the old Torrin answers to those things, but I don't know the current Torrin's.

We've spent time together since I came back, but it hasn't been spent going over the details—we've been too overwhelmed by the weight of the big things.

I know Torrin, but I don't know the daily version of him. The seemingly inconsequential details that, when stacked together, are just as significant as the big stuff. Who he is on the surface is just as important as who he is beneath it all.

So I don't know what he likes for breakfast, but I do know that whatever it is, I probably don't have it. That isn't going to stop me from trying to give him what he wants though.

I think about it for another minute. What do my parents have in the morning? What do I remember my parents' friends having?

I feel a smile when I remember—coffee. It's an adult staple, right? After throwing open a few cupboards, I find them mostly empty. I throw open the rest, even the ones meant for silverware and dish towels, and don't see anything that looks like coffee. Not that I could have done anything with it since, I realize, I don't have a coffeepot. Not that I would know what to do if I had one because—though I probably could have figured it out with a little trial and error—I've never made coffee in my whole life.

A pot of coffee. I never would have thought it would feel like some test I need to take to graduate into adulthood.

I grumble and head back toward my room. Maybe if I just stare at him long enough, I can figure it out. Is he still a sugar-for-every-meal guy? Or has he morphed into one of those Seattleites who only eats food that looks like it was grown for unicorns?

I've barely been standing there for two seconds when a sleepy smile stretches over his face. "I missed you." His eyes are closed, and he's still lying in bed like he's holding me.

I smile too. Torrin's bare upper half is a stark contrast to the soft pillow and smooth sheets tangled around his legs. "I was gone for five minutes."

"Yeah, and you were gone for ten years." His eyes open. "I've done my time when it comes to missing you."

It's impossible not to shift when he looks at me like this. When I do, I try to remember why I'm standing here watching him. "Yeah, so, I think someone's usually supposed to make coffee in the morning, but I don't have coffee because I'm still a child who thinks it tastes like ass." I pluck at the hem of my shirt as I look at him. In my bed. Half naked and staring at me the way every person wants to be looked at by another person at least once in their lifetime. It's like a dream, but it doesn't quite feel like one, because in my dreams, I feel more intact than crumbling. "But I think I've got milk and cereal, so how about a bowl of Cheerios to wake you up?"

Torrin flashes me a thumbs-up. "Cheerios sound awesome."

"Coming right up."

I smile as I wander back down the hall. Cheerios. I don't know if this is what he has some, most, or all mornings, but at least for this morning, it's what he wants. It's awesome. That's a start.

I'm just reaching for the yellow box on top of the fridge when I hear something. It isn't my neighbors moving around upstairs or someone dropping off their recycling. It's a familiar sound—though not in this context.

I move toward the window, clutching the unopened box of cereal to my chest. I don't make it far before it falls out of my arms and hits the floor. I shouldn't have opened the curtains. I should have kept these ones closed.

Outside past the gate, I see what's behind the familiar noise—it's the media. I feel like they're right outside my window even though they're stationed a little ways back thanks to the police barrier going into place.

They found me. *How* did they find me? I've barely been a resident for twenty-four hours, and already they're here, ready with their scalpels and bone saws to dissect me, piece by bloody piece.

I won't be able to leave my apartment without passing them. I won't be able to do anything outside of this one-thousand-square-foot space without them seeing it or following me or documenting it.

My heart drops all the way into its grave six feet under. *Torrin.*

Do they know he's here? They can't. But they will. Soon. If I don't figure out something.

I'm thinking of ways to get him out of here, avenues for him to escape through as I stumble down the hall.

He knows something's wrong before I face him. His expression goes from serene to troubled in half a blink of my eyes. "What is it?"

I freeze-frame this moment and archive it at the front of my memory. This moment can't last, but the memory of it can. "They're here."

He doesn't ask who. He doesn't ask how many. He doesn't ask where. His expression creases as he throws off the sheets and jumps out of my bed. "Good. I've got a confession to make."

The way he says it, the way he powers past me . . . I know. What's he about to do and what he's going to say.

"Torrin, don't." I jog after him, panic digging its claws into my throat.

"They want a story? I'll give them a story."

The muscles of his back are tense, and as I follow him, I realize there are so many more parts of him I haven't seen. So many lines and grooves and dips I want to touch and explore. I could spend one full night acquainting myself with each of them.

That will have to wait though because what I want and what's best for him are two opposite things.

"No, stop." When he's reaching for the door, I lunge forward and grab his wrist. It stops him. Momentarily. "People look at me and see a man—Earl Rae Jackson." When I say his name, Torrin's jaw locks. "They see what he did and judge him and cross their fingers they'll never run into someone like him someday." I pause to catch my breath. "I don't want the world to look at me and see Father Costigan, because you know that's what will happen." I slowly come around in front of him, putting myself between him and the door. "You go out there and start shouting about the way things are between us, shirtless at seven

on a Saturday morning, and that will not put an end to anything." I grab his other wrist and step into him. I don't
look away. I don't stutter. I just keep telling him the hard
truth. "It's only going to be the start of a long, painful process where in the end, we'll both come out looking like we
swim in the same cesspool of morality as the Earl Raes of
the world. I can't do that to you. Please don't ask me to."

Torrin's eyes cut to the door. His chest is moving as
fast as it did during certain parts last night. He's so torn I
can see it about to split him down the middle. "Do you
think that's what I want for you? Another reason for the
media to not leave you alone?" The muscles banding down
his neck break to the surface. "But I don't know what to do
anymore. They won't leave you alone. But the thing is
. . ." He exhales and lowers his hand around my back. "I
can't leave you alone either. I don't want to keep pretending we're old friends. I don't want to keep sneaking in
through dark windows and doors. I don't want to keep pretending, Jade. It's killing me."

The heat from his hand is already coming through my
shirt, seeping into my skin, spreading to my head and
messing with my sense of reasoning. I squeeze my eyes
closed and try to concentrate. "I know. It's doing the same
thing to me, but they aren't going to leave us alone just
because you ask them to. It'll get worse. Every kiss, every
touch, every private moment . . . they'll find a way to take
those from us, to twist them into something ugly and
shameful. I can't let them do that to us. I can't let them
corrupt what we have."

"Then what are we supposed to do?" His wrist twists

in my hand to free itself. He lifts it to slide my hair behind my ear.

I stare at the door, my stomach knotting when I think about what's waiting. It's not just the media I'm afraid of. "I know they're not going away until I tell my story, and I can't tell my story until I know what that story is. I need time to figure it out. And I won't drag you into this mess while I'm taking my time and trying to put myself back together."

His forehead lowers to mine, and our eyes close. "And what if I want to be dragged into it?"

"I'd ask you—beg you—not to."

He exhales. "Why?"

I don't pull back, but I open my eyes. His are already open. "Because that's a choice I want us to make when the time's right. I don't want us to be forced into making that choice."

"No one's forcing me to do anything."

My hands form around the sides of his neck. "No, but if you do this, you're forcing me."

That gets his attention. The creases iron out of his forehead, and the anger rolling through his eyes fades away.

"Look at me, Torrin." I step back so he can, and I hold my arms at my sides. He looks at me, but I don't think he sees what I do when I look in the mirror. "I was reintroduced to the world weeks ago after years of being away from it. The smallest, most insignificant things send me into a tailspin. I have flashbacks and nightmares and images in my head that would traumatize a sadist." I pause, remembering why I'm saying this. Why this is so important to me. *Him.* He's important. He deserves the best and the most, and until I can give that to him, I can't do this. "I need to get myself right so I don't do this—us— wrong. I'd be a fool to think I can just get over this or move on or get back to my old life. It's going to take time. *I'm* going to need time. Can you give me that?"

I've only seen Torrin cry once, and that was the day I found him camped out on his front steps when everyone else was inside after his dad's funeral. I didn't say any-thing when I walked up to him that day. I just sat down beside him, wound an arm around him, and let him cry.

This is the closest to crying I've seen him since then.

Like that gray afternoon on his front steps fifteen years ago, he doesn't say anything. He just closes the space between us, wraps his arms around me one at a time, and draws me close. His head tucks mine against him, and he holds me for an eternity. At least the only kind of eter-nity Torrin Costigan and I can have.

The finite kind.

"What am I supposed to do?" His voice is hoarse like someone's been choking him.

"Go back to being a priest. Unsuspend yourself. Be that light. Be wonderful and infectious and compassionate and all the things that drew me to you." I lean back and look up at him. I have to say good-bye, but at least this time I get to say it. "Go be *you*. And I'll try to figure out who I am while you're doing that."

His arms slide away from me and fall heavily at his sides. He manages a smile because I think he knows that a frown will kill me "Anything else?"

I smile back because I think a frown would kill him too. "Yeah." I tip my chin down the hall. Away from the media. Away from the storm. "Take the back door."

He manages a tiny laugh, and I know how lucky I am to have this as my last memory of him. Shirtless, doused in sunlight, his smile eclipsing into a laugh. I've lived a full life, and I'm not even thirty. Whatever comes next, I'm prepared to accept it.

As he turns to go, I grab him just before he gets away. "And one more thing."

Then I kiss him good-bye.

Twenty-Six

"THANK YOU FOR taking the time to sit down and go over a few last details." Detective Reyes closes the folder in front of her. "I know this has been a trying process for you."

A week after my night with Torrin, Detective Reyes called to ask if I'd be open to going over my case again. I agreed, but not without setting the date out as far as I thought I could push it without pressing my luck. The week between her call and today went faster than I would have liked.

"No problem. Thank you for all of your patience."

"Well, the police couldn't manage to find you for ten years." She leans back in her chair looking like she's trying to get comfortable, but she doesn't seem like the kind of person who could ever just get comfortable. "Waiting a couple weeks for the rest of your story was really the least we could do."

I smile because she's making a joke, and I'm getting better with conditioned responses. I'm relearning at the pace of a turtle with three broken legs, but at least I'm moving forward.

Detective Reyes offered to drive to my place to go over the last few things, but I told her I'd meet her at the station. It's a small thing that feels like a big one. When we first settled at her desk to talk, I felt everyone watching me. I suppose most of them were involved in my case either at the beginning, the end, or both, and all of them are familiar with my dad, so I should have been ready for the stares.

Reyes must have picked up on my discomfort because she didn't ask if I wanted to move; she just stood and waved me back down a hall. She offered either a break room or an interrogation room, and I went with the interrogation room.

The interview took less time than I'd expected, making me wonder why we couldn't have just gone over her handful of questions on the phone.

As I start to push my chair back from the table, Reyes lifts her pen. The file stays closed. "Real quick—there was a solar panel salesman who came to Earl Rae's house two days before your rescue. Do you remember that?"

I have to dig around in my head for a moment because I've been working on replacing those memories with the new ones I'm making. I don't have to dig long because I haven't managed to bury them very deep yet. "Yeah, I do."

"You saw him?"

My eyebrows come together. "No, Earl Rae put me in the closet. He always did when anyone showed up at the house." I know I've mentioned that before, so I'm surprised she's asking.

"So you never saw the salesman?" She spins the pen between her fingers. "Was there any way he could have seen you?"

Unless he had Superman X-ray vision? "No. And no."

Reyes nods and continues. "The black Converse you were kidnapped in. They had little hearts you'd penned onto the rubber toe?"

I nod.

"Where did those go?" she asks.

My favorite pair of shoes. I still miss them . . . and it wasn't me who penned those black hearts on the toes—it was Torrin. "That was all gone when I woke up. I was wearing something else. He told me he'd burned it all."

Reyes's expression is flat, but that pen keeps spinning slow circles in her fingers like she's working out something. "So those shoes couldn't have been lying around the living room right around the time you were rescued?"

"No. No way."

She makes a sound like she's stumped and trying to work through a problem that won't add up. She's not really looking at me—she's watching the twirling pen.

"Okay, so weird string of questions." I curl my sweater more tightly around me because it's cold in this room. Something about what I can almost feel Reyes is working out is making me cold too. "Why are you asking?"

She keeps watching the pen, and I start to feel like I'm twirling around the room with it. "Well, that solar panel salesman?" Her head shakes once. "He wasn't exactly a salesman."

My lungs go limp right before they feel like they're about to burst. "Oh my god . . . it was him. Wasn't it?"

She doesn't nod, because she knows I don't need a confirmation. I know it was him.

"After telling us what he remembered about Earl Rae at the gas station, he wasn't happy that things weren't moving at lightning speed, and we weren't breaking down doors that day, so he decided to track down Earl Rae. On his own. Without telling us," Reyes grumbles. "When he told us about his little covert op, he said that he'd caught a glimpse of you in the hall—along with your shoes in the front room. Two days later, we were breaking down that door." Reyes looks at me. "That's how we found you."

I feel a lot of things right then. Mostly I'm just kind of overwhelmed from learning that it was him—he was that close—and that I might still be on the end of that chain of it wasn't for him. But I also feel worry. This feeling grows as the other recedes. He lied. To the police. I know that's never a good thing, and in certain cases, it's a crime. I'm going to guess a lie about seeing a missing girl that resulted in the police assembling a couple dozen people to storm a house would fall into that category.

I stare at the table, hoping I'll sound as convincing as I have to be. "You know, maybe he could have seen me. It took Earl Rae a little while to get me in the closet, and he could have seen me then." I swallow and keep going. He's saved me in so many ways—I have to get this right. I have to save him now. "And Earl Rae could have been lying about burning all my stuff. It's not like I was ever able to confirm it."

Reyes is silent for so long my hands start to shake. Why didn't Torrin tell me? Why didn't he tell me so I could change my story? Why didn't he tell me? That's the question that keeps playing through my head, but I guess the simple answer is that he didn't tell me because he didn't want to. For whatever reason—be it he didn't want me to know or he didn't want me to lie for him or he didn't think it was that big of a deal—he didn't tell me. That's enough for me to accept.

"But he didn't see you. Earl Rae had every single window in that house boarded up." Reyes lets the spinning pen fall from her fingers. When it hits the table, it makes a sharp sound that echoes around the room. "And your shoes are ashes that blew into the wind years ago."

I stare at the folder and wonder why it's still closed. Why she isn't making notes like she was earlier. "He found me." I lean forward in my chair. "Does how he did it matter?"

"Well"—Reyes shrugs—"only if you believe in things like the law, and telling the truth, and not perjuring yourself in order to get a SWAT team to pound down the door of some guy you remembered saying something creepy to your girlfriend ten years ago."

God, she makes that sound bad. He isn't just someone who lied either—he's a priest who lied. That would make it a hundred times worse if this were released.

"Please, don't," I say, but my tone is more reminiscent of begging. "He saw me. I remember."

Reyes lifts her hands as I start to warm up. "Jade, it's okay." She keeps them lifted for another second before setting them down. "I knew Torrin was lying when he came barreling in here, ordering every man in the department load up and show up at Earl Rae's house."

I blink at her. "You knew? How?"

Reyes checks the cameras stationed in the room. She told me they weren't rolling or anything since this was a courtesy interview and not an official interrogation, but I get the feeling she's double-checking because she doesn't want what she's about to say filmed.

"I didn't work your case at the beginning." Her gaze shifts from the cameras. "I didn't get it until recently, but I know the detectives who worked it after you went missing. They told me all about Torrin Costigan and how during that first year, he was in here every day looking for an update or delivering one himself. He called them on their days off and called them even after they retired. He didn't know the meaning of giving up." Reyes slides the folder down the table. "That kind of person does not get a glimpse of the girl he's been looking for for ten years and turn around and walk away. Torrin Costigan wouldn't catch a glimpse of a *shadow* of you in a hall, or see your old shoes or a strand of hair he suspected was yours, and let the door close in his face, walk down the front porch steps, and wait two days for you to be rescued."

Reyes pauses like she's waiting for a confirmation from me, but I'm not opening my mouth and saying anything else that could get him in trouble.

"If Torrin Costigan saw you that day, nothing would

have stopped him from bringing you home. And yeah, we might have found Earl Rae's body one day, but the bullet in his head wouldn't have been from his own doing."

I shift in my seat, unable to find a comfortable position anymore. "Why didn't you tell anyone?"

Reyes shrugs. "Because he was right. You were there."

"He never told me . . . my dad, he never even told me. I had no idea." My head feels thick with confusion. "Why didn't they tell me?"

Reyes's eyes narrow a little as they glance at the door. "Your dad doesn't know. As far as the official report goes, it was an anonymous tipster who gave us what we needed to find you."

My eyes widen, but I stay quiet because even though my first instinct is to assume Dad would go bad cop all over this place if he ever found out, I remember something he's been telling me my whole life—he's a dad first and a cop second. I was home—the how that went into that wouldn't matter much to him.

"And as for why Torrin hasn't told you or anyone that he was *the* one responsible for bringing you home, I think it's because he doesn't want the notoriety or the recognition or anything that comes with that. All he wanted was to find you. All he cared about was bringing you home."

I have to bite my lip to keep from crying. He found me. He didn't just look for me. He didn't just keep believing. He *found* me.

He failed better until he got it right.

Those ten years I thought I was so very alone, I really

wasn't. He was still there, looking. Searching. Finding. That tether might have stretched and pulled and neared its breaking point, but he never let go. He was with me then too.

"Listen," Reyes says, "I didn't tell you any of this at first because I knew you had enough coming at you. I wasn't going to tell you at all because it doesn't change anything about who he is and who you are."

I wonder if this is the whole reason she asked to meet. Not so I could tell what was missing from my story but so she could tell hers. "Then why are you telling me now?"

"I thought you'd want to know." She taps the table with her palm. "I thought you'd want to know that when everyone else was giving in to the statistics, he was looking for you. I thought you'd want to know that when everyone else said you were never coming home, he brought you back. He refused to believe you were gone—he just wouldn't accept it. I thought you'd want to know because I sure as hell would." She shakes her head, and for a moment, she's not here in this room—she's somewhere else, with someone else. "I'd want to know that a man was willing to give up everything for the fraction of a fraction of a chance that I was in that house and the fraction of a fraction of a chance that I was still alive inside. That kind of love, friendship, whatever you want to call it, is worth crossing lines for."

I inhale, understanding. She's rooting for the happy ending. She's advocating the fairy tale. Seems strange coming from a tough police detective.

"Even if that person is a priest?" I glance at her.

She lifts her eyebrows and stands. She doesn't blink when she answers. "Even if that person is the motherfucking pope." When I wrestle with a smile, she raps on the table a few times before heading for the door. "There are thousands of priests in the world to spread good, do good, and be good . . . but there's only one him."

She's almost out of the room when she stops, catching herself with a snap. "Oh, I left something for you at the front desk, so grab it before you leave. Some evidence that belonged to you that we collected at Jackson's." She looks at me with something meaningful in her eyes. "Something I thought you'd want a chance to finish."

Twenty-Seven

Ten Months Later

IT'S MY BIRTHDAY. I'm turning twenty-eight. It's the first one I've celebrated in ten years. It feels a little like a rebirth.

That's probably why I scheduled what I did for this morning.

"Are you sure you're ready for this, sweetie?" Mom's sitting on the edge of my bed as I finish with my hair. I got it cut a little shorter, and I still haven't gotten used to what to do with the different length.

"I'm ready." I stare at myself in the mirror for a minute, looking for that light in my eyes. It takes a while to find it, but at least I can now. When I leave the bathroom, I do a little spin before slipping into my shoes. "So? How do I look?"

"Beautiful. Just don't rub up against anything or drink anything or eat anything." Her eyes scan me, and she motions for me to do another twirl. I do. "White's dangerous."

"No, white's appropriate for the situation." I run my hands down the smooth fabric and focus on my breathing. I'm nervous, but I have an arsenal of tools at my disposal now for when that happens. Deep breathing, redirecting the negative energy into something positive, focusing on an anchor memory that grounds me. I do all three now.

"Why's that?" Mom comes over to help me adjust a few things. Turns the pearl necklace so the clasp is hiding. Smooths the seam running down my side. Combs a stray hair back into place.

"Because everyone's expecting me to wear black. White's going to take them all by surprise."

"Why's everyone expecting you to wear black?"

I shrug, smiling at my light dress. "Because black absorbs everything around it, making it what it is, unlike white, which reflects everything and doesn't let anything past. I want everyone to know I'm not defined by what happened—it doesn't make me what I am today. I am who I am, not what's happened to me."

Mom lifts a brow at me and smiles. "And here I thought you picked the dress because it fit you like a dream and was on the sale rack."

I lift a shoulder. "And maybe that too."

I've gotten a job at the public pool, teaching swimming lessons to adults who can't swim, while I work on knocking out a few college prereqs at the community college in town. I love the job, but it doesn't pay much. So I shop sale racks and yard sales because I insist on paying my own way. It's important for me to be able to take care of myself.

"Are you as nervous as I am? You don't look it," Mom asks, placing her hand across her stomach.

"I'm so nervous I'm one frayed nerve away from peeing my pants, which, by the way, you did not mention in your list of what not to do when wearing white."

Someone knocks on my door. They're ready.

She bites her lips and glances at the door. "You'll do great. And we'll all be right there for you."

I give her a side hug, which turns into her pulling me into a full-body one. She squeezes me so tightly it's like she's just been told this is the last time she'll be able to see me.

"I'm so proud of you, Jade."

I wind my other arm around her and squeeze her back. "I'm proud of me too."

When she sniffs, I lean back and find her crying. Well, she's trying *not* to cry, but it doesn't change that she would be if she weren't putting on The Brave Face for me.

"Wow. Even you're looking at me like it's a funeral."

She shakes her head and pulls a tissue from her purse. "I'm just worried. This is a big day. A lot's happened. It's only been a year." She dabs at her nose and eyes and glances at the door where another knock's sounding. "Are you sure you don't want to wait? Make sure this is really what you want?"

I lower myself so I'm at her eye-level. "Exactly. It's been a year. I'm ready."

"She's ready." Dr. Argent rises from the rocking chair and sends me a wink. "And she already knows she doesn't have to say anything she's not prepared to say."

"See? I won't say anything I'm not ready to say." I give Mom a little shake. "I'm good."

"We should get going. They're waiting." Dr. Argent moves for the door and puts her hand on the handle. She's waiting for me to give the nod that I'm ready. We've spent a lot of time talking about doors and windows, past and present, dark and light.

Since I'd pitched her card in the garbage at the hospital, I had to call them to get in touch with her. I guess she'd been waiting for my call because they forwarded me automatically to her cell. She's helped me a lot—well, she's helped me help myself. I guess that's what two-hour sessions twice a week will do, but she's right—I am ready. For whatever's coming. For whatever came. I'm ready.

Ready, however, is different than feeling whole again. That is still a work in progress.

When I nod, she opens the door and waves me through it. When I start to leave, Mom falls in right behind me, hanging so close she'll crash into my back if I slow down.

I hear a bunch of noise coming from my living room, but I also hear Dad's and Sam's voices. That makes it easier to keep going when I want to turn around and tuck back into that closet I've spent more than my first night in. I focus on the good and let it propel me forward instead of letting the fear pull me back into its cave.

I glance in the kitchen as I come to the end of the hall. I can't help but smile at the coffeepot propped on the counter. Maybe one day I'll get a chance to use it. I've figured out how finally.

When I turn into the living room, I roll to a stop. All of my stuff's still here: the couch, tables, old chair, pictures, and throw pillows, but it looks entirely different. Not only are there at least a dozen unfamiliar faces squeezing around each other in the small space, there are twice as many foreign objects. Lights, cameras, other tech-looking things I can't name . . . all of it's overflowing in my little room.

I feel my heartbeat quicken and my palms dampen. Am I ready for this? Am I *really* ready for this? The reporters camped outside have shrunk in number but not in tenacity. I don't get followed for quite as long by quite as many of them anymore, but I still can't have a single private moment in public without feeling like a camera's watching me.

I finally agreed to this big interview with this giant station with this legend of a reporter because once my story's out there, I'll be left alone. Or at least a little more left alone. I guess it'll still be months before the cameras leave my front door, and years before I can stuff a hot dog in my mouth without having to worry about a camera snapping at the worst possible time.

I can do this. I want to do this.

I repeat that to myself as I position a smile into place. I say it silently as I force my feet to break through the roots keeping them in place. Sometimes I have to pretend I feel brave before I actually do. Sometimes I never make it past the pretending part. But those days are getting fewer and further between.

"Miss Childs." The reporter who is just as flawless and poised in person as she appears on TV notices me and approaches. She's wearing a dark skirt suit with a few pieces of gold jewelry popping out.

I glance at my mom with a raised brow, and she sighs. Even the reporter has shown up to the interview like she's attending a funeral. Black.

No more black. I'm done with it. At least willingly letting it into my life. I'm done letting it strangle me without fighting back.

"I can't tell you how honored I am to be the one you're ready to tell your story to for the first time." She holds out her hand when she stops in front of me, and I shake it without thinking about it. I can shake people's hands and brush by them and not feel like it's a giant invasion of privacy.

"Thank you for coming here. I know it must have been a huge inconvenience." My voice wobbles a little, but if she notices, I can't tell.

"If you wanted to do this interview on the moon, it wouldn't have been an inconvenience." She smiles, and I get the feeling it's a real one.

This is part of the reason I requested her—because of the genuineness she seems to embody in a profession I can't exactly say with a lot of confidence personifies that quality. Plus, she actually seems to give a shit about what she reports and the people she interviews. Giving a shit is important.

Dr. Argent taught me that.

"We're ready when you are, but feel free to take as

much time as you need. I know this has to be difficult for you."

I swallow. I try not to think about the questions she's going to ask me. I try not to think about my answers. "A little."

"Everyone I've ever interviewed has been nervous, so you're not alone. Just try to forget about all of this stuff and pretend it's just you and me having a conversation." She leans in and points at someone playing with a big camera that's facing the chair I'll be in. "If that doesn't work, just look at Cameron's beard. That always gets a laugh."

Hearing his name, Cameron sighs and strokes what I guess some people might consider a beard. "The beard again? Really? Aren't you a reporter? Fresh material should not be a foreign concept."

The reporter chuckles and starts toward the chair she'll be sitting in across from me. "That is not a beard. That is a thirteen-year-old's peach fuzz."

Mom and Dr. Argent are laughing, but Mom's trying to rein it in, I guess for Cameron's sake. Or Cameron's beard's sake.

My feet are able to move, and even though every step becomes harder to take, I keep going.

Dad and Sam are standing off to the side, leaning against the back wall. They flash me a couple of thumbs-ups when I look over. Mom and Dr. Argent join them against the wall. This way, they'll be right here, just in the corner of my eye.

Everyone's here—even Patrick and Maisy are milling

around somewhere, but now that she's two, she has a tough time with the whole staying still thing.

I guess *almost* everyone's here. One is missing. Today isn't just my birthday—it's a Sunday. Since it's eight o'clock, he's probably just about to start early mass. Torrin's suspension ended ten months ago, and he's gotten back to doing what he does best—being him. He's helped people, he done the right thing, he's spreading good like it's going extinct, and he's shone a light everywhere he's gone.

I've managed to find a flicker of my own that burns on occasion, but he will always be my light.

The reporter waits for me to take my seat before she settles into hers. I cross my ankles and fold my hands into my lap. A couple of people approach, and while one dusts my nose with what I assume is powder, the other holds something by my face that looks like he's measuring it or something. I don't know. I just let them do what they need to while I focus on keeping calm.

My armpits are already damp, and I start to rethink my color choice for today. By the end of this, I'm going to have sweat stains running down to my belly button.

The same team moves over to the reporter. After they finish powdering and measuring and adjusting, they wander behind the lights and cameras.

It's just the two of us now, and when a few more lights switch on, everyone around me fades. I can't make out the forms of my family or Dr. Argent to my right. I can't see my kitchen across the hall. I can't see anything, and I feel the world start to shrink in around me again. It's

336

happened hundreds of time. It comes in around me from all directions, trying to fold me into something no bigger than a speck of dust.

The reporter crosses her legs and checks a clipboard with what I guess are the list of questions she's prepared to fire at me, and now I'm really shrinking. The lights are blinding. I can even feel the heat coming from them like it's scorching my skin.

I need an anchor. I need to find it. I need to remember I'm tied to it so no matter how far I feel like I'm falling or how small I feel I'm shrinking or how hollow I feel I'm being carved, I can remind myself I'm not alone. I'm tied to something. Connected. Grounded. Safe.

I close my eyes and search for it—it's there on the tip of my brain, but the panic keeps shoving it out of my reach.

Opening my eyes, about to tell the reporter I can't do this, I see the photo. It's sitting on the end table still, in this inner circle with me. It's the one of Torrin and me at Westport. It's in the same shattered frame because after painstakingly gluing it back together, I realized that the view of the photo might have changed but the spirit of it had not.

Try again. Fail again. Fail better. Those words he quoted to me months ago have saved me from waving the surrender flag in life's direction countless times since then. I've failed so many times I've lost count—but I've failed better and better each time.

Progress . . . one failure at a time.

I take a deep breath, let it spread, then I feel it. My

anchor. What I'm tethered to. It's him. It's always been him. It always will be him.

"I'm ready," I tell the reporter.

After giving me a moment to change my mind, she cues the cameras with a twirl of her finger. Cameron lowers behind the camera facing me, and even though I guess I'm now officially being taped, I don't feel any different. I don't feel nervous anymore. I feel ready.

Ready to tell my story.

"Jade Childs, thank you so much for taking the time to speak with me today and tell the story of your ten-year captivity with Earl Rae Jackson. The world is anxious to hear your account."

The reporter's voice fills my living room, and I notice my family seem to take a collective shift. Now that I've adjusted to the lighting, I can make them out again.

"Before we dive into the interview, I want to ask you one question. You've been at the epicenter of a media storm for one year and have kept quiet the entire time. You're breaking your silence now." The reporter leans forward. "What words do you want to break your silence with?"

I glance at my hands, considering her question. My answer rises from somewhere deep inside. From a place I thought had decayed and could never be brought back to life. I've been finding more and more of those pieces—bringing them back into being. I've been gluing myself back together, one shattered piece at a time.

When I look up, I stare right into the camera. I think I'm supposed to look at her when I answer, but I want to

338

look into the world's eyes when I say this. "When people look at me, most of them see a victim. But I'm a survivor." My eyes drift to my anchor before they shift back to the camera. "I want everyone to know that a new life—a fresh start—is possible no matter who you are or what you've been through."

"Everything you've been through . . ." The dot, dot, dot is written on her face as she leans forward. "How do you do it? What gets you out of bed every morning?"

I've had to answer that question for myself so many times, the answer's always on the tip of my tongue. "I fail. A lot." I temper my words with a careful smile. "But I remind myself of something someone I respect quoted to me that had helped him in a dark time." My smile isn't so careful anymore. It's eclipsing into a real one from thinking of him. "Try again. Fail again. Fail better."

Twenty-Eight

I SURVIVED THE interview. Now I just need to make it through the next part, and the rest of my birthday will be a breeze.

It's another clear day as I wander past the cemetery gates, but this time, I'm not passing through them to unfurl my anger. I'm not coming to mourn either. I'm coming for a different reason—to say good-bye.

I'm not here searching for flowers to leave or to kick dead weeds from a gravestone. I'm here to make peace with this part of my past. I'm ready to leave it behind me for good.

I could tell my family was worried when I left the apartment as soon as the interview was over. I didn't wait for the crew to pack up and leave even. I'd thanked the reporter, shaken her hand, and left. It's my birthday, and a rebirth doesn't just happen on its own. It doesn't come from one interview—it comes at a much steeper price.

It's one I'm willing to pay.

Being a sunny Sunday morning in summer, the cemetery's virtually empty of people. I guess the living don't want to spend this kind of a day with the dead.

My pace doesn't slow down as I get closer. It doesn't speed up either. My heart follows the same pattern, as do my lungs. In a way, I made peace with this a while ago, but standing in front of his gravestone and saying it seems important.

When I stop in front of Earl Rae Jackson's gravestone, I look around for those dried weeds. I know they've been chopped up by a lawn mower or become a part of the soil by now, but I can't help but feel that they're still here.

My neck still burns when I think about him. Dr. Argent said it's a phantom pain I'll probably live with most of my life. Kind of like the scar I'll always bear there. But while some scars can never be removed, some can.

Those ones are the ones I'm concerned about when I think of the man whose body is decaying below my feet. Those scars are the reason I've come here.

Earl Rae might have taken away ten years of my life. He might have permanently violated my views on safety and trust and human nature. He might have given me nightmares I'm too afraid of to talk to Dr. Argent about. He might have taken me away from the people I loved. He might have broken me so I couldn't even remember what free felt like when I had it.

He might have taken ten years.

But he couldn't have another minute of my life.

I glance at his gravestone for the last time.

"Good-bye," I say, before walking away and leaving Earl Rae Jackson where he belongs.

Six feet under. Behind me.

Twenty-Nine

I'VE MADE IT just in time. It's eleven thirty on the dot, and I've managed to make it through an interview that's going to be internationally streamed and say what I needed to at the cemetery.

I hadn't been sure I was going to be able to make it today, but it wouldn't have been right to miss the one thing I'm actually looking forward to on the first birthday I've celebrated in a decade.

St. Marks is always packed no matter what service is being held, but the second Sunday morning one is sometimes a standing-room-only ordeal. Thankfully, today some kind old couple notices me searching for a seat and squeezes together a little tighter and waves me over.

"Thank you," I whisper because the choir's lining up in the front.

"That dress is just lovely, honey." The elderly woman pats my knee when I settle beside them. "Pretty enough to wear on a wedding day."

I smooth my hands down it. "Well, I am in a church."

"And there is a priest." The woman points at the front where a familiar figure is climbing the stairs toward the altar.

Instead of going another round that could make me blush any more than I already am, I smile and turn around in my seat.

Torrin moves behind the altar, and his hands rest on the sides of it. He looks natural, at ease, like he could be having a conversation with his old soccer teammates about the upcoming game. He's so good at this. Good at what he does and how he influences people into action.

It's part of what makes it hard to come most of the Sundays I do. If he weren't so great at this, it would be easy. Easy to tell him and easier to let him make his decision based on that.

It's not easy though because if I tell him what I want to, I know what he'll do. I know the consequences. Wouldn't it be one of the most selfish things I could do? Taking away a person who affects so many lives because I want him to crawl into bed with me every night and hold my hand when we walk into the grocery store?

Torrin's still in my life. We're still friends. We still get to see each other and be around each other and call each other. Sure, we have to be careful we don't see each other "too" much or, when we are together, get "too" close, but I still get to see him.

I already *have* him in my life . . . but I want more. I want everything that comes with that promise he made me one night on the sidewalk in front of our houses.

I want it . . . but I'm not ready for it—not until I finish collecting those missing pieces. And in the meantime, a city of people need him.

As Torrin starts to speak, I lean in like those extra two inches will make all the difference in the twenty feet keeping us apart. I don't usually sit so close. I make it a point not to sit in the front row or the back row. I sit in the middle so I blend in. To the other churchgoers and to him. I never succeed though, at least with him.

He always seems to know where I am before he moves behind the altar. Today he's giving a sermon about the pain humans can cause us but that God heals all wounds. I don't usually listen all that closely—I come to be close to him; in the same room, sharing the same air—but today, when he talks about the physical wounds we humans can inflict on one another, he rubs that right cheek of his and pauses, practically smirking in my direction.

I roll my eyes at him, and he gets on with the sermon. This is why I come. For these kinds of moments. The ones no one else catches but mean everything to us.

The woman leans into me when Torrin takes a seat as the choir breaks into a song about redemption. "Don't you just love Father Costigan?"

I look at him and smile. Like he can feel it, his head turns. Probably no one else can tell he's smiling, but I can. I've known Torrin Costigan for what feels like my entire life.

"Yes," I answer her. "Yes, I do."

Thirty

I'M SPENDING THE rest of my birthday right here, sitting on an old beach blanket at Westport and watching the waves spool in. The sun's falling, but there's still plenty of good light. My family's off somewhere inspecting tide pools with Maisy, and I'm just . . . living. The sand between my toes, the sticky breeze on my face, the sun bouncing off my skin. I feel it all. I'm no longer a voyeur going through life without a spectrum of senses to guide me.

Eleven years ago, I was taken. One year ago, I was found. Today, I have my life back.

"Happy birthday to you. Happy birthday to you. Happy birthday, dear Jade, happy birthday to you." Torrin's walking toward me slowly, holding a cupcake and shielding a candle from the breeze. The flame is flickering, and when it starts to go out, he slows down and waits. When it fans back to life, he starts moving again.

He's changed from his usual Sunday attire to jeans and that same Henley he wore the first night he spent the night at my apartment. It was the last night he stayed there too, and seeing it makes me remember the way it clung to him when I tugged it off, the way it felt between my fingers.

I clear my throat in an attempt to clear the image. I'm not successful. "I thought you had to attend a church potluck tonight since you're kind of the leader of the church and all."

He's watching the flame intently, but his eyes dart my way for a moment. "I said I had an urgent family emergency to attend to and got out of it."

I scoot over when he reaches the edge of the blanket. "So you lied?"

His brows come together. "You're as much my family as my real one is."

That makes me smile—I share the same sentiment. "If not in title, in experience."

As he lowers onto his knees, his eyes flicker my way. He crawls closer, still shielding the candle from the breeze trying to blow it out. "Maybe one day in title too." Before I can figure out how to reply, he holds out the cupcake. "Make a wish."

"It already came true." I grin at the cupcake because it's my favorite kind. I used to love vanilla, but now I'm more of a lemon fan.

His brows come together.

I answer his unsaid question with a shrug. "You're here."

His smile erases the creases of confusion. "Then make another wish."

I squeeze my eyes together and tip my head like I have to think really, really hard about it. But I already know what I'm going to wish for. It's what I wish for every night.

When I get ready to blow the candle out, Torrin slides around so his whole body is shielding the candle from the breeze. Leaning forward, I blow like I'm trying to blow out a barn fire. The candle goes out.

For all of five seconds.

Then it makes some kind of spark and sizzle sound before coming back to life. I blow it out again. When I blow it out the third time, I give him a little glare.

He only laughs and moves aside so he's not deflecting the wind anymore. This time, the forces of nature blow out the light.

It flickers back to life though.

"It just keeps coming back. Doesn't matter how many times you blow it out, it comes back. It lights right back up." He holds out the cupcake for me. "I thought you'd like it."

I take the cupcake and set it down. The candle's still burning bright. "I love it."

He slides the hair whipping around my face behind my ear and sits beside me. "So how does it feel to be twenty-eight?"

I give a little groan at the thought of being closer to thirty than twenty. "The last birthday I had, I turned seventeen. I like the sound of eighteen a lot more than twenty-eight."

Torrin laughs and slides closer. When he leans back,

one of his arms goes behind my back. It doesn't touch me, but I can feel it there.

"What are you working on over there?" He leans over to get a look. "Are those sketches of me?" His brows come together. "Really, really good sketches of me?"

I pick the board and drawings back up from the blanket and pull the pencil from behind my ear. Since he's here, I might as well try to finish them. "I don't know about really, really good, but yeah, they're you. I drew them before . . ." I steal a look at him before lowering the pencil to the paper. "I never got a chance to finish them though, and one of the detectives returned them to me so I could."

"They look finished to me."

"No. Your eyes. I could never get them right. Didn't matter how many times I tried or different ways I drew them, I couldn't get them right." I bite the eraser as I examine his eyes two feet away. No wonder I could never get them right.

"You got everything else right. Why don't you think the eyes are?" Torrin leans in and studies the sketch at the top of the stack. The one I'm already starting to adjust.

"I wasn't just trying to get the shape right. Or the lightness of them just perfect." I shrug as my pencil flies across the paper. "I was trying to draw them the way they are when you look at me."

Torrin's gaze shifts from the paper to me. "So they look different now than they did when I was looking at that piece of paper?"

I glance at him staring at me. My pencil stops moving. "Yes. You look at me differently than you look at anything else."

His mouth starts to pull up. "I look at you different how?"

I have to glance away to concentrate on that. I study the horizon, tapping the pencil point against my cheek. "You know that feeling of something missing? You don't know what it is exactly, you just know it's not there? That hollow spot inside that you don't know what to fill it with, you just know it's empty?" When I notice him nod, I turn my head so I'm looking at him. I never want to look away. I never want him to look away, because I feel the same thing when I look at him. "That's how you look at me. Like I'm your what's not there. I'm what fills that hollow spot." I lower the pencil because I don't need to get the sketches right anymore—not when he's right in front of me again. "That's how you look at me."

He leans in closer, and even though I know I shouldn't, I tip closer too. We don't stop moving until the breeze is whipping my hair against his cheek and tangling it in his stubble.

"I look at you like that because that's exactly what you are. You fill all my hollow spots. You're my what's missing." He lets that settle between us, letting a little more of me get tangled up in him, then he slowly leans back.

I stay where I am because I'm not ready for this moment to be over. I hold on to it until it's floated so far away I can't see it anymore.

"How was your day?" he asks softly, but I don't miss

the concern buried in his voice.

He's been "concerned"—a.k.a. freaking out—ever since I told him about agreeing to the interview. I didn't tell him about the cemetery visit though. I didn't want him worrying about today any more than I knew he already was.

"Let's see. It was exhausting, relieving, emotional . . . pick an adjective, and that probably sums up how today was." When I lean back, I spread my arms behind me, crossing mine beneath his.

"So this would probably be a pretty great time for a birthday present, right?" Torrin looks at me from the side, his eyes excited. He's still a kid when it comes to birthdays, and I love finding that out about him. I love every new thing I learn about him and everything I remember about him from before.

"This wouldn't just be a good time; it would be an *ideal* time," I say, glancing at him from the corners of my eyes.

He's grinning, but his grin fades a little when he leans in closer. The candle still flickering below us catches the lights of his eyes. "I love you."

My head turns, and I feel my eyes widen. "Torrin . . ."

It's the first time he's said it like this. It's the first time he's said it since the night I disappeared.

"I didn't think it was a secret." He looks me straight-on and doesn't look ashamed. He doesn't look like he's said or done anything wrong. "I told you I loved you for the first time thirteen years ago. It didn't come with an expiration date. It never will."

The breeze whips around me and feels like it's trying to lift me up. "I thought you weren't allowed to love someone like that anymore."

"My job is to love people." He stretches his legs in front of him and stares at the ocean. "There's no line drawn between who I can and can't love. The calling is to love all people." The corner of his mouth twitches. "I just might not mention I happen to love you a little or a lot more than the rest."

I stare at the ocean with him until I feel the waves churning something inside me too. "Those journalists have accused me of being your forbidden mistress, your submissive, and everything in between, but they've never printed the truth." I taste the words in my mouth first, testing them. They feel right. "The woman who loves you."

His head turns, and he watches me for a moment. "I'm ready, Jade. To walk away, to start a new life. For whatever comes—good and bad. I'm ready."

"I know you are." I dig my toes into the sand. Delaying the inevitable for two more seconds. "But I'm not."

He exhales slowly, but he doesn't say anything else because I think he knows. I'm healing, but there's still more to do. Some days it feels like the more I fix, the more I realize is broken. Those are the bad days. The good ones are the days I remind myself that no matter what, everything can be fixed. Those are the days that get me through the others.

"I've been through a year of intensive counseling, some serious soul-searching, daily meditation, and some really sad attempts at yoga." I nudge him. "And I still know something's missing. I'm not whole, and until I am, I won't let you give everything up for me."

"I *want* to give up everything for you. Broken, whole, I don't care."

I take a slow breath. I know he can and does love me exactly the way I am, but his end of the love equation isn't the problem—it's mine.

He kicks at the sand. "You're whole already," he says, looking at me like he's trying to prove it. "I know that. But I can wait for you to figure it out on your own. I'm really good at waiting."

I kick some sand over his toes. "You have ten years of experience."

"I suppose I do," he says, smiling at the horizon. He keeps staring at it as his hand lifts to his chest. "So . . . I had another birthday present for you . . ." When his hand curls around something hanging beneath his shirt, I swallow. "But I'm guessing this isn't the right birthday for this gift."

I can see the chain around the back of his neck, the outline of the ring beneath his shirt. My hand curls into the sand when I find myself wanting to hold it out to him. "Not this one. Not yet."

"I'm ready to make that choice—no one and nothing is forcing it. I'm ready to walk away."

"Don't walk away—not yet. Stay where you are. I'll be right here." I slide just a fraction of an inch closer so our shoulders are just barely touching. But even with this slightest of touches, my body responds as if he's crawling over me the way he did that night in his bedroom, that night when I'd never been happier. "I'm not going any-where."

"But if I do that—stay where I am—you know what that means, right?" His eyes drop to the distance between us. "Father Costigan can't give you a ring. He can't give you intimacy. He can't give you his last name or a family or a home."

My chest contracts—then it slowly releases. "I know, but Torrin Costigan can love me."

"And this is enough for you? Being what I am? Being like this?" He looks at my mouth in a familiar way. He wants to kiss me, but he can't. Not with the way our lives are now. Not on a public beach for anyone to see.

"All I've ever wanted is you. You're enough. In whatever way I can have you." I lean forward. "Besides, look at me. I'm a psychologist's dream or nightmare—depending on the day. I'm at the epicenter of an interna-tional media storm. I'm in love with a priest." I fight my smile but lose the battle. "Is *that* enough for you?"

He lowers his face toward mine. He doesn't blink. "You, Jade Childs, have always been more than enough."

I don't lean back. I stay right where I am, our faces in line so I can feel his warm breath wash across my lips. I've never mentioned to him what I found out that day in the interrogation room with Reyes, and I'm not sure I ever will. I think he doesn't want me to feel like I owe him any-thing or have that skew my decision when it comes to us. I think it's important to him that when I'm ready, I make that decision because I want to be with him and not because I want to pay him back for the ten years he never gave up—for the decade he refused to let go of me.

"Thank you," I say, but my eyes are relaying a million other things that I hope he sees. I think he might.

"For what?"

I could go on and on, detailing everything I'm thankful to him for, but it all comes down to the same thing. "For saving me."

His face moves a little closer, and I can almost feel his forehead leaning into mine. "You're welcome."

I see devotion and loyalty and love and desire when I look into his eyes. I see the boy I loved's eyes in the face of the man I love. I see a person who sacrificed ten years of his life to save mine. I see everything I've always wanted and everything I hope to one day deserve, and the man beside me stares at me in a similar kind of way.

It's the best birthday I've ever had. Maybe because I never thought I'd celebrate another one. Or maybe because I'm alive to have a birthday when the odds put me in the one-in-a-million range. But I guess this is the best birthday ever because he's here to share it with me. He isn't my husband or my fiancé or my boyfriend . . . or even my secret lover. He's my friend. My best friend.

For now, for me, that's more than I ever could have imagined having again. For now, this is exactly what I need. Torrin Costigan is worth the wait until I've completed the process of putting myself back together.

"Everyone thought I was dead."

Torrin's brows pull together like it's a painful memory. Then he shakes his head. "Everyone was wrong."

"You found me alive." I smile when I want to kiss him. He smiles when I know he wants to kiss me back. "But then you brought me back to life."

He exhales, and just before he leans back, his forehead presses against mine. It's fleeting and forever all at once. In the advancing twilight, that little light still flickering below us lights up his whole face. It illuminates the distance between us too.

"Someday?" he asks.

I nod and scoot a little closer. My hand finds his just beneath the surface of the sand and forms around it. No one watching would think anything of it. But he knows what it means. So do I. "One day."

Thank you for reading COLLARED
by NEW YORK TIMES and USATODAY
bestselling author, Nicole Williams.

Make sure to check out Nicole's next book,
HATING HIM, releasing this June.

Nicole loves to hear from her readers.
You can connect with her on:

Facebook: Nicole Williams (Official Author Page)
Twitter: nwilliamsbooks
Blog: nicoleawilliams.blogspot.com

Other Works by Nicole:

CRASH, CLASH, and CRUSH (HarperCollins)

UP IN FLAMES (Simon & Schuster UK)

LOST & FOUND, NEAR & FAR, HEART & SOUL

FINDERS KEEPERS, LOSERS WEEPERS

THE FABLE OF US

THREE BROTHERS

HARD KNOX, DAMAGED GOODS

CROSSING STARS

GREAT EXPLOITATIONS

THE EDEN TRILOGY

THE PATRICK CHRONICLES

Made in the USA
San Bernardino, CA
20 April 2016